BEAUTY AND THE BARON

Deborah Hale

MILLS
BOON

First published in Great Britain 2013
by Mills & Boon, an imprint of Harlequin (UK) Limited.
Harlequin (UK) Limited, Eton House, 18-24 Paradise Road,
Richmond, Surrey TW9 1SR

© Deborah M. Hale 2003

ISBN: 978 0 263 89851 4

Harlequin (UK) policy is to use papers that are natural, renewable and recyclable products and made from wood grown in sustainable forests. The logging and manufacturing process conform to the legal environmental regulations of the country of origin.

Printed and bound in Spain
by Blackprint CPI, Barcelona

Chapter One

⚜

Northamptonshire, England, 1818

"Who shut the curtains on such a lovely day?" Angela Lacewood darted into the drawing room at Netherstowe, her bonnet pulled back off her head and a pair of thick gloves in one hand. "It's like a tomb in here!"

She'd been working out in the garden, basking in the lavish sunshine of late May when the butler had summoned her to receive an unexpected visitor. Why anyone would be paying a call at Netherstowe when the family was traveling abroad, Angela could not guess. Nor did she much care, to be truthful.

She would deal with them as quickly as possible, then reclaim her privacy.

As she crossed the darkened room to open the curtains, her eyes not yet accustomed to the dimness of indoors, a deep masculine voice reached out of the shadows, like a foot to trip her up.

"Leave the curtains be! I shut them and I wish them kept that way until I go."

Startled by the brusque order, Angela dropped her gloves and took a stumbling step too near her aunt's favorite footstool. Her foot caught on the low hurdle and she pitched to the floor.

Or would have done, had not a powerful pair of arms unfolded out of the darkness to catch her.

"I beg your pardon. I didn't mean to frighten you." The voice clearly belonged to the same person as the arms, for it wafted into her left ear from so intimate a distance it might almost have been a kiss. But could that voice—smooth, rich and beguiling—be the same gruff one that had frightened her into a humiliating stumble?

Perhaps they did have one thing in common, after all, she decided. Both made her heart flutter and her breath hasten…for quite different reasons.

"W-who are you, sir, and why have you come to Netherstowe?" The questions had scarcely tumbled from her lips when Angela guessed the answer to the first. Her pulse raced faster still, though from fright…or something else, she could not be certain.

The visitor set her on her feet again, but not before she felt the moist caress of his breath against her bare throat. For an instant she sensed a hint of reluctance to let her go. Or was it her own reluctance to break from her first time being held in a man's arms?

Even if that man were the devil himself.

"Lord Lucius Daventry, Miss Lacewood."

He executed a stiff bow over her hand. "At your service."

Not the devil perhaps, but as close as she was likely to encounter deep in the sleepy countryside of Northamptonshire. Even so isolated from London society, Angela knew her guest had been dubbed "Lord Lucifer" by wags of the ton. Lately, the village folk had begun to use that name— though never in his lordship's hearing.

"I beg pardon for startling you, and for taking liberties with your domestic arrangements." He gestured toward the window. "My eye is sensitive to bright light."

Could that be the reason he seldom ventured abroad by day? Gossip ascribed far more sinister motives to his lordship's nocturnal habits.

Her own vision had adjusted to the room's dimness enough for Angela to make out the sharp shadow of a curious demimask that gave Lucius Daventry a diabolical appearance to match his reputation. A large patch of black leather concealed half of his upper face, from cheekbone to temple, with a narrow slit to expose his left eye.

Was it only his eye that could no longer abide the light? she wondered. Or was it his pride as well? Before Waterloo, his lordship had been hailed as the handsomest beau in Britain. Though she'd had little experience on which to base a comparison, Angela had thought that reputation scarcely did him justice.

"To what do I owe the honor of your call, sir? Lord and Lady Bulwick and my cousins departed a fortnight ago for their tour of the Continent. I do not expect them back for some months."

Hard as she tried to purge the sweet ring of satisfaction from her voice, Angela could not. Weeks and weeks of lovely spring and summer with the whole house to herself and nobody to criticize or patronize her. That was as near *heaven* as she was apt to get for some years.

"And my brother is away at school," she added as a hasty afterthought.

Usually Miles was foremost in her mind, but today she'd consciously turned her thoughts in other directions. It did no good to fret about her brother's future when she had no means to help him.

Lord Daventry shook his head. "It is you I've come to see, Miss Lacewood."

"Me? Whatever for?" Too late Angela tried to bottle up her unmannerly question by pressing her fingers to her lips. Really, though, she'd asked the man his business twice, already. And twice he had failed to enlighten her.

Nor did he this time.

"May we sit?" he asked, instead.

"Of course." As Angela sank onto her aunt's favorite chair, her tardy manners caught up with her. "Would you care for some refreshment, my lord? You must excuse me for being such a poor hostess. I've never had company of my own to entertain before."

"Nothing, thank you." His lordship chose a

seat some distance from her, and more deeply in shadow. "This is not exactly a social call."

The man was beginning to vex her. First interrupting her jolly afternoon in the garden, then giving her a fright, and finally stirring up all kinds of bewildering feelings she had no desire to experience.

"If not a social call, then, what exactly *is* it, sir?"

Aunt Hester would have had a fit of the vapors to hear her addressing a gentleman of wealth and title in such a tone, but Lord Daventry did not lose his cool aplomb.

Angela wondered if he ever did.

"All in good time, Miss Lacewood, if you will be so patient as to indulge me. For my grandfather's sake," he added, in a tone that betrayed more emotion than he had shown since ordering her to keep the curtains closed.

"Your grandfather?" Angela surged up from her seat. "Is something the matter with the earl?"

Her guest motioned for her to resume her seat. "The two of you have become great friends these past few years, have you not?"

Did the man *ever* answer a direct question when one was put to him? Angela wondered. Perhaps she should demonstrate how to accomplish such a feat.

"I cannot answer for your grandfather, but I am fonder of him than of anyone…except my brother."

The dear Earl of Welland had a knack for making her feel clever and graceful and capable—all the things Angela had given up hoping she would ever be.

"Be assured, Miss Lacewood, my grandfather also holds you in the highest regard. It was good of you to visit him so often while I was…absent."

On the Continent, serving under the revered Duke of Wellington. Was Lord Daventry aware how much she knew of his service in the cavalry? All his letters she'd read aloud to the earl, marveling at the adventures of which he'd made light with wry, self-deprecating wit.

"I did hate the thought of him over there in that big house," she said, "with no company but the servants."

"My grandfather is rather a pet project of yours, is he not? I gather you have a number of other such persons in the parish."

Though her caller did not raise his ripe, resonant voice or sharpen his tone, Angela felt a subtle sting in his remark. Did he imagine she'd implied some criticism of him for putting his service to king and country ahead of filial duty to the grandfather who had raised him?

"There are others besides your grandfather in need of a little cheer, sir, which I do my best to provide since I have not the means to dispense more practical comforts." How often Angela had regretted that lack. "Loneliness takes no account of rank or wealth." Against her inclination, her tone sharpened. "But if by *project* you mean to suggest I condescend to my friends or think well of myself for what little service I do them, I hope you are mistaken."

Why was she bothering to justify her motives to this arrogant man? Her penchant for nurturing what Aunt Hester called "Angela's strays" had long been considered a joke by the family. Even she did not fully understand what compelled her to care about people for whom no one else spared a thought.

Could it be because so few thoughts had ever been spared for her that she felt such kinship with the neglected?

His lordship's fine wide mouth lifted for an instant in the ghost of a smile. "Come, Miss Lacewood. I vow, you're as prickly as a hedgehog. I meant no slight on your kindness, truly. You have far better right to think well of yourself on that account than others who pride themselves upon the happy accident of birth or beauty, which they've done nothing to merit."

It was a bald sort of compliment, neither lavish nor lyrical. Angela thought she detected within it a backhanded rebuke of himself. Yet, the very frugal nature of his praise pleased her, somehow. If it had been a whit more extravagant, she might have supposed he meant to mock her.

"If I seem prickly, sir, it is because I find myself quite out of my depth." She fumbled to untie the ribbons of her bonnet. "You have arrived out of the blue to call on me, who never receives guests. You say this is no social visit, yet rather than reveal its purpose, you question my friendship with your grandfather. I feel as though I'm engaged in a game of blindman's bluff."

Lord Daventry clasped his large, long-fingered hands together and rested his chin upon them. "Some consider blindman's bluff a diverting pastime, Miss Lacewood."

"Not those who must always play the blind-man." She had good reason to know.

To her astonishment, his lordship laughed.

Once, Angela had run her hand over a sable collar her cousin Clemmie had received as a Christmas gift. She'd never forgotten the lush tex-ture of it. His lordship's laughter reminded her of that fur—rich and deep, with a provocative whis-per of darkness lurking beneath.

"Touché, Miss Lacewood! I begin to see why Grandfather cherishes your acquaintance so."

Cherish. Surely she'd heard that word before. Angela knew what it meant...in an abstract fash-ion. Hearing it spoken by Lucius Daventry, ca-ressed by his tongue and lips, was to hear it for the first time as Nature had intended it to be uttered.

A chill, part dread, part reluctant anticipation, quivered through her, for suddenly she glimpsed the reason behind Lord Lucifer's visit. Like his namesake had to other mortals throughout the ages, he had come to make her a bargain.

And to steal her soul.

He was making a botch of it.

The knowledge put Lucius Daventry in a vile temper, though he flattered himself that he hid the fact from Miss Lacewood, the way he hid most of his emotions. Few things vexed him worse than performing poorly at any task he set himself. This one more than most, for so much depended upon his success.

The young lady wanted to know why he'd come. The longer he delayed telling her, the less likely she would be to oblige his request. And he must win her cooperation.

If only he could secure his own!

Lucius Daventry was not accustomed to being of two minds about anything. He'd always prided himself on setting high goals, then committing all his energies to achieving them...until today.

Miss Lacewood was the problem. He had come to Netherstowe expecting to find the poor little pudding of a child he remembered, grown into stout, dowdy womanhood. Such a creature would surely have been eager to accept his offer without placing his heart in jeopardy.

Instead he'd found the dumpy little caterpillar transformed into an exquisite Regency butterfly. When she'd fallen into his arms, Miss Lacewood had reminded him of how long it had been since he'd held anything so soft and fragrant. Her tantalizing beauty and her charitable nature posed a grave threat to his lordship's hard-won peace. Though it shamed Lucius to admit it, even to himself, the lady frightened him worse than a unit of French cavalry at full charge.

For the sake of his grandfather, Lucius was prepared to brave his worst fears. Though perhaps he might not have to...

"No doubt there are gentlemen much younger than my grandfather who also value your acquaintance, Miss Lacewood. I hope you will pardon my curiosity for inquiring if there is any one in particular paying you his addresses?"

For a moment she made no reply. Lucius wondered if he had trespassed too far on her privacy.

When it came, her answer held none of the indignation he'd armed himself to repel. Instead, Miss Lacewood spoke in a tone of gentle reproach that slid beneath his defences.

"Must you mock me, sir?"

"Indeed, I do not!" Lucius sprang from his chair, retreating to the deepest shadows of the drawing room, where he paced in the restless manner of a wild beast caged. "Why would you suppose I mock you?"

"Why would you suppose I might have an admirer?"

Pulling off her bonnet, Miss Lacewood set it on the footstool that had launched her into his arms. Then, she rose from her chair and withdrew to the opposite side of the room, where a few stray sunbeams had pierced small gaps in the closed curtains. One lit on the crown of her head, like the magic wand of a fairy godmother, gilding her tawny tumble of curls.

The answer to her question was so manifestly obvious Lucius could only stand dumb and gaze.

If he'd had to choose a single word to sum

up her appearance, it would have been *generous*. Eyes large and luminous, the warm brown of a yearling fawn dappled with golden sunshine. Lips so lush they fairly demanded to be kissed. Features with a rounded softness that put him in mind of peaches ripe for the plucking.

Her beauty cast a spell over him, lulling to sleep the stern guard he had set to govern his tongue.

A bemused whisper of his true thoughts escaped. "I only wonder that you do not have a hundred."

Her eyes fixed on him then and something stirred in their russet depths, a power that made him fear for his cherished self-control. "I would say you flatter me, sir, but I do not think you are much given to flattery. Unless there is something you want from me?"

Her wariness called to his own, whispering vain promises of sympathy. Promises Lucius knew he dared not trust.

"I *do* want something from you, Miss Lacewood."

He had roused the slumbering censor. No further word, inflection, gesture or look of his must convey to this woman any more or less than he wished to convey. The thoughts that sang like cold steel in his mind and the emotions that seethed in his heart must be his alone to know.

"I want something, and I am willing to compensate you handsomely for it."

"Indeed?" She tensed. "I suspected as much. What is it you desire?"

Her alarm was so palpable his lordship's nostrils flared as though greedy to catch the subtle redolence of it. Try as she might to hide behind a mask of bravado, she feared him.

What woman wouldn't?

Better fear than pity. Since Waterloo, that had become Lucius Daventry's creed.

"Let us first speak of what I will give you in exchange."

"As you wish." Miss Lacewood took a step nearer the window. Perhaps she planned to blind him by ripping the curtains open if he menaced her. "I must warn you, though. My situation may be modest, but so are my needs. I doubt you have anything with which to tempt me."

I wish I could say the same of you. The words prickled on his tongue like lemon juice, demanding he spit them out. By an act of will, Lucius managed to swallow them, only to find they had a seductively sweet flavor.

"Judge for yourself, my dear." The latter word had a toothsome taste as well. If he did not exercise some restraint soon, he might become a glutton for such dainties. "I believe your brother wishes to take up a commission in the cavalry."

A tremor ran through Angela Lacewood such as his lordship had seen soldiers give when they tasted cold steel in the belly. She managed to answer with a steady voice, however, which Lucius could not help but admire.

"Your information is correct, sir. Ever since he was a young lad, Miles has longed to return to India, as an officer in our father's old regiment."

"Commissions are costly." Lucius leaned against the back of the chair on which he'd been seated earlier. "As is the proper kit to outfit an officer bound for India."

"So I have discovered, sir."

"Lord Bulwick will not support your brother's ambition?" Lucius knew the answer well enough. He asked merely to enhance the value of his offer in Miss Lacewood's eyes.

"His lordship is only a relation by marriage." Clearly Miss Lacewood was parroting back the answer her entreaties to her uncle had received. "He feels he has fulfilled his obligations by taking my brother and me into his household after our parents died. He wishes Miles to find a post in the city."

Lucius nodded. He'd expected no better from the odious Lord Bulwick. "I would purchase a commission for your brother and see that he is suitably outfitted for it."

"And what would you expect from me in return?" Angela Lacewood squared her shoulders.

Lucius found himself wishing he could see those shoulders bare and admire their contours, for he had no doubt they would equal her graceful neck in beauty.

How might Miss Lacewood react if he approached her with slow, deliberate steps, then raised his hands to push down the brief sleeves of her gown?

Swoon dead away perhaps? Run screaming? It was a dangerous weakness for him to entertain such fancies.

Dangerous? Perhaps. But he had once courted Lady Danger and been seduced by her lethal charms.

"I would ask only one favor of you, my dear." Emerging from behind his fortress of furniture, the baron approached Miss Lacewood with slow, deliberate steps. "A trifle, really."

Some subtle cant of her posture and a rapid sideways glance told Lucius the young lady wanted to retreat from his steady advance. Yet, she managed to hold her ground. "One man's trifle is another man's treasure."

"So it is." Lucius halted his advance.

There was not much distance between them now. If he held out his hand and she held out hers, they might touch.

"Your words are most apt in this case," he added. "What I require from you will cost only a little time and less effort on your part. But it will bring a treasure's worth of pleasure to someone else."

"To you?"

"No." At one time it might have, but those days were past.

"To whom then?"

"Perhaps you will guess when I tell you what I want."

"I shall be glad to hear…at last."

Balancing on the balls of his feet, Lucius sank slowly to his knees. It was a ridiculous and unnecessary bit of ritual, but he felt compelled to it all the same. "Miss Lacewood, I am asking you to become my fiancée."

The lady did not move, speak or even blink. She stood there like a golden statue, staring down at him.

Her eyes were alive, though. Alive with wariness and aversion and other things the baron could not so easily identify. It took every crumb of his considerable will to hold her gaze in his, issuing her a mute challenge to accept his offer.

At last she drew a deep breath and wet her bountiful lips with a dart of her tongue that made Lucius ache with sensations he struggled to ignore.

"I am sensible of the honor you do me by proposing, my lord." She shook her head. "But I cannot marry you."

Lucius heard himself laugh for the second time in half an hour. It must be some sort of record. For a moment all the cares that weighed on him eased.

"I understand, Miss Lacewood." As slowly as he had sunk to the floor, the baron rose again until he looked down into her eyes. "But, you see, that is *not* what I am asking."

Chapter Two

Angela could not decide whether she was sorry or relieved that she'd left her gloves back on the footstool with her bonnet. If she'd been holding them in her hand when Lord Daventry had baited her with yet another riddle, the urge to strike him with them might have been too fierce a temptation for her to resist.

He *was* playing blindman's bluff with her! Keeping her in the dark about his intentions and his feelings. Swooping in close to tease her with a tiny kernel of information calculated to set her lurching after him. Then dancing out of her reach once again, while she groped a fistful of air.

"Did you wake up this morning, sir, and say to yourself, 'This looks like a marvelous day to go vex my neighbor!'?"

His lordship laughed again, clearly oblivious to his increasing danger of being throttled. "If that notion had entered my mind, I can assure you, Miss Lacewood, you'd be at the very bottom of my list of potential victims. Forgive me for not being more plainspoken. My years spent in polite society did little to foster that commendable ability."

He sounded genuinely contrite in a wry sort of way. His green eyes, previously hard, cool and impenetrable as jade, had softened until they beckoned her like the garden on a dewy summer morning at sunrise.

Against her will, Angela felt herself relent. "I should have known better than to presume you were proposing marriage to someone like me, my lord."

"On the contrary." A harsh note crept into his hypnotic voice. "Someone like me would not presume to propose marriage to you, Miss Lacewood."

"But you said…?"

"I asked you to be my fiancée, not my wife. And before you accuse me of vexing you intentionally again, I beg to point out that one need not follow the other as a matter of course."

Ninety-nine times out of a hundred it did, though, unless a couple wished to bring scandal on themselves and their families.

Once upon a time, Angela had indulged in childish fancies of marrying a man like Lucius Daventry—titled, wealthy and so very handsome. A sort of fairy-tale prince to whisk her away from Netherstowe, where she often felt of little more consequence than a scullery maid.

Since then, she'd experienced enough of the

world to realize how unlikely it was that any man would offer for a dowerless, unaccomplished country girl who had never ventured out in society. She'd also come to understand that marriage might not be the refuge she'd once imagined it to be. For those reasons, she'd resigned herself to a life of placid spinsterhood, making herself sufficiently useful to her relations that they would not grudge her bed and board.

While sunshine, fresh air, music and friendship were still free for the taking, she would be content. If only Lord Daventry had not come with his unorthodox proposal to stir up the embers of her silly girlhood longing for some-thing more.

"Intentional or not, I fear you are confusing me again, sir." Not only with his words, either.

Never before had she felt herself so aggravated by a person one moment, then so powerfully drawn to him the next. Really, it was enough to drive a girl straight to…the pantry! How she would love to soothe her wrought-up feelings with a thick slice of pound cake, so rich as to be nearly indigestible.

"Whatever you want from me, Lord Daventry, I seem unable to grasp it." Her mouth watered so much at the thought of cake that she had to swallow before continuing. "No doubt there are plenty of other young ladies who'd be delighted to oblige you."

Her guest parted his lips to speak, but Angela cut him off. "I bid you good-day, my lord. Remember me warmly to your grandfather."

She pivoted on the toe of her slipper to dash off. Before she could stir a step, his lordship caught her hand to detain her. A curious sensation rippled up her arm—hot and cold at the same time. Rather like her bewildering reaction to the baron himself.

Before she had a chance to withdraw her hand from his, Lucius Daventry blurted out the words she had prevented him from speaking a moment before. "Please, Miss Lacewood, stay and hear me out. I need your help. My grandfather is dying."

His words struck Angela a harsh backhand blow. She flinched from it at the same instant her knees grew weak. If his lordship had not held her hand in such a tight grip, she might have wilted to the floor.

"Dying?" She raised her free hand to her brow in a vain effort to stem the chaotic whirl of thoughts in her mind. "That can't be. When I visited Helmhurst yesterday he looked better than I've seen him in some time."

But the earl was not a young man. And he'd been mildly ailing for as long as Angela could remember. "I must go to him at once!"

Another notion reared up from the tempest of her thoughts.

"Why did you not tell me straight away?" Wrenching her hand back from Lord Daventry's, she was surprised to find the warm air of the sitting room chilly against her skin where he had touched. "It was most unfeeling of you, subjecting me to a litany of paradoxes while keeping me in ignorance of your grandfather's condition!"

The baron clenched his jaw tight, but some subtle shift of his brow betrayed the injury her reproach had inflicted upon him.

Stifling a qualm of guilt that squirmed in her belly, Angela turned away from him. She must get to Helmhurst, and her dear friend the earl, as soon as possible.

She had scarcely taken a step toward the door before Lord Daventry loomed in front of her. "I cannot let you go, Miss Lacewood."

"You had better." She tried to duck around him, but he caught her in his arms.

"Let go of me this instant!" she cried, ignoring her ridiculous desire to linger in his hold, which felt oddly like an embrace.

"I cannot let you go," he repeated, "until you have calmed down. My grandfather is in no immediate danger, and I do not want him to guess what his doctors have told me."

Angela eased her token struggle to free herself, yet her breath came fast and shallow, as though she had wrestled against him with all her might. "How can you say the earl is dying one minute, then claim he is in no danger the next?"

"No *immediate* danger," Lord Daventry corrected her. His respiration seemed to have picked up tempo, too. "You should pay more careful heed to my words, Miss Lacewood. Though my grandfather does not appear in any worse health than usual, his doctors assure me he has, at most, three months to live."

A bank of dark, tearful clouds suddenly shadowed the coming summer that had stretched ahead of Angela with such promise only moments ago.

Lord Daventry relaxed his grip on her.

"I do not want that time blighted for him in any way by the knowledge of how grave his condition is. If you wish to see him again, I must have your word that you will honor my wishes."

She wanted to feel some sympathy for the baron, but he made it impossible. Planting her hands against the breast of his well-tailored coat, Angela pushed herself out of his grasp, despising the passing flicker of disappointment she felt when he let her go with so little resistance.

"If the earl knows nothing of this, you may rest assured I would not speak of it to him, even without your bidding."

"You need not say a word to betray everything, Miss Lacewood. Your face is an open book for anyone curious enough to read it, your eyes even more so."

A cold wave of dismay washed over Angela.

Was Lord Daventry telling the truth or only baiting her again? And if the former, might he decipher the contrary, far too intense feelings he provoked in her?

Lucius Daventry's emotions had been a seething stew bubbling in a tightly lidded pot. Angela

Lacewood had jarred that lid more than once during their interview—each time venting a scalding blast of steam. For all Lucius hated anyone unsettling his composure, he had to admit those momentary discharges of pressure had probably kept him from exploding.

Now if only the searing imprint of Miss Lacewood in his arms did not make his body burst into flames!

She lowered her gaze, perhaps to protect herself from his searching scrutiny. "I am able to put on a cheerful face when I wish, sir, and your grandfather's sight is not what it once was. I would never do anything to cause him distress."

"I believe that, my dear."

The last word slipped past Lord Daventry's censor. He hastened on, hoping she would not pay it any heed. If he succeeded in convincing her to help him, which seemed unlikely at present, he would have to accustom himself to uttering such endearments.

A spasm of alarm gripped his heart at that thought.

"What I need to know is how far you would be willing to dissemble in order to make my grandfather happy in his last months?"

The words stung his throat as he expelled them. It had taken him several long nights staring into the cold, dark beauty of the starry sky to cultivate his present stoic acceptance of the situation. Perhaps his ruse with Miss Lacewood would provide a welcome distraction for him in the weeks to come.

If only he could convince her to help him.

Her eyes widened and her gaze flew back to meet his. A flicker of triumph in their golden brown depths told Lucius she had finally reconciled all the contradictions of his strange proposal.

"You want to pretend we're getting married, to please the earl?"

"Just so. Grandfather has been remarkably unsubtle in his quest to bring us together."

The glimmer of a smile bewitched her lips for an instant. Evidently the earl had been making a nuisance of himself matchmaking with Miss Lacewood, too.

"There is nothing else he wants so much in this life," Lucius continued. "Until now I have turned a deaf ear to his constant litany of your virtues, for I have no intention of marrying. Not even for my grandfather's sake."

The young lady could not disguise her relief. "But you would become *engaged* to me?"

Lucius nodded. "With the understanding that you will break the engagement once…it has served its purpose. In exchange for your cooperation, I will assist your brother in gaining the commission he desires."

She stared at him in silence for a moment. Despite his earlier protestations, Lucius could not divine what she was thinking or how she might respond.

"I require no such inducement from you, my lord," she said at last. "If I choose to do what you ask, it will be because I also wish to make the earl happy."

"Nevertheless, Miss Lacewood, I would insist." Lucius declined to insult the young lady by telling her it would be a kind of insurance, to guarantee that she'd break the engagement once it had outlived its usefulness.

After all, it was a woman's prerogative to change her mind in matters of this nature. A mild local scandal might result, but little more. When a gentleman jilted a lady, on the other hand, it became the tattle of the ton—likely to end up in the law courts or, worse yet, the newspapers.

If what his grandfather had told him about Angela Lacewood were true, Lucius doubted she would betray him by insisting they go ahead with a marriage he did not want. A nobleman with a comfortable fortune could never be too careful, though. He would feel less uneasy about the whole enterprise if he had some influence he could exercise over her when the time came.

"Now that you understand my intentions, Miss Lacewood, is it possible you might oblige me?"

As he awaited her answer, it seemed to Lucius that all of his internal organs had contracted into one tight, heavy ball such as might blast from the mouth of a cannon. Finding that his palms had begun to sweat, he thrust his arms behind his back.

"It is…possible, my lord," she said at last.

Lucius expelled the breath he had not realized he'd been holding.

"But I will need more information upon which to base my decision," she hastened to add. "What would this engagement of ours entail, exactly?"

"How in blazes should I know!" Lucius flared. This whole business had wound him far too tight. His struggle to project an unruffled facade had not helped.

"Whatever it takes to make grandfather believe we mean to get married, I suppose." He was vexed with himself for failing to plan beyond this interview, which had not gone at all as he'd expected.

"Would we have to go out in society together?" Miss Lacewood looked as though she were wringing her hands. At second glance, Lucius realized she was twisting a slender ring on her little finger. "I mean, such society as one finds in this quiet corner of the country?"

Since he wasn't certain what answer she wanted, Lucius gave her the one he preferred. "I don't see why we should have to. I seldom get invited anywhere these days and almost always decline when I do. I don't expect that to change simply because I've acquired a fiancée."

A certain stiffness in her posture seemed to ease. Had she approved of his unsociable answer? Perhaps they might get along well enough after all.

"Would I be allowed to visit Helmhurst even more frequently than I do now?" This time there could be no question what she wanted to hear.

Though the notion of sharing the last few precious months of his grandfather's company with another person did not appeal to him, Lucius made himself nod. "As much as you wish."

Miss Lacewood made no effort to hide her bittersweet satisfaction with his answer.

It was beginning to look as though he might just succeed in winning her cooperation. The prospect made Lucius light-headed and off balance.

"Anything else?" he asked. The corners of his mouth arched upward and he could do nothing to stop them.

She greeted his question with a blush so intense Lucius could see it in spite of the dim light in the room.

"Kiss?"

The tremulous murmur of her query hit him like a hard, unexpected blow to the belly. Lucius ordered himself not to stare at Miss Lacewood's wide, full lips. Under no circumstances should he imagine what it might be like to kiss her. Or speculate whether she'd been kissed by another man.

All at once, Lucius fancied he could hear bugles in the distance sounding retreat.

"I should never have come here." He wheeled about and strode for the sitting room door, snatching up his cloak and wide-brimmed felt hat from the back of a chair where he had left them.

"This was a ludicrous idea—quite unworkable. I'm sorry to have troubled you, Miss Lacewood. I will see myself out."

As he marched toward the entry hall, Lucius flung his cloak around his shoulders and jammed his hat on, pulling the broad brim low to shade his face.

Behind him he heard footsteps hurrying to catch up.

"Please, Lord Daventry, will you wait a moment?"

Lucius did not slacken his pace, though he fancied he could hear the Iron Duke bellowing, *"The little baggage has you on the run, eh, Daventry? Stand and take it like a man, why don't you."*

When he reached the front door, Lucius wheeled to face his pursuer.

Clearly Miss Lacewood had not anticipated this, for she failed to curb her headlong chase. As he pivoted toward her, she barreled into him. If the door had not been at his back, they might have crashed onto the floor of the entry hall in a tangled heap. Instead, Lucius felt his arms rise to enfold her for the third time that afternoon.

Her wild tumble of curls tickled his nose. They smelled as fresh and sweet as the garden from whence she'd been summoned by his call. If sunbeams could have substance and texture, surely they would feel like Miss Lacewood's golden tresses.

She raised her face to his, and for one mad, fleeting instant Lucius wanted to give her the kiss she'd asked about. The kiss her lips had been made for.

But before he had the chance, words gushed

from between those provocatively parted lips. "I'm sorry!"

It brought him back to his senses with the cold shock of ice water.

"I'm so sorry I bumped into you." She sounded thoroughly rattled. "And I'm sorry if I embarrassed you with my question."

She lifted her hand to his face.

Lucius flinched at the soft, pitying caress of her gentle fingers.

"I'm sorry," she repeated in a whisper as her hand strayed closer to his mask, making the mangled flesh beneath it burn.

Though part of him longed to thrust her away with all his strength, Lucius exercised every crumb of his considerable restraint to detach Angela Lacewood from him.

"That, my dear, is precisely the problem."

Sorry? Angela fumed as she watched Lord Daventry ride away, the wide brim of his hat pulled low to his brow and his dark cloak billowing behind him. She was sorry, to be sure.

Sorry that insufferable man had come calling with his distressing news, his bewildering proposal and his abrupt departure! Yet it was only when he had disappeared altogether from sight that she marched back into the house.

For the first time in her life, Angela slammed the heavy front door of Netherstowe behind her. She had never been given to venting her feelings. Indeed, she'd spent most of her life trying to avoid

•

strong emotions of any kind. They served no purpose but to cause a variety of unpleasant physical
sensations—racing heart, breathlessness, bilious
stomach, headaches.

In the past hour, Lord Daventry had whipped
her emotions to such a pitch it was a wonder she
hadn't broken out head to toe in bright red spots!

From below stairs wafted the comforting
aroma of freshly baked gingerbread. Angela
gulped a deep, soothing breath of it and immediately felt her agitation begin to ease. Determined to put Lord Daventry out of her mind, she
followed the mouthwatering smell down to the
kitchen.

There, true to her nose, she discovered two
large pans of gingerbread cooling on the counter,
permeating the air with their spicy sweetness. The
cook, a tiny scrap of a woman, was endeavour-
ing to wrestle a large roasting pan into the oven.

"Here, Tibby, let me help." Angela scrambled
to bear some of the pan's considerable weight.
"What's for supper?"

"A roast of mutton and batter pudding," replied Mrs. Tibbs as she shut the oven door. She
pushed a few lank strands of grizzled hair back
up under her cap. "It'll be a while yet. Do you
fancy a cup of tea and morsel of gingerbread to
stay your stomach until then, my pet?"

Angela nodded readily as she pictured Lucius
Daventry buried beneath a sweet, stodgy moun-
tain of gingerbread, seed cake and lemon tarts.
She fetched cups and saucers, while Tibby cut her

a *morsel* of warm gingerbread that would have satisfied a starving field laborer.

"I hear tell Lord Lucifer ventured out in broad daylight to call on you," said Tibby a few moments later, as she poured the tea. "I told Hoskins he ought to have stood guard by the sitting room door to see that no harm came to you. He just laughed, the old fool. Won't hear a word against his lordship."

"While you never have a *good* word to say about him," Angela reminded the cook, as if she needed to. In an effort to distract Tibby from the subject, she added, "This gingerbread is heavenly! Just what I needed after working up a sharp appetite in the garden."

Never would she admit, least of all to a notorious tattle like Tibby, that it was not her hours digging in the garden but his lordship's unexpected call that had sent her scurrying for the kitchen.

"What did Lord Lucifer want with you?" The cook peered over the rim of her teacup at Angela, her small black eyes glittering with curiosity.

"I wish you wouldn't call him that," Angela protested. She should have known Tibby would not be diverted easily from her favorite subject of gossip. This quiet corner of Northamptonshire provided few quite so piquant. "The poor man was wounded in the service of his country. We should take pity on him, rather than pay heed to all that ridiculous talk about deviltry."

She had never quite managed to reconcile the dutiful grandson of the earl's fulsome accounts or the brave but sardonic cavalry officer of his own letters with the sinister reputation Lord Daventry had acquired since retiring to Helmhurst.

Their meeting this afternoon had only per-plexed her further.

"Humph! You wouldn't call it ridiculous if you'd ever met him walking abroad after dark." Tibby shivered. "Mrs. Hackenley vows he put a curse on their well and the Babbits had two swine disappear without a trace."

Angela's mouthful of tea sprayed out over her gingerbread in a fine mist. "Tibby! Surely you aren't accusing the heir to an earldom of being a common pig thief, on top of everything else?"

The cook raised her sharp, thin shoulders al-most to her ears. "I don't say he is, and I don't say he ain't."

Her eyes narrowed to mere slits and her voice dropped to an eerie whisper. "But I hear tell pigs' blood and entrails is used for…sacrifices."

The back of Angela's neck rose in gooseflesh, but something compelled her to scoff, "Nonsense! His lordship doesn't go out much in the daytime, because his eyes are sensitive to strong light."

Tibby digested that scrap of information. "You still haven't told me what he wanted with you."

If she didn't tell Tibby something, it would probably be all over the neighborhood by to-morrow morning that Lord Daventry had been recruiting her to join his coven, or something equally daft. Though Angela herself had sensed a dark, even dangerous, side to the man, she *knew* he could not be as evil as ignorant gossip painted him.

"Did I not mention it?" She tossed the words off in the most casual tone she could feign. "His lordship came to ask for my hand."

Tibby's pointy little chin fell, leaving her mouth agape. Her eyes looked in grave danger of popping out of their sockets and rolling across the table.

Angela struggled to keep a sober face as she ate more of her somewhat soggy gingerbread. The mellow sweetness on her tongue and the warm weight of it in her stomach were providing their accustomed comfort. Or perhaps it was Tibby's excessive suspicion of Lord Daventry that made her own earlier misgivings about the man seem so foolish.

Whatever the reason, Angela found herself becoming more favorably disposed toward Lucius Daventry by the minute.

"Lord-a-mercy!" The cook crossed her flat bosom. "What did he say when you refused him? I heard him stomping off, then the door slam shut. He hasn't put a curse on Netherstowe, has he?"

"Calm yourself, Tibby." Angela washed down the last of her gingerbread with a mouthful of tea. "His lordship didn't say a word about a curse."

Mrs. Tibbs blew out a shuddering breath.

Some unlikely impulse of devilment made Angela ask, "What makes you so certain I refused him?"

"You can't mean to wed such a creature?"

"Why ever not?" Was she trying to convince Tibby…or herself? "It isn't as though I have my pick of suitors. I haven't a penny in the world. I'm not clever or accomplished or beautiful. This could be my only chance to have a home of my own."

Why was she talking as if Lord Daventry had offered her a real marriage? Angela wondered. Certainly she dared not tell Tibby the truth and risk word finding its way back to the earl.

"Not beautiful?" sputtered the cook. "Do you never look in a glass, girl? You're clever enough to suit most men, and you've the kindest heart in the world. If her ladyship would only take you to London or Brighton as she ought, you'd soon have your pick of swains."

Angela shook her head, "You're too partial. I know my own shortcomings well enough." Her aunt and cousins had made her well aware of them over the years. "I'm sure there are plenty of young ladies who'd be delighted to tolerate Lord Daventry's eccentricities for the chance to be mistress of Helmhurst."

"More fools, them," muttered Tibby.

"I think his lordship would make an ideal sort of husband. Sleeping most of the day, then wandering abroad at night."

Angela's conscience warned her she should not tease poor Tibby, who'd been a better substitute mother to her than Aunt Hester ever had. Yet, she had never been able to keep herself from defending anyone under attack. Not even if that one was

the powerful Lord Daventry and the attack nothing more than silly gossip.

"Don't fret yourself, Tibby. I didn't accept him.
In any case, I'm not altogether certain he still
wants me. I must have offended him somehow,
for he said proposing to me had been a ludicrous
idea. That's when he stomped off."

What *had* provoked him so? Angela wondered.
She'd only asked if their sham engagement would
involve the odd kiss. Did he consider the possibility so very unpleasant?

"Well, that's all right then." Tibby dismissed
the whole matter with a wave of her hand. "As
long as there's no curse, and you didn't accept
him. Now tell me everything he said."

Angela scarcely heard Tibby over the sudden
uproar of her own thoughts. Had Lord Daventry
assumed her question indicated distaste on her
part for the possibility of kissing him, because
of his reputation…or his injuries?

She shot to her feet. "I must speak with him,
at once."

"No, you mustn't!" cried Tibby. "You said he'd
changed his mind. You don't want to risk offend-
ing him worse, do you?"

"I'll be back in time for dinner," Angela called
over her shoulder.

As she dashed up the stairs, Tibby called after
her, "Don't do anything foolish, now, because you
feel sorry for him. You've too soft a heart for your
own good!"

A soft heart? Angela popped back into the sitting room to retrieve her bonnet and gloves. She hadn't shown Lucius Daventry much sympathy this afternoon.

Just because he hid his hurts behind a facade of cool irony did not mean he felt them less keenly or deserved less compassion than others who freely bared their wounds. She of all people should know that.

If only she could convince Lord Daventry to give her another chance.

Chapter Three

Damn his fool pride! Lucius chided himself as he strove to ignore the hopeful light in his grandfather's eyes.

"Carruthers tells me you went out riding this afternoon." The earl glanced up from his book. "In the direction of Netherstowe."

Lucius glared at the ancient valet who stood behind his grandfather's chair. "Plenty of places lie east of here besides Netherstowe."

"True." The faint specter of a smile passed across the earl's face as he cocked one gray brow. "But that is where you went, isn't it?"

"What if I did?" Lucius turned to stare out one of the tall narrow windows of Helmhurst's library. A thick bank of clouds had blown in from the west, shrouding the sun's earlier brilliant glare. "Perhaps I was curious to discover whether Miss Lacewood bore any resemblance to the paragon you've been touting so continuously."

He'd discovered that Angela Lacewood bore a

strong resemblance to the sunshine from which he shrank—too warm and bright for a creature of the night to bear.

"And what was your verdict, my boy?" Beneath the mild, polite-sounding inquiry, Lucius detected a gloating note in his grandfather's voice.

He meant to dismiss the young lady with some wry quip, only to hear himself murmur, "You scarcely did her justice."

"I beg your pardon?" said the earl, though Lucius suspected he had heard.

Turning back toward his grandfather, Lucius spoke louder, exaggerating his words. "Pleasant enough, I suppose, if one's tastes are that way inclined."

The earl closed his book. "And yours are not?"

Lucius knew his grandfather well enough to read the subtle signs of disappointment on those wrinkled patrician features.

"Once, perhaps." Moving toward the old man's chair, Lucius shot Carruthers a look that bid him leave the two of them alone.

"Ring if you need anything, my lord," muttered the valet as he shuffled out of the library.

Lucius settled himself onto the footstool by the earl's favorite chair. How many hours of his boyhood had he spent on that footstool, while his grandfather had read to him?

A raw place in his heart gave a twinge. Too soon his grandfather would be gone and he would be all alone in the world. By his own choice, but alone just the same.

"I suppose you won't leave off asking until I tell you about it." A rueful sigh escaped from Lucius. "The truth is, I went over to Netherstowe to propose to your delightful Miss Lacewood."

Perhaps if he admitted what had occurred—an expurgated version of events, at least—it would lay the earl's matchmaking schemes to rest once and for all. Then Lucius would proceed to do everything *else* in his power to make his grandfather's last months happy.

"Well done, dear boy!" The earl's face remained impassive, yet it lit with a joyful radiance that Lucius regretted he would soon have to snuff out. "You'll never repent your choice, I promise you. My young friend is a rare jewel."

Lucius did not tell his grandfather that he already repented his interview with Angela Lacewood. She had provoked a vague sense of discontent within him, one he could not afford to entertain.

"She has certainly improved since I saw her last." Lucius knew he must disabuse his grandfather of the ridiculous notion that Miss Lacewood had accepted him, but he could not bring himself to do it straight away. "She used to remind me of a plump brown rabbit with her round face and long teeth."

"Winsome little creatures, rabbits," said the earl. "Soft. Timid."

"Not quite as helpless as they look, though." Lucius remembered having one as a pet in his younger years. "Those back legs can deliver a nasty scratch if you're not careful how you pick them up."

The earl gave a soft, wheezy chuckle. "Even the meekest of creatures must defend itself when cornered."

He reached out and patted his grandson's hand. "Turned you down, did she? Well, never mind. I proposed to your grandmother four times before she got tired of refusing me. Fortunately we Daventry men are a patient lot."

Lucius glanced up at the portrait of his grandmother that hung above the library mantelpiece. Though not strictly beautiful, she'd had a certain glow the artist had managed to capture.

"You had so little time with her," Lucius mused aloud. "Did you ever wish you'd married a lady with a more robust constitution?"

For a moment, he wondered if the earl would answer so intimate a question. They had never been given to speaking of such matters. Lucius could not suppress a sense of gratitude to Angela Lacewood for having opened a door that had previously been closed between them.

"At first," the earl admitted. "But less and less as the years passed. Certain people burrow themselves deep into one's heart, and their going leaves a greater void on that account. Better a heart riddled with such holes, I think, than one perfectly intact...untouched."

His grandfather made it sound so simple. Lucius knew better.

When a man's heart was in danger of becom-

ing nothing but a collection of holes, wasn't he
obliged to protect the tattered remnants he had
left?

"About Miss Lacewood, Grandfather..."

He'd better have out with it—admit he'd fled
like a coward before Angela Lacewood had a
chance to refuse him a second time. Somehow
he must make his grandfather understand that he
could not go begging her repeatedly.

Before he could finish what he'd started to say,
a discreet knock sounded on the library door and
the earl's valet peered in. "Miss Lacewood to see
you, my lords."

The earl set his book aside and rose to his feet
rather unsteadily. "Bring her in, Carruthers, by
all means. The dear girl hardly needs to stand on
ceremony after all these years."

Angela Lacewood breezed into the library,
looking a trifle windblown but all the more attractive for it. "I hope you don't mind my arriv-
ing out of the blue, my lord, but this seems to be
a day for unexpected visits."

When she held out her hand to him, the earl
raised her fingers to his lips. "The only thing
more pleasant than anticipating a regular visit
from you, my dear, is receiving a surprise one."

As she lavished the earl with a fond smile of
dazzling intensity, Miss Lacewood cast Lucius
a fleeting glance in which he perceived sorrow,
valiantly restrained. So she did have some skill in
masking her emotions, as she'd claimed.

Lucius was grateful that her pretense of felicity appeared to convince the earl.

Carruthers fetched her a chair and set it close to his master's. When she thanked him with greater warmth than so small a service merited, the desiccated old stick beamed from ear to ear as he tottered back out of the library.

To his bafflement, Lucius felt a sharp, savage little twist deep in his gut. Surely it could not be anything so absurd as…envy?

"Do sit down, my dear." The earl indicated the chair his valet had brought for her. "You sound a trifle winded."

Angela had run most of the way from Netherstowe, yet it was only when she'd caught sight of Lucius Daventry again that she had found herself unaccountably breathless.

"Thank you, my lord." She lowered herself onto the seat, as the earl settled back into his favorite chair. "You're always such an attentive host."

Lord Daventry did not resume his seat on the footstool from which he had risen so abruptly when she'd entered the room. Instead he skulked some distance away with his hands clasped behind his back, regarding her with an expression of thinly veiled wariness.

Clearly her unexpected arrival had put him on his guard, the way his appearance at Netherstowe had put Angela on hers. Forgetting for a moment her intent to show the man some compassion, she wondered how he liked this taste of his own medicine.

Perhaps he feared she might break down and tell the earl of his doctor's dire prediction. If so, Lord Daventry had vastly underestimated her.

The next words out of his mouth disabused Angela of that notion. "Shall I give the two of you some privacy to enjoy your visit?"

Though the stiffness of his question irritated her, she saw past it and silently chided herself. Lord Daventry had been enjoying a quiet, private moment with his beloved grandfather, which she had interrupted. How many more such moments might they have in the coming weeks?

"Please don't go, my lord!"

"No indeed," insisted the earl in a voice that must have once been rich and resonant like his grandson's but which now put Angela in mind of threadbare satin. "It is not as though Miss Lacewood has come courting *me*. I should be the one to withdraw and give the two of you a private moment."

He shook his head and gave a soft chuckle. "But I don't intend to."

Angela fought a losing battle against the stinging blush that crept into her cheeks. At the same time, a yawning emptiness gaped within her, one that she sensed was but a foretaste of the bottomless void her dear friend's passing would create in her life.

"I leave subtlety to the young," said the earl. "You have time for it. At my age, I fear one must be indelicately frank if one expects to achieve one's aims."

He wagged his forefinger at Angela. "So no maidenly evasion about what brought you to Helmhurst, my dear. I hope you won't hold it against my grandson that he told me he proposed to you."

"Grandfather!" barked Lord Daventry.

The earl dismissed his grandson's protest with a slight wave of his hand. "Carruthers and I extracted the confession under torture, of that you may be certain."

For some reason the dry quip made Angela's eyes prickle with tears she dared not shed.

Perhaps Lord Daventry sensed her distress, for he provided her a reasonable cover. "Please, Grandfather, you are embarrassing Miss Lacewood."

She raised a hand to shield her brow, which gave her the moment she needed to compose herself.

"Is that so, my dear?" The earl sounded both surprised and contrite. "Well, you must pardon me as an old friend and an old fool. You know I'd never willingly do anything to distress you."

Angela reached for his hand. She would not see the earl's final months marred by the least shadow that was within her power to dispel.

"I've never doubted your kind intentions toward me, sir." She hoped he would attribute any slight moisture in her eyes to excessive modesty. "It's just that this has all taken me so greatly by surprise. I had no idea Lord Daventry knew of my existence, let alone that he entertained…tender feelings for me."

She stole a glance in the baron's direction only to find his gaze averted. His demeanor appeared as imperturbable as ever, yet it reminded Angela of the smooth surface of simmering water just prior to boiling.

She almost fancied she could hear his thoughts—
Tender feelings, indeed!

Somehow, believing she had flustered him, even a little, restored a bit of her composure, which he had so thoroughly rattled.

The earl seemed to enjoy sporting with his grandson, too. "You may depend upon it that I have made my grandson favorably aware of your existence, dear child."

"I hope you have not sung my praises so loud that Lord Daventry finds I cannot live up to your account of me."

"On the contrary," replied the earl with obvious relish. "He said I failed to do you justice."

"Really, Grandfather!" cried Lord Daventry, confirming Angela's suspicion about the simmering water. "If you mean to go on like this, then perhaps one of us *should* make himself scarce."

"Nonsense." The earl showed no sign of repentance. "What is wrong with relaying a word of praise to a young lady so vastly deserving of it."

He turned to Angela. "No wonder you refused him, my dear, with that attitude. I expect his marriage proposal had all the romantic trappings of a legal writ."

"Enough of this." Lord Daventry stalked toward the library door. "I shall leave the pair of you to abuse me to your hearts' content."

A sickening tide of shame propelled Angela out of her chair to come between Lucius Daventry and his means of escape. "Please, my lord, don't go."

Though she knew her next words would probably vex him, she could not fathom why. Not that it mattered, for she could not bite them back. "I'm sorry. We didn't mean to torment you, truly."

"Speak for yourself, girl." The earl leaned farther back in his chair, resting his chin against his clasped hands. "I have been chaffing my grandson like this since he was half his present size. He's never taken an ounce of umbrage until today, which may betray his partiality for you."

Angela cast the earl a look of pretended severity. "I think you had better stop it before you change his opinion of me."

She raised her eyes to Lord Daventry. "Shall we punish your grandfather by going away to talk in private?"

The corners of the baron's firm lips raised ever so slightly. "It would serve him right, the old meddler."

"Away with you, then." The earl made a great show of picking up a book from the small table beside his chair. "Be warned, though, I am apt to sulk."

He was only teasing, Angela knew, but since this was all meant to be for his benefit, she did not want the earl to miss a moment of their performance.

"In that case—" She addressed herself to Lord Daventry "—I came to tell you that I hope you did not mistake my hesitation in accepting your proposal as a sign that I meant to refuse. From what your grandfather has said, I fear you have."

"I could scarcely blame you," the baron replied. "My grandfather is right—it was badly done on my part and far too precipitous. I...apologize."

"Does that mean you wish to withdraw your offer?" she asked, not entirely certain how she hoped he would answer.

Before Lord Daventry could reply, the earl spoke up. "Not unless he wishes me to hurl this book at his head."

Perhaps the baron heard the gleeful ring in his grandfather's voice, for his compelling green gaze searched hers, wordlessly inquiring if she could tolerate the two of them going on like this for... as long as necessary.

He had said her face was an open book. Now Angela hoped he could read her unspoken response, for suddenly she knew what answer she wanted from him.

"My offer stands, Miss Lacewood." He held out his hand to her. "And not because I entertain any fear of my grandfather braining me with his volume of *Rasselas*."

When she placed her hand in his, Lord Daventry bowed over it, grazing her fingers with his lips. The chaste gesture made Angela feel as if she were a saucer brimming with syllabub—frothy and intoxicating.

"In that case, Lord Daventry, I accept." Before she realized what she was doing, Angela raised his hand to *her* lips to seal their bargain.

"Marvelous!" The earl applauded their convincing performance.

That was all it had been, Angela told herself, a command performance to entertain and edify a very special audience.

During the coming weeks, she must take care to remember that, and not fall under the perilous illusion that Lord Lucifer was capable of caring for her.

Or she for him.

The sensation of Angela Lacewood's divine lips grazing the back of his fingers brought all manner of provocative, unwelcome memories whispering through Lucius. In his younger years, when his looks had made women swoon, he'd been something of a rakehell, gorging himself on a banquet of pleasures afforded by his wealth, his title and his handsome countenance.

Since the war, and the disfigurement that made women swoon for the opposite reason, he had become as devoted a celibate as he had once been a libertine. Until just now, Lucius Daventry had not realized how little he'd missed the shallow diversions of his youth.

But, his lovely, new fiancée threatened to rouse the sleeping hunger within him, damn her!

The earl held out his hands to Lucius and Angela. "I believe this calls for a toast!"

Lucius made every effort not to drop Miss Lacewood's hand too abruptly, while battling an equally fierce inclination to kiss it again.

Toast, indeed! They could toast his peace of mind like a crumpet over the glowing coals of his rekindled lust.

"Tell Carruthers to fetch us a bottle of our best champagne from the cellar," the earl ordered Lucius. "On second thought, have him hunt up three or four so the servants may also drink to your happiness."

The gleam of delight in his grandfather's eyes countered the reservations that gnawed at Lucius. Three months would pass by far too quickly. Besides, what was a gift worth without a little sacrifice?

"You don't want to set the cook drunk, and have her burn our dinner," he said as he set off to relay the earl's instructions.

"Drink half a dozen toasts and we'll never notice." The earl beckoned Miss Lacewood toward him.

Lucius hesitated at the library door long enough to see her stoop and ask, "May I call you Grandfather from now on?"

The earl pulled her into his embrace, "My dearest girl, nothing could make me happier!"

As Lucius watched them together, a foolish, wistful ache settled deep in his belly. With dogged effort, he reinforced his flagging composure and hurried off to order the wine.

He returned to the library a few minutes later to hear his grandfather ask Miss Lacewood, "How soon shall we set the date? June is always a pleasant month for weddings."

Set a date? A bottomless sensation engulfed Lucius, as though the library's parquet floor had suddenly opened up beneath his feet.

Before he could stammer out something that might have exposed their ruse to the earl, as well as making himself sound a complete ass, Miss Lacewood came to his rescue.

"We dare not make plans until my aunt and uncle return from the Continent. In fact, I probably shouldn't have accepted Lord Daventry's proposal without their permission."

Lucius privately applauded her quick thinking.

"Old Bulwick?" scoffed the earl, who bettered his neighbor's age by at least two decades. "Nonsense! You've reached years of discretion?"

"Decidedly on the shelf," Miss Lacewood admitted. "I don't doubt my aunt and uncle will be delighted to see me make such a fine match, at last. However, they can be somewhat…jealous of their privileges."

"Yes, yes," the earl grumbled. "Since you'll be remaining in the neighborhood, I suppose we ought not to offend your relations by wedding you off in their absence."

Carruthers appeared just then, bearing a tray

with three tall slender glasses and a bottle of champagne. With a murmur of thanks, Lucius set about uncorking and pouring the wine.

Once in possession of his glass, the earl raised it toward Miss Lacewood in a salute. "Let us drink to the most beautiful addition to the Daventry family in many a year—my dear Angela. I hope I may take the liberty of calling you by your name, since you propose to call me Grandfather."

She nodded, lowering her gaze while a self-conscious little smile hovered on her lips.

"To Angela." Lucius raised his glass, adding his voice to his grandfather's. Her name sparkled on his tongue with an intoxicating sweetness that rivaled the champagne.

The earl sipped his wine and gave an approving nod.

"Anxious as I am to see you settled, perhaps a long betrothal is not a bad thing in your case. The two of you need some time to become better acquainted before you marry."

Before Lucius could voice his agreement, the earl added, "Of course, I know why you've gone and gotten yourselves engaged in the first place."

Lucius felt his jaw go slack as his fiancée sputtered her champagne.

Chapter Four

Champagne dancing its way down her throat was one of the sweetest luxuries Angela had ever enjoyed. Champagne surging back up, its innocent little bubbles scouring the back of her throat and nose, was another matter entirely!

When she heard the earl declare that he knew the true reason behind her engagement to his grandson, she could not stifle a gasp, which set her choking on her wine. Her eyes watered and she struggled to catch her breath between bouts of violent coughing.

She managed to hold on to her champagne flute long enough for a steadier hand to take it from her. A moment later she felt Lord Daventry gently tapping her on the back.

"Are you all right, Angela?" he asked. "Can I get anything for you?"

If she'd been able to reply, she might have told him it did no good posing questions to someone who was coughing too hard to speak. All

the same, the warm concern of his tone eased
her enough that she was able to catch her breath
again. Before long, she had her coughing under
control.

"Poor child!" The earl sounded flustered. "I
hope you didn't think I was implying any sinister motive to your betrothal. I only meant that I
know you've both undertaken it to please me, in
which you have heartily succeeded, I assure you."

Angela felt doubly foolish. She should have
known the earl was not referring to his doctors'
grim predictions. Now her excessive reaction to
his remark might rouse his suspicions.

Fortunately, a lifetime of practice smoothing
over her many blunders came to Angela's rescue.
"It had nothing to do with anything you said,
my lord, truly. This was the first time I'd drunk
champagne, that's all. The bubbles tickled the
back of my throat."

"First taste of champagne?" The earl shook
his head at his grandson. "And Bulwick fancies
himself a gentleman?"

The hand with which Lord Daventry had been
patting Angela's back came to rest there for a
moment, in what he might have meant as a com-
radely gesture of approval for her quick thinking.

Her reaction to his innocent touch was anything but innocent. A dark, ravenous energy
stirred within her and began to rove through
her flesh. Her thoughts swarmed with long-suppressed curiosity about the mysterious rites of
lovers.

To her vast relief, those immodest fancies did not blaze on her face for the gentlemen to see.

"Sip slowly, my dear, if you are not used to it," the earl advised her in a most solicitous tone before taking a drink himself.

Lord Daventry left Angela's side to refill her glass. His brief touch had made her hunger for more. When he returned with her champagne she made a deliberate effort to brush her fingers against his when he handed the flute to her.

Was it possible he felt something of the strange force he had excited in her? she wondered as he lifted his gaze to hers and held it for a taut, expectant instant.

The earl's voice broke in on their fleeting private moment. "Perhaps I should be ashamed of myself for meddling in your lives." He regarded Angela and his grandson with transparent satisfaction. "But I'm not. This modern notion of *love matches* is folly if you ask me. Let a young man choose his own mistress, I say, but let him be guided by his elders in the choice of a wife."

"You needn't preach to me, Grandfather. I quite agree." As Lord Daventry retreated to the mantel with his own champagne, he tossed the remark off in such a casual tone that Angela decided she must have imagined the potent flicker of awareness between them.

Hoping to quench her own futile preoccupation with his lordship, Angela savored a deep draft of her wine, and then another.

"Wise boy," the earl commended his grandson.

"It occurs to me that if I must postpone the happy occupation of planning a wedding, we might at least celebrate your betrothal properly."

"Forgive me." Lord Daventry lifted his glass, from which he'd scarcely taken a drink. "I thought that's what we're doing."

Either the earl did not hear, or he chose to ignore his grandson's comment.

"A ball!" he cried, then immediately toasted his idea with another drink. "I've become an awful old recluse these past few years, turning down invitations and never going out anywhere. It's time I rectified that by hosting a gathering."

A ball? For her? Under ordinary circumstances the prospect would have filled Angela with alarm. At the moment it sounded a perfectly jolly idea. She suspected that might be due to the glass of champagne she'd emptied so quickly, but she didn't care.

A ball. The very word conjured up visions from fairy stories, for Angela had no firsthand experience to counter them.

Invitations to her cousins, Clemence and Camilla, had never included her. Aunt Hester thought the local Assembly Hall quite beneath the notice of her household, so Angela had never been allowed to go there. Uncle sometimes hosted house parties at which there might be a little dancing. But they were nothing compared to a real ball at a great house like Helmhurst.

With herself as the guest of honor.

"A ball?" Lord Daventry's voice slashed through

her soap bubble and rainbow daydreams. "Have you taken leave of your senses, Grandfather?"

That miserable man! Angela's lower lip thrust out. He wouldn't let her have any fun at all out of this engagement, would he?

Before the earl could reply, Angela took up her cudgels on his behalf. "Where are your manners, Lucius Daventry? That's no way to speak to your grandfather. And what's wrong with a ball, if I may ask? You make it sound like some sort of debauchery."

She had just enough discretion left to keep from calling him *Lord Lucifer* to his face, or suggesting that a night of debauchery might accord well with his wicked reputation.

What if Tibby was right about Lord Lucifer after all? Angela wondered as she met his baleful glare. What if he did put curses on people?

Good Lord! Lucius cursed under his breath. A single glass of champagne and the silly chit was foxed.

He could barely refrain from groaning, especially when his grandfather appeared to endorse the young lady's tipsy talk.

"Angela's quite right, my boy." The earl lobbed his words back at Lucius. "In the first place, I taught you better manners than that, and in the second, I believe this engagement of yours is the perfect excuse for a little festivity."

All his old friends...and enemies strutting about his quiet sanctuary, staring at his masked face, whispering to one another about what had happened to him. *Poor Daventry. Such a shame. And he used to be so handsome—the toast of the ton.*

Why didn't the old man just order one of his limbs amputated for amusement? Lucius wondered. Perhaps his helpful fiancée could wield the surgeon's saw, damn her!

Angela rose from her chair and walked toward Lucius with a weaving gait that looked graceful but precarious.

"If a ball to celebrate our engagement will amuse your grandfather, isn't that reason enough for us to agree?" Her large liquid eyes and lopsided smile beseeched him in a manner he found difficult to resist. "After all, wasn't that the whole point of—?"

He had to silence the fuddled little fool before she blurted out everything. Perhaps because he'd thought more about kissing in the past several hours than he had in the previous three years, Lucius seized on the one means to quiet his fiancée that would least arouse his grandfather's suspicions.

Catching Angela's hand, he pulled her into his arms and kissed her as if he meant it. That would teach the little goose to mind her tongue!

He had not forgotten *how* to kiss a woman, Lucius was gratified to discover, as he claimed Angela's delectable lips. What he had forgotten, or tried to forget, was how it *felt* to kiss a woman.

Unless this one was somehow different from all the others.

The aftertaste of champagne he imbibed from her had the most delicate bouquet, with heightened sweetness and sparkle. His head began to spin as though he'd guzzled an entire bottle. He finally parted from her as reluctantly as a drunkard from his favorite bottle.

His kiss had the effect he'd hoped in temporarily robbing Angela of speech. Lucius had not anticipated that it might have a similar effect upon him.

Meanwhile, the earl continued to sit with his back to them, sipping his champagne and turning a deaf ear to whatever minor liberties the newly betrothed couple might be taking.

"D-did it ever occur to you," Lucius asked, when he had finally regained command of his vocal organs, "that I might prefer to keep my engagement a private matter?"

Though he addressed his grandfather, Lucius shot Angela a look that he hoped would penetrate her tipsy haze and the dumbstruck outrage of his sudden kiss.

The more public their engagement, the more difficult it would be to break when the time came. Not that Lucius cared much on his own account, but the scandal might ruin Angela's chances of contracting a proper marriage later on.

Why did the prospect of her wedding someone else bring such a sour taste to his mouth?

"Privacy is one thing, my dear boy," replied

the earl, "but this smacks of something furtive. Surely you don't wish to encourage any ridiculous tattle that you're ashamed of this connection?"

"Of course not!"

Lucius stalked over to the side table where the champagne bottle rested. He needed another drink. He also needed to put some distance between himself and Angela, lest the urge to kiss her again should overpower him.

"I doubt anyone will think such a thing simply because you fail to host a ball. It's well-known I've retired from society."

The earl gazed heavenward. "That has fueled enough unsavory gossip to tarnish our family name for a generation. I, for one, am anxious to lay such malicious talk to rest. A lavish celebration of your betrothal to a sweet, beautiful young lady like Angela should go a long way to rehabilitate your reputation."

For such a frail old stick, his grandfather had a will of iron, Lucius mused with a mixture of annoyance and admiration. The earl would not be balked. He would keep answering every objection Lucius threw up, raising the matter tomorrow and the next day and the next until he wore his grandson down.

It didn't help that his grandfather had recruited an ally in Angela Lacewood. From halfway across the large room, her wistful, coaxing gaze found Lucius with the power and precision of a well-aimed artillery barrage.

Surely she didn't believe he would be *ashamed* to wed a beauty like her?

Lucius bolted another drink of champagne. He had one last scrap of ammunition. Though it was of a powerful calibre, particularly against Angela's soft heart, pride made him shrink from deploying it.

"Do either of you understand what you're asking of me? To spend an evening under the glare of chandeliers?"

The looks on both their faces told him he need not mention the glare of so many curious stares.

"Apologies, my boy," the earl murmured. "I hadn't considered that."

His grandfather looked so disappointed Lucius rather wished he'd held his tongue. As Angela had been about to say before he'd stopped her with his kiss, the whole point of their sham engagement was to make the earl's last months happy. Compared with what he'd already undertaken in that cause, what was one little ball?

"I know!" cried Angela. "What if we *don't* hold it indoors under all those bright lights?"

Once again she approached him with unsteady steps. Was she not afraid he might kiss her again?

"Helmhurst has some of the most charming grounds in the country. Why don't we hold the ball outside, under the stars?" As the soft shine of starlight shimmered in her eyes, Lucius knew he was lost.

"By Jove!" The earl clapped his hands like a

child delighted with a new plaything. "What a clever idea, my dear!"

"That champagne has put lots of clever ideas in my head." Angela held Lucius in her gaze. "Could we not make this outdoor ball a masquerade, as well?"

A masquerade? What could he say to that? His appearance might not draw a single curious glance among a throng of masked guests.

"If you are both so resolved upon it—" Lucius looked from his grandfather to Angela "—I suppose I have no choice but to surrender. A ball you want, then a ball you shall have. So novel and magnificent a ball it will give the ton something pleasant to gossip about for a change."

"Do you mean it?" Angela looked ready to throw her arms around him, but at the last moment she curbed her tipsy elation in favor of grasping his hand instead. "Thank you!"

Lucius almost succeeded in convincing himself that he approved of her tardy display of discretion.

Was it the champagne making her throw caution to the winds? Angela wondered in a curiously detached sort of way as she clung to Lucius Daventry's hand. Or was it the unsettling effect his presence continued to work upon her?

So much about his stance and manner demanded she keep her distance. Yet, some contrary force, of which he seemed unaware, called to her. As potent as it was puzzling, that force left her with no choice but to respond.

If his lordship had intended the swift, heart-stopping kiss he'd thrust upon her to punish her for opposing him, or frighten her into being more compliant in future, he had made a grave miscalculation. From the moment he'd left her clinging to the mantelpiece to keep from melting to the floor, she'd begun to wonder how she might provoke him into another one.

When he'd executed a sudden about-face, agreeing to host a ball for her, Angela had wanted very much to kiss *him*.

But she couldn't, no matter how much champagne she had in her belly. For many years she had made the mistake of trying to give affection where it was not wanted. Bitter experience had cured her of that tendency.

"I knew you'd come around, my boy." The earl could not have sounded better pleased if his grandson had agreed to the ball straightaway.

Lord Daventry extracted his hand from Angela's eager grip. "If there's one lesson I learned under General Wellington, it's to know when I'm outgunned."

"Don't sulk," said the earl. "You'll have a splendid time. We all will."

Before Lord Daventry could phrase a pithy reply, a familiar, discreet knock sounded on the library door and the earl bid his valet to enter.

"The household wishes to thank milords for the champagne and to extend our compliments to Lord Daventry and Miss Lacewood on the happy news of their engagement." The only sign that Carruthers had partaken of the celebratory refreshment was a rather glassy stare. "Also, milords, Cook begs to inquire whether Miss Lacewood will be staying to dinner."

"Indeed she will." Belatedly the earl cast a glance at Angela. "You will, won't you, my dear? We can discuss the guest list for this ball of ours."

A wave of dismay broke over Angela as she exchanged fond smiles with her dearest friend. Nothing would induce her to shadow his remaining time with the knowledge of how brief it would be. But the champagne had loosened her tongue and eroded her natural discretion.

She had better not stay to risk a blunder from which Lord Daventry might not be able to rescue her.

"I wish I could." She shook her head. "But I promised Tibby I'd be home for supper. She'll worry if I don't get back soon."

Seeing the earl's disappointment, she added, "Tomorrow night, perhaps? Now that I'm to be one of the family, may I invite myself to dinner?"

"From now on, a place will be set for you every evening," the earl assured her. "Carruthers, order the gig harnessed so Lord Daventry can drive Miss Lacewood back to Netherstowe in time for her dinner."

"That's not necessary." Angela was not certain she could trust herself alone with Lucius Daventry in her present condition. "I've been coming and going from Helmhurst on foot for years."

"Never this late," the earl countered. "Besides, it looks apt to rain."

The set of his countenance told Angela he was no more likely to be swayed over this than he had in the matter of the ball.

"Very well, then. Thank you." She stole a quick glance at Lord Daventry.

Though he had raised no objection and his features betrayed nothing beyond polite resignation, Angela knew he could be no better pleased with the arrangements than she.

Indeed, Lord Daventry's silence spoke eloquently for him. He uttered scarcely a word as Angela and the earl said their goodbyes and made plans for the next day. With mute courtesy he escorted her to the forecourt, where a trim two-wheeled carriage with a leather canopy awaited them.

The distance between Helmhurst and Netherstowe was much greater by road than cross-country. Lord Daventry appeared ready to maintain his silence the whole way. As they drove along the deserted country road, rain kept up a gentle patter against the canopy, while the horse's hooves beat a muted rhythm. Dark, weeping clouds dimmed the waning daylight to a level the baron seemed able to tolerate but which Angela found dismal.

Her light, bubbly humor, induced by the champagne, had since soured and gone flat. Lord Daventry's brooding, stone-faced silence reproached Angela more harshly than words could have done. In Lord Bulwick's household, displeasure was frequently expressed by not speaking.

Angela's accustomed response to such wordless censure had always been to make herself as inconspicuous as possible until she was tacitly forgiven, soothing her injured feelings with sweets from Tibby's pantry. But there was nowhere to hide in the little gig and not so much as a peppermint drop or lemon pastille to comfort her.

A tempest brewed in Angela's breast until she could no longer contain it. "Go ahead and say what you're thinking, Lord Daventry!"

Her sudden outburst startled the horse, who tossed its mane and whinnied.

Lucius Daventry kept looking straight ahead at the road. "I haven't the least idea what you're talking about, Miss Lacewood."

Angela knew she should not say anything more, but it was such a great relief to vent her feelings that she couldn't turn back. "If you expect me to believe that, you must think me insufferably stupid, in addition to everything else."

"Everything else?"

Though she could only see the masked half of his face in profile, Angela could picture his other brow raised.

"You know," she insisted, "bothersome, unreliable and…about as pleasant to kiss as that horse!"

The flesh of his lean, angular cheek tensed. Could he be fighting back a smile?

Lord Daventry pulled hard on the reins. The horse and gig came to a stop on a lonely strip of road that skirted the base of a tall hill.

The baron looked more than a little menacing as he turned to face her. Suddenly Tibby's dire warnings about Lord Lucifer did not seem quite so ridiculous.

"Very well, Miss Lacewood. Since you demand to know what I'm thinking and since you seem determined to attribute all manner of disagreeable opinions to me, I am compelled to set the record straight between us."

Angela braced herself.

Lord Daventry looked so severe. Perhaps he thought even worse of her than she'd suspected. Bad enough imagining someone's low opinion of her. Were there enough jam buns in the whole county to soothe her crushed feelings once she'd heard the blunt truth from his lordship's own lips?

"I think you are every bit as meddlesome as my grandfather, in your own way," the baron began. "And I fear the two of you will use this betrothal to reform a reputation I would prefer to keep. Not to mention turn the life with which I am perfectly content upside down and inside out."

Compared to what Angela had been expecting, this sounded almost like praise.

She opened her mouth to reply, but Lord Daventry raised his hand. "You ordered me to tell you what I think, Miss Lacewood. Kindly have the courtesy to hear me out."

So there was more to come. Angela pressed her lips together.

"I think you had better avoid champagne in future unless you *wish* to commit an indiscretion. And finally, though I have never touched lips with a horse, I believe I can say with some authority that yours are far preferable to kiss."

As abruptly as he had stopped the gig, Lord Daventry flicked the reins again and turned his attention back to driving. Angela sat beside him, steeled for a blow that had never come.

Perhaps his gruff but temperate words emboldened her. Or perhaps the aftereffects of the champagne continued to loosen her tongue. "You've kissed a lot of women, haven't you?"

"At one time," he replied after a significant hesitation. "See here, I'm sorry I kissed you, but not because I found it unpleasant. Now, can we talk about something else?"

Did that mean he'd found it pleasant? As pleasant as she had?

They turned into the long lane that wound its way to Netherstowe. Before Angela could think of another topic of conversation, the gig had drawn to a halt before the front entrance.

Lord Daventry climbed out, then came around to Angela's side of the carriage to help her down. In spite of the rain, they stood there for an awkward moment of parting, forgetting to release each other's hand.

Angela stared up at the baron, pondering the mysteries guarded by his inscrutable green gaze. "If you ever need to kiss me again…I won't mind."

A flash of savage intensity blazed in his eyes just then, like a jagged bolt of lightning across a dark sky. "Let us hope the need will never arise."

If he had spit in her face, Angela could not have felt more thoroughly mortified. Wrenching her fingers from his grasp, she ran into the house and slammed the door behind her for the second time that day.

Had Lord Daventry thought she was begging him for something he could not give her? Well, she hadn't been!

Had she?

Angela wished she could be certain.

Chapter Five

"**W**hat do you want with me?" Miles Lacewood squinted into the dimly lit study his housemaster had made available to Lucius for this meeting. "And who are you?"

Was it only yesterday he had been posed those same questions by the boy's sister at Netherstowe? His tightly guarded emotions had been pushed and pulled in so many directions since then, it seemed to Lucius that a fortnight must have passed.

"Lord Daventry of Helmhurst," he introduced himself, "a neighbor of your uncle's."

The boy's eyes widened. He was a well-made lad, tall for his age, with the same fair coloring as his sister. "What brings you to my school, sir? Nothing's happened to Angela, has it?"

Not the kind of calamity young Mr. Lacewood anticipated, perhaps.

"Your sister is perfectly well, if that's what you mean. But something has occurred which will be to her benefit, and to yours, I hope." As always, Lucius chose his words with care. He did not want to speak of marriage or wedding when he intended neither. "Miss Angela and I became engaged yesterday."

"You must be joking." The boy had not meant to give voice to his thought, Lucius could tell, but the shock of the news had forced it out of him.

Young Lacewood had better learn to govern his tongue if he hoped to get on in the army.

"What makes you think I'm in jest?"

"I…that is…" The lad struggled to remedy his blunder. "I wasn't aware that you and Angela knew each other…so well."

"For some years, your sister has regularly visited my grandfather at Helmhurst."

The boy shrugged. "She never mentioned meeting you during those visits."

The implied misgivings about a connection between him and Angela Lacewood rubbed Lucius the wrong way. "Does your sister tell you about everyone she meets?"

The boy considered his lordship's question for a long moment. "Evidently not."

"Enough of this," snapped Lucius. "I assure you, we are betrothed. You may confirm the fact with your sister whenever you wish."

He turned his head, as though something in the housemaster's book-cluttered study had caught his attention. In fact, Miles Lacewood's frank stare at his mask unsettled Lucius. He sought to shield himself from it as he would have shielded his injured eye from the sun's relentless glare.

"You are completing your final term here," he continued. "I understand you would like to join your father's old regiment once your schooling is finished."

"The Twenty-Ninth Light Dragoons, sir." In his eagerness, the boy seemed to forget both his surprise over his sister's sudden engagement, and his wariness of Lord Daventry. "If only I could persuade Uncle Bulwick to buy me a commission. He's set on my going into the city, though."

Miles Lacewood wrinkled his well-shaped nose as if he could smell the drainage ditches of London's East End.

Lucius wished the lad did not remind him so forcefully of himself in his younger years. "While you'd rather be off in India, riding, playing polo and pigsticking?"

"I know there's a sight more to it than that, sir." The boy's whole face radiated enthusiasm for the soldiering life, just the same. "My father was killed at Laswaree when I was four years old. I still remember how splendid he looked in his uniform and how he used to hoist me up onto this saddle for a ride."

Lucius envied the boy's memories of his father. "I sympathize with your eagerness to follow in his footsteps. Growing up, I felt the same way about my father."

Something compelled him to add, "You know,

if our fathers had lived, I believe they might have encouraged us to pursue other paths in life."

How many officers' widows, desperate to sanctify their loss, had primed their sons to take up arms as they grew to manhood? Lucius wondered.

His own, certainly. Mrs. Lacewood, too?

"It wouldn't matter." The boy shook his head. "Soldiering is all I've ever wanted to do."

"In that case—" Lucius quenched a pang of guilt over what he was about to propose "—I am willing to purchase a commission for you, if you wish it."

"No!"

The boy's abrupt turnabout from his earlier show of eagerness caught Lucius by surprise. "Didn't you just say…?"

"I said I wanted to join my father's old regiment." The longing for it ached in Miles Lacewood's candid brown eyes, which reminded Lucius too much of Angela's. "I didn't say I would sell my sister for a commission."

"Sell your…?" Lucius fancied he could feel the slap of leather against his cheek. "That remark shows a decided want of delicacy, young man!"

"Delicate or not, that's why Angela agreed to marry you, isn't it?" The boy took a step toward Lucius, obviously afraid but refusing to be intimidated. "So you would do this for me?"

Lucius swung about to meet the lad's indignant glare. His pride smarted at the suggestion that no woman would marry him except to gain advantage of fortune, though he had insisted the same

thing to himself time and again. Had it been a futile attempt to toughen himself against the day he
would hear the indictment from someone else?

"You credit your sister's concern for your wel-
fare, my boy, but you underestimate both her good
sense and her integrity." Lucius found himself
grateful to Angela for making what he was about
to say true.

"Whatever her private reasons for accepting
my proposal, she refused my offer to buy you a
commission. I insisted. Though if you'd prefer to
work as a glorified clerk in some airless little of-
fice in the city, be my guest."

"No!" Miles Lacewood cried for the second
time in a very few minutes. This time a pleading
note had replaced his earlier indignation. "Perhaps I was too hasty. I did not want Angela obligated to you on my account. If you had a sister, I
believe you would understand, my lord."

"I do understand. The attitude does you credit,
my boy." Lucius had seen too many men eager to
sacrifice the happiness of their sisters or daughters for their own advantage.

"If you care for Angela and she for you, then
I am grateful enough that you have made her an
honorable proposal." The boy flashed a frank,
good-natured smile and held out his hand to Lucius. "I've always secretly hankered to have a
brother."

So had he. Yet Lucius found himself hesitant
to grasp Miles Lacewood's hand. He could not

help feeling it would confirm all those innocent falsehoods the boy seemed anxious to believe.

He did not *care for* Angela Lacewood, no matter how much she had preoccupied his thoughts in the past twenty-four hours. Neither did the young lady care for him, in spite of her charitable offer to suffer another of his kisses as a means to convince the earl of their mutual devotion. He hadn't made Miss Lacewood the kind of honorable proposal her brother believed.

She would never have accepted him if he had.

This was not a convenient time for an attack of scruples, Lucius decided as he forced himself to shake hands with Miles Lacewood. "Then let us sit down and talk some more about this commission business."

The boy considered for a moment. "I suppose it wouldn't hurt to talk."

Lucius Daventry recognized a tone of surrender when he heard it. So far his campaign was progressing according to plan, with one slight but troublesome exception—his inconvenient fascination with Angela Lacewood.

If he was not very careful in future, Lucius feared his beautiful fiancée might begin to wield an undesirable influence over him.

For the first time in years of frequent visits to Helmhurst, Angela found her senses on heightened alert. She scanned the wide gallery, vigilant for any half-opened door or someone lurking behind a piece of statuary. She listened for the faintest footstep or squeaking door hinge behind her.

What foolishness! she chided herself. In the middle of a bright morning, with golden spring sunshine pouring through the tall windows that lined the outer wall of the gallery, she was in no danger of encountering Lucius Daventry.

Just because he had ventured out in daylight yesterday did not mean his lordship meant to break from his customary habits altogether. In the three years since he'd returned home from the war, she had only glimpsed him from a distance once or twice.

All the time she'd been paying her visits to the earl, Lord Daventry had been somewhere on the floor above in a shuttered and curtained room, enjoying his daytime slumber. He was probably asleep upstairs at this very moment.

The thought of it lulled her apprehension of meeting him again so soon after their awkward parting of the previous night. Yet at the same time it stirred a potent awareness of his presence in the house, as well as an unseemly curiosity.

Did his lordship sleep in a nightshirt? Or did he sprawl naked beneath the bedclothes, wrapped in the subtle but provocative musk of sleep? While Angela made her way toward the earl's library, her imagination hovered over the slumbering form of Lord Lucifer.

"There you are at last, my dear!" cried the earl when she stepped into the room. "I was beginning to fear you'd had second thoughts about marrying my grandson, and had deserted me as a result."

"Never!" Angela protested. "I overslept this morning, that's all."

After a night tossing and turning with second, third and fourth thoughts about the wisdom of accepting Lord Daventry's offer. Only the fear that backing out so soon would make it too awkward to visit Helmhurst had decided her to proceed with their unorthodox engagement.

"What shall we do today?" she asked brightly, hoping to distract the earl from any further talk of Lord Daventry. "Read? Play chess? Shall I write a letter for you?"

"No, no, no." The earl planted his hands on the arms of his chair and pushed himself to his feet with some effort. "Have you forgotten, my dear? We have a ball to plan."

"The ball, of course."

Angela fetched his walking stick and offered him her elbow for support on the other side. All the while, she tried to summon up the enthusiasm she'd felt for the project last night when the earl had first proposed it.

Perhaps her eagerness had been born of too much champagne.

The earl started for the library door with steps that seemed stronger and steadier than they had in some time. "This is a fine morning to take a stroll around the grounds and talk over our plans."

The sunshine, fresh air and mild exertion would do him good, Angela reflected. They might

sharpen his appetite and make him sleep more
soundly. Planning for the ball would give him
something to look forward to. Something to occupy his energy without overtaxing it.

The earl's enthusiasm for this match between
her and his grandson was obviously proving a
tonic. Could it be that, taken together, they might
provide powerful enough medicine to extend his
days beyond the physicians' grim reckoning?

"I take it Lord Daventry will not be joining
us?" Angela strove to keep her tone casual as she
slanted a glance toward the staircase.

The earl's valet appeared in the entryway bearing his lordship's old-fashioned tricorn hat.

"Heavens, no." The earl donned his hat as they
stepped through the open door into the morning's
lavish sunshine. "My grandson is long gone."

Gone where and for how long? Angela found
herself wondering. The earl's cheerful announce-
ment *should* have brought her a swift sense of
relief, but it didn't. Instead a queer pang of disappointment twisted her insides. Lord Daventry's
absence mocked her shameful fancy of hovering
over him while he slept.

Though she knew any sign of interest from her
would only please the earl, Angela resisted betraying her curiosity about his grandson's where-
abouts.

The earl needed no prompting, though. "He
was up and away long before I left my bed. Said
nothing to the servants about where he was

bound, but I'm told he took no luggage, so I expect him home tonight."

They wandered down the wide path of golden-brown crushed rock that wound through Helmhurst's formal garden, abloom in a vivid tapestry of spring flowers.

"I don't care much where he's gone." The earl chuckled. "Just so long as he has. I rather like being an old hermit, but the boy is too young for that. He needs something or someone to draw him out again."

He gave Angela's arm a fond squeeze. "You are proving to be that someone, my dear. Just as I'd hoped."

Angela averted her face slightly as if to drink in the manicured perfection of the garden, when in fact she hoped the brim of her bonnet would hide her face from the earl long enough for her bright blush to subside.

"I wish I could take credit for Lord Daventry's absence, if it pleases you, Grandfather." How she loved being able to call him that. "But I doubt I had anything to do with it."

"Nonsense! What else could be responsible? Yesterday, for the first time in three years, my grandson ventured abroad by day. He returned home engaged to you. Today he's off again. Logic informs us that you must be behind it somehow."

"Perhaps," Angela agreed, albeit reluctantly. Better the earl should credit her influence than guess that Lord Daventry might have gone off to further consult with his grandfather's doctors.

The earl stopped and took a deep breath of the fresh spring air. "You know, I'm not such a blind old fool as to believe the pair of you love each other. But I believe you *can,* in time."

He did believe it, too. The certainty radiated from him as if the bright promise of spring sunshine had taken up residence in his heart.

Angela could not bring herself to meet his steadfast gaze. A great lump of unshed tears settled in the back of her throat.

Fortunately, the earl appeared to misunderstand her chagrin. "Don't think I fault you for accepting his proposal on other grounds, my dear. A woman must think of her future, no matter what sentimental twaddle one hears to the contrary these days."

"I have no designs upon your grandson's fortune, sir!" Thank heaven she could say that with a clear conscience.

The earl dismissed the notion with a swish of his walking stick. "Of course not, my dear. I should be the last to think it. But you have enough good sense not to hold his comfortable income against him. As I said last night, I know you accepted for the same reason he proposed—to please an old man who dotes on you both."

He would drive her to tears yet, drat him!

"Is it such a bad reason?" She could say that much, surely, without blurting out the truth.

"The best in the world, as far as I am concerned." The earl winked, then immediately turned sober. "Only do leave your heart open for something more, won't you?"

"I'll try." More words, ones she hadn't meant to give voice, came tumbling out. "If Lord Daventry will let me."

"Don't ask his leave." The earl began to move forward again, with greater strength in his step to match the force of his words. "What a lady does with her heart is her own business."

She should distract the earl from the whole disconcerting subject of hearts and her relationship with Lord Daventry. Talk about the ball might do it.

Before Angela could come up with any suitably diverting remark, the earl continued. "It may take some doing, but I expect you know that. In spite of his fortune and title, my grandson has not had an easy lot in life, poor fellow. Being raised by a dusty old stick like me, to begin with."

"You know that's not true," Angela insisted. "Why, he's devoted to you, far beyond what most men are to their fathers."

The earl looked pleased yet somehow regretful. "You may be right, though that is more to his credit than to mine. At the very least I should have taken better care in his religious education. You don't give any credence to that silly gossip about my grandson being involved in unholy practices...do you?"

"No!" Angela hoped she sounded more certain than she felt. "Of course not!"

The earl lifted his stick, pointing toward a hill

half a mile to the east. "That's where he goes, I believe, most nights after we've had dinner and spent a quiet evening together. After I retire to bed."

Angela stared toward the hill, the base of which she and Lord Daventry had skirted on the previous evening when he'd driven her home. "H-have you ever asked him what he does there?"

The earl lowered his stick by slow degrees until it hung at a dispirited angle. "Never. I'm not sure I could stomach his answer. And he has never volunteered the information."

As they walked on a little farther in silence, it seemed to Angela as if the distant hill cast an invisible shadow over the vibrant garden.

At last the earl spoke again. "My grandson has never told me what happened to him at Waterloo, either. That is how it's always been between us. We are both very fond of each other in our ways, I believe, but so much left unsaid."

Angela understood, perhaps better than the earl might have realized. Lord Daventry had an air about him that firmly discouraged anyone from trespassing on his privacy. Even when the man had something important he *wanted* to convey, like his proposal to her, he had gone about it in such a riddling, roundabout manner that she'd almost given up listening.

Surely the earl wasn't hoping his grandson would take *her* into his confidence? The very notion set Angela's heart in a rapid, shallow beat.

Like the earl, she wasn't certain she could bear to hear what Lord Daventry might tell her.

"This is no fit talk for such a fine day," the earl scolded himself. "We have a ball to plan—remember?"

Those words were as sweet to Angela's ears as a cup of warm chocolate in Tibby's kitchen at the end of a hard day.

"So we do." She glanced around her. "*Is* it feasible to hold one out of doors, do you think? When I proposed the idea last night, I had rather a lot of champagne in me."

"Tipsy or sober, it was a brilliant suggestion, my dear."

They had come to a fork in the path. The earl tugged Angela toward the south lawn.

"What ballroom in the kingdom can compare to this?" He raised his walking stick in a sweeping gesture.

Angela had passed this way many times. A few years ago, when the earl had been stronger, the two of them had often played pall-mall here on summer evenings. Now, looking at the south lawn in a new light, she had to agree it was perfectly suited to what she'd imagined.

The broad, tiled terrace would make an ideal area for dancing, while the lawn itself was so smooth and flat it could easily be set with clusters of small tables and chairs. As for the ornamental trees that ringed the lawn…

The earl pointed toward them. "What would

you think of hanging small tin lanterns from the branches?"

"Like fairy lights—marvellous!"

They enjoyed a leisurely walk, planning where the musicians should set up and where the supper buffet should go. They discussed the guest list at length, though most names the earl mentioned Angela only knew by reputation. Suddenly she was pleased on her own account that she'd suggested a masquerade.

All these illustrious guests might be less intimidating dressed up in fanciful costumes. In her own disguise, she might be able to pretend she was someone else. Not some countrified spinster living on the charity of wealthy relations, but a fine lady worthy to be the bride of a baron. If that didn't work, she could at least hope her mask might hide the worst of her alarm.

Deep in her heart, Angela felt a faint flicker of kinship toward Lord Daventry, for whom every day must be a masquerade.

Though not the pleasant kind she and the earl were planning.

Chapter Six

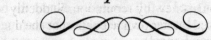

Lucius Daventry raised one arm to protect his weak eye against the blinding sunlight. With his other hand, he twitched back the heavy curtain that draped the window of his traveling coach and peered out. Spotting the familiar spire of St. Owen's in Grafton Renforth, he gave a grunt of satisfaction and let the curtain fall again. He would be home soon, and one benefit of this cursedly bright day should be a fine, clear night— perfect for his purposes.

Lucius yawned.

For the past forty-eight hours, he'd been venturing out into the world by day, then retiring to his bed at night. After three years as a night dweller, it felt unnatural, somehow.

He always slept fitfully during the night, when an eerie stillness settled over Helmhurst. The muted daytime sounds of the place—servants coming and going, distant voices—lulled him into a peaceful, dreamless slumber he had never expected to enjoy again after Waterloo.

For the next few months, he would have to skulk about the shadowed fringes of the waking world in order to make the most of his remaining time with his grandfather. With a twinge of regret, Lucius contemplated the hundreds of hours he had not used to full advantage during the past three years. Instead, while he'd been sleeping in his darkened chamber, Angela Lacewood had been enjoying his grandfather's society.

Lucius wanted to resent her for usurping his place, but his long-dormant sense of honor insisted that was not fair. Miss Lacewood had only taken on what he had abdicated. The lady would be within her rights to resent *his* intrusion on her accustomed afternoon visits with the earl.

She'd have to get used to the new order of things, Lucius told himself, as the carriage slowed and turned. They all would.

A few moments later, the carriage came to a stop in front of Helmhurst's entry. Lowering the brim of his hat and raising his arm, Lucius thrust the carriage door open and gained the sanctuary of the house in a few long, swift strides.

He handed his hat and cloak to a waiting footman. "My grandfather?"

"In the library, I believe, my lord."

Lucius took a few steps toward the east gallery, then hesitated. "Is Miss Lacewood with him, still?"

"I believe so, sir."

Why had he asked? Lucius wondered. It wasn't as though the young lady's presence would deter him from joining his grandfather. Perhaps it was simply a leftover compulsion from his military days to be forewarned about what awaited him wherever he was bound.

The level of light in the east gallery was almost bearable this late in the day. Lucius looked forward to the approaching summer solstice, after which the hours of daylight would begin to ebb again, allowing him greater freedom.

When he entered the library, his grandfather called out, "You see, my dear Angela, our prodigal has returned. Just as I prophesied. I hope you had a pleasant journey, my boy."

That was as close as the earl would come to inquiring where he'd been all day. In three years, his grandfather had never once asked where Lucius went at night.

"I didn't go for pleasure." Lucius made his way to a tall table beside the mantel which held two cut-glass decanters and an array of gleaming glassware. "I concluded my business to my satisfaction. The drive there and back was smooth and swift. What more could one ask for?"

Despite the early hour, he poured himself a liberal splash of brandy. With luck, the drink would ease his headache. "Care to join me, Grandfather? Miss Lacewood?"

What in the world had prompted him to ask her? Given how she'd reacted to a single glass of champagne last evening, Lucius hated to think what a jolt of well-aged brandy might do to her.

"Later, perhaps, my boy," replied the earl.

"Nothing for me either, thank you, Lord Daventry."

The clipped precision of Miss Lacewood's diction made Lucius glance her way, straight into her stony glare. Did she think he *wanted* to loosen her tongue with drink again so he would have a fresh opportunity to silence her with his lips?

What if he did? She'd claimed she wouldn't mind a kiss now and then, if the need arose. Or perhaps that had only been the champagne talking.

As she held his gaze, Angela Lacewood spoke again. "Will you settle a small wager for us, Lord Daventry?"

"A wager, eh?" Lucius fortified himself with a bolt of brandy. "I didn't think you were a gambling man, Grandfather."

"One must take a flutter now and again, dear boy, or life becomes sadly predictable." The earl regarded Lucius and Angela with an indulgent smile, as if they were a pair of precocious children whose antics amused him. "If I win, Angela will allow me the honor of purchasing her a costume for our masquerade."

The look that came over her face told Lucius this was the first Angela had heard of the stakes in their *wager*.

"I promised no such thing!" she cried, confirming his guess.

The earl gave a wheezy chuckle. "But you will, won't you? The stakes hardly matter if you're so certain you'll win."

Angela cast a cautious look at Lucius. "Very well, then. But what is to be my prize *when* I win?"

"Name it," the earl challenged her.

Her delicate brow furrowed as she pondered the possibilities. Lucius watched the subtle shifts of her features as she considered and discarded several in rapid succession. He recalled something she'd said the previous afternoon when he had fumbled his way through that farce of a proposal.

My situation may be modest, but my needs are few.

With all his heart, he envied Angela Lacewood her singular contentment.

"Come now," the earl prompted her. "There must be *something* you desire that is in my power to provide."

Her forehead unpuckered at last and she flashed a smile so brilliant it almost made Lucius flinch. "A pound of barley candy from the confectioner's shop in Rugby...."

An absurd twinge of regret stung Lucius. If only he'd known, he could have fetched some back with him. It was the sort of thing a lover should do for his lady, after all. And such a gesture, played for his grandfather's benefit, would have charmed the old fellow no end.

"Done!" The earl slapped the arm of his chair.

"And…" Miss Lacewood added in a tone that sounded significant.

"And?" The earl's bristling white brows rose.

"You and Lord Daventry will accompany me to church on Sunday."

Into the stunned silence that greeted her words, she added, "Matins or evensong, whichever suits you. The stained-glass windows mute the light, even on the brightest day. I'd like to introduce you both to our new vicar. He's only a young man, but quite a good preacher."

"We accept," declared the earl with the kind of reckless zeal Lucius had often seen come to grief at the tables.

"Grandfather…" He tried to protest, but the earl dismissed his objection with a look of pretended severity.

Lucius gave up.

"Oh, very well." He took another drink. "What is this wager of yours, anyway?" He wasn't at all sure he liked the idea of the two of them speculating about him.

Miss Lacewood exchanged a look with the earl. "Your grandfather and I had a difference of opinion about the reason for your journey."

"Did you?"

She nodded. "He believes your business had something to do with me. I disagree. Which of us is correct?"

Lucius found himself reluctant to disappoint her, even weighed against the prospect of making a spectacle of himself by attending church. "My grandfather is right, Miss Lacewood. I went to see your brother at his school, to talk over the idea of my purchasing a commission for him."

"Splendid!" cried the earl.

Whether his grandfather was referring to the commission for Miles Lacewood, or winning this strange wager with the boy's sister, Lucius could not be certain.

He glanced up from his drink to see his fiancée approaching. She wore a cream-colored gown in a gold-and-brown flowered print that flattered both her complexion and her eyes. Her hair was piled high on her head in a spume of golden curls.

As she passed near his grandfather's chair, Lucius found himself wishing the earl's walking stick might trip her up, so he could toss aside his glass and catch her in his arms again.

Today Angela Lacewood proved vexingly steady on her feet.

"I told you that was *not* necessary, Lord Daventry."

In the grip of potent, ungovernable emotions that felt as if they must belong to someone else, Lucius could not make sense of her words for a moment.

"The commission, you mean." He struggled to marshal his wits. "I told you I would insist. From what I saw of him today, I'd say your brother would make a pitiful excuse for a cit."

"I believe Uncle Bulwick will see that for himself, given time." Her firm, quiet tone informed Lucius that while she had no wish to distress his grandfather with an open quarrel, the subject was far from closed.

Lucius lowered his own voice to a coaxing murmur. "Would you prefer to be beholden to your aunt's husband than to me?"

Her gaze faltered. "I...suppose...I'm used to being beholden to my mother's family."

Though Lucius thought it unlikely his grandfather had overheard their exchange, the earl called out, "Do let him have his way, Angela. It's a gentleman's duty to do all he can to help his wife's family. There would be gossip if he failed to. You don't want that, surely?"

She turned toward the earl's chair, raising her voice so he would be sure to hear. "I suppose not."

Looking back at Lucius for an instant, she added, "Very well, Lord Daventry, I am in your debt."

Lucius sensed something deeply suggestive in those words, though he doubted she had meant them to be. They struck a bittersweet chord that resonated deep within him.

Miss Lacewood might consider herself in his debt, but unless he kept better guard on his heart, Lucius feared he might wake up one day to discover that he had fallen under her power.

Before he could betray his feelings with an unsanctioned glance or word, she slipped away to kneel beside his grandfather's chair.

"I know I promised to stay for dinner tonight,

but I've just remembered an urgent errand. I hope you'll excuse me."

The earl expelled a sigh that would have done credit to the celebrated actor, Mr. Kean. "I was looking forward to a pleasant dinner with the three of us. But if we must manage without you, I suppose we must."

"I believe you overrate my company." Angela chuckled. "But I give you my word I'll join you tomorrow night, no matter what else might intervene."

"We will hold you to it," the earl warned her. He glanced up at his grandson. "Order the gig harnessed, my boy, so you can drive Angela home."

An awkward succession of evening drives to Netherstowe stretched ahead of Lucius. He wanted to protest, but on what grounds?

Before he could say anything, Angela rose from her crouch beside his grandfather's chair to retrieve her bonnet. "Absolutely not. I accepted your kind offer of a drive last night because it was dark and raining. This is a fine evening. I won't waste an hour of Lord Daventry's time carting me back to Netherstowe when I can be there in a quarter the time on foot."

Lucius repressed the urge to cry, Hear! Hear!

Perhaps the earl sensed his unspoken endorsement, for he frowned at his grandson. "Stuff and nonsense! In my day it was not considered a waste of time for a gentleman to squire his lady home of an evening."

Miss Lacewood came to the rescue. "Don't scold Lord Daventry for my decision. I assure you, I enjoy the walk, especially at this time of year." As if to prove her resolve, she headed toward the library door.

"Rest well." She raised her hand in a parting wave to the earl. "I'll see you at the usual time tomorrow. If Lord Daventry's at home, he can help us choose a date for the ball."

Then she was gone, and it seemed to Lucius that something vital was missing from the room. Like the sky on a crisp winter night without the bright cluster of stars in Orion's belt.

He and his grandfather ate a rather subdued dinner that evening, followed by an uninspired chess match which Lucius deliberately fumbled in the closing moves to let the old man win.

At last the pedestal clock in the far corner of the library struck eleven.

"Time for bed." The earl rose from his chair and stretched. "You've had a long day, my boy. Will you be coming up, too?"

"Another drink first, I think, Grandfather." Lucius strode toward the brandy decanter, though they both knew it was only an excuse to linger here until he could slip out of the house.

A solemn, weary look came over the earl's face. "She's a marvelous girl, Lucius. You will give her a chance, won't you?"

The appeal was so different from anything Lucius had expected that he found it impossible to counter with any of his usual smooth evasions.

Fortunately, the earl did not wait for an answer, but tottered off to bed without a backward glance.

Lucius paced the library, trying to keep his grandfather's parting words out of his mind. He glanced toward the brandy decanter but resisted the impulse to occupy himself with the drink he'd pretended to want. Having gone without his accustomed rest today, he didn't care to have his wits or his senses muddled by spirits.

After what felt like an eternity but which the library clock insisted was no more than ten minutes, Lucius snuffed the candles and stole out of the house.

Once outside, he fairly guzzled a deep breath of cool, dewy-sweet night air. To think there were fool physicians who declared it unwholesome!

All day he had been mewed up indoors, held prisoner by the pitiless sun. Now he was free again, with the dark breeze playing through his hair and whispering its cool, seductive caress over his face.

His hands trembled with the eagerness of a green boy peeling the clothes off his first conquest. He lifted them to remove the hated mask, which he had worn today for many more hours than he was accustomed. It felt hot, itchy…suffocating.

The rush of pure, delicious relief when it came off rivaled what he had once felt in the throes of passion. Or so Lucius told himself.

Tilting his head back, he drank in the delicate shimmer of a star-strewn sky without even a sliver of moon to outshine the soft spectral luster. It made him pity the poor fools who wasted their nights wrapped in the blind darkness of sleep. Yet he was grateful they did.

The muted beauty of the night was only one of its charms for him. The other was its promise of privacy. He had no inclination to share it with anyone.

His earlier weariness lifted from him, as a compound of star shine and night air set up a stimulating sparkle in his veins. With a buoyant step, he set off toward the hill that occupied the most eastern part of his grandfather's estate.

In the distance an owl hooted. The night wind played a ghostly lullaby through the leaves. In the underbrush, a faint rustle betrayed the scuttling movement of some small nocturnal creature. The familiar sounds greeted Lucius as he climbed the well-wooded path that led to the top of the hill.

Then, from behind him, he picked up faint sounds he was *not* accustomed to hearing on his nightly walk. His ears strained to catch them over the muted tread of his own footsteps.

There! What was that?

The muffled snap of a twig under another foot? The soft rasp of someone else's breath?

Was he being stalked?

Lucius curbed his long stride slightly and prepared himself to swing about and confront whoever was following him.

He would make certain they regretted trespassing on Lord Lucifer's privacy.

The devil had long legs! Angela cursed under her breath as she scrambled to pursue the elusive shadow of Lord Daventry without drawing his notice.

At least the fast walking had warmed her up. Though the night was not cold, a slight chill had settled into Angela's flesh as she had waited in the shadows of Helmhurst to see if her fiancé would venture out for the night.

Just when she'd been about to abandon her vigil and trudge home in disgust, she had caught sight of the baron's tall, spare profile against one of the lighted windows of the house. Immediately her heart had begun to race, and once again she'd doubted the wisdom of her plan.

But some compulsion, as irresistible as it was foolhardy, had pulled her along in his wake. Toward the hill, and whatever awaited him there.

For the earl's sake, and for her own, Angela was determined to find out what drew him here, night after night. If it turned out to be something quite harmless, she would tell the earl and set his mind at rest. And if it proved to be something sinister, surely that would cure her of the unwelcome feelings Lord Daventry had provoked.

"Whooo?" challenged a ghostly voice from above her.

Angela stifled a scream as she realized it was only an owl. Or was it? Weren't witches said to keep creatures like owls, cats and bats as their familiars?

Bats! Angela's shoulders flew up to brush the lobes of her ears.

Stop being so silly! she ordered herself. No educated person in nineteenth-century England believed in witches.

There was no reason to be frightened. She would relish a walk down this wooded path in the daylight, serenaded by a chorus of wrens and thrushes, charmed to discover a half-hidden cluster of wild violets. But the coming of night seemed to work a dark enchantment on her familiar, beloved countryside.

Was that a pair of pale, luminous eyes peering at her from the underbrush? Angela shivered, though she no longer felt cold.

As she stopped for a moment to catch her breath, she strained to listen for the sound of Lord Daventry's footsteps ahead of her. All she heard was the phantom whisper of the night wind through the leaves.

Dash it all! While she'd been jumping at every noise and shrinking from every shadow, he must have gained a vast lead on her. She hurried forward, hoping to close the gap between them.

She'd only taken a few steps when a lofty shadow of frightfully solid substance towered in her path. This time she could not check the scream that ripped from her throat. The menacing black form seized her in a powerful grip.

She pummeled it with her fists and struggled to escape.

As it enveloped her, she caught the faint scent of shaving soap and brandy.

"Miss Lacewood? What the devil are you doing here at this hour?" Lucius Daventry's resonant voice cleaved the night air.

The knowledge that it was *only* the baron did less to calm Angela's fears than it might have done. After all, the man sent a thrill of fear through her even by day, in the civilized confines of his grandfather's library. On a deserted path, late at night, it was far more difficult to dismiss his lordship's sinister reputation.

Fear had a curious effect, though, when taken to an extreme, which Angela never had before. For some reason, it triggered an equally potent discharge of anger.

Against all her natural prudence, she heard herself cry, "I'm trying to discover what the *devil* you do here at this hour!"

His grip on her slackened and his voice dropped to an eerie whisper. "What do you *think* I do here at night?"

Her rage seemed to have spent itself in that one futile blast. This time, when Angela coaxed her words out of a constricted throat, they emerged as a timorous squeak. "I...don't know."

"Are you certain you want to find out?"

If she declined, would he release her so she could flee back to Netherstowe as fast as her legs would carry her? Surely, he must. But if she turned back now, she would renounce any right to find out about this secret part of his life.

If, contrary to all suspicion, Lord Daventry's clandestine activities turned out to be innocent, he would take her refusal as proof she thought the worst of him.

"Well?" he asked again. "*Do* you want to know?"

"I do." Only after she had spit out her answer did Angela realize the significance of those words. Words the baron never wanted to hear her speak in front of a vicar.

He seemed not to notice, or perhaps not to care.

Releasing her from his grasp, except for one hand firmly closed around her upper arm, Lord Daventry marched her toward the crest of the hill.

"Very well, then. Come along, and you shall see."

What might she find there, and what might he do to her once she knew the truth?

In a lifetime of missteps and mistakes, Angela feared she had just made her biggest mistake yet.

Chapter Seven

What had he done? Lucius asked himself, followed immediately by, what would he do now?

Challenging Angela Lacewood to confront this part of his life had been a huge mistake—almost as big as the one he'd made by involving her in this ridiculous charade of an engagement.

The only thing he'd expected less than finding his fiancée spying on him, was having her call his bluff.

With a firm grip on her upper arm, he pushed her toward the crest of the hill. "Come along, Miss Lacewood, and you shall see."

She must be thoroughly convinced he was not involved in any of the diabolical practices gossip attributed to him. Otherwise she would have turned tail and fled back down the hill to safety, like a sensible young lady.

What gave her such reckless confidence in him when he had done nothing to win her trust? On the contrary, he'd gone out of his way to put Miss

Lacewood on her guard. As she'd done to him without even trying.

Lucius couldn't decide how he felt about her unmerited faith in him. Somehow it rendered him less in control of their curious relationship, yet at the same time it touched him in a way he was helpless to prevent.

Angela stumbled on the uneven ground, but his solid hold on her arm kept her from falling. Lucius slowed his pace.

A tall structure rose in front of them, blotting out the faint flicker of the stars.

"Don't move," he ordered as he let her go.

Though he'd expected no answer but compliance, one floated out of the darkness—tremulous yet quietly defiant. "If I'd wanted to leave, I would have done it before this."

Lucius fumbled with the door latch. "I only meant you shouldn't walk around in the dark without me holding on to you."

"I see. What is this place? I had no idea there was a building here."

"As far as I can tell, it's an old lookout tower."

With a series of movements so familiar he could have performed them blindfolded, Lucius pushed open the door and reached for a flint and candle. They rested on the lip of a narrow wall sconce just inside the base of the tower.

With a practiced motion, he struck a spark to the candlewick. A tiny flame kindled, sending shadows dancing over the curved stone wall and the winding stair that clung to it.

"Damn!"

His curse echoed through the empty tower as Lucius dropped the flint and the candle. Its flame flickered and died.

"What happened?" Angela called in an anxious voice. "Are you all right?"

Of course he was not *all right!* Lucius wanted to bellow. He would never be all right again.

He settled for a vague growl about butterfingers.

"Oh, never mind." Angela sounded much less anxious—almost cheerful. "I do that sort of thing all the time."

Under his breath, Lucius muttered, "I do not."

Alarm, not clumsiness, had made him drop the candle when he remembered that he'd removed his mask. Now he rummaged in his pocket, pulled it out and secured it back in place. That done, he groped about on the floor for the flint and candle, which he relit.

"Come along." He beckoned Angela inside, resenting the need for the candle to light their way up the stairs.

Bad enough to hear her voice and catch her scent while only imagining her face and figure. Now the capricious candlelight mocked him with the truth…that Miss Lacewood looked even more lovely than he could imagine.

The night air and their walk up the hill had coaxed a rosy glow to her cheeks. The wind had teased wisps of golden hair to escape the confines of her bonnet and curl around her face. Darkness, and perhaps a touch of fear, had made her eyes look wider and darker. As for her lips, he did not dare dwell on them if he wished to retain his flagging composure.

She stepped over the doorsill, staring around her with obvious alarm. Perhaps she'd come to her senses at last and begun to cultivate a healthy fear of him.

"Are there any bats?" She grasped his free hand and drew closer to him, as if for protection.

Bats! She was more worried about some insignificant winged rodent than about being alone at night in such a deserted spot with a man of his reputation?

Lucius could not decide whether to curse… or to laugh.

"A few," he admitted. "They'll all be off getting their dinner now. Not that they'd do you any harm if they were here."

Angela shuddered. "I detest bats!"

"They're no worse than mice." Holding the candle high, Lucius nudged her toward the stairs. "Bats just have a more menacing reputation, that's all."

Two steps ahead, Angela came to an abrupt halt and turned back toward him.

"You should know all about that." A bewitching glint of mischief danced in her eyes.

He could not mistake it, for they were standing nose to nose, with scarcely a breath between them. It was everything Lucius could do to keep from dropping his candle for the second time that night. Before he could trust himself to utter a word, Angela turned away again and continued up the stairs.

Over her shoulder, she called, "I don't much care for mice, either, come to that."

Lucius forced himself to ignore the delicious sway of her backside and tantalizing glimpses of her ankles as he hurried after her.

"What's all this?" Angela asked as she climbed up to the second floor of the tower.

Lucius vaulted the last few steps two at a time to find her staring at the high, curved table that hugged a vast portion of the wall. He had left it in some disarray, strewn with long rolls of paper, open books and various instruments for measuring and drawing. After the talk he'd had with his grandfather's physician, his mind had not been on his work the last few nights he'd come here.

This night promised to be no better.

"It's my workroom."

"I can see that." Angela picked up a yellowed copy of *Conaissance des Temps*. "But what sort of work do you do?"

Lucius headed for a set of stairs that clung to the opposite wall. "Come this way."

For no good reason, a sense of anticipation brewed within him at the prospect of sharing his secret passion with her.

He tried to mask it with a brusque warning. "Watch your step, now. I won't be coming behind to catch you if you slip."

Though he could hear the soft pad of Angela's footsteps following him, no audible word of reply left her lips. Lucius found himself wishing he could see her face, so he would know whether his remark had offended her, as he feared.

The trapdoor loomed above him.

Handing the candle back to Angela, Lucius deliberately softened his tone. "Would you mind holding this for me?"

"Aren't you worried I'll drop it and burn up all your papers?"

"I'm willing to risk it."

"Very well, then." Her fingers brushed his as she took the candle.

For the first time in years of climbing the steep, narrow stairs, a wave of vertigo threatened Lucius. Resolved to ignore it, he pushed the trapdoor open and crawled through. Then he turned and grasped Angela's hand to hoist her up behind him. Once she was safely through, he closed it again.

Angela shielded the flickering candle flame against a breeze that blew through the door of the small shelter into which they had ascended. "Now what?"

Lucius hefted a long wooden box from its resting place and carried it out to the middle of the tower's flat, open roof. After pulling a swath of thick coarse canvas from around a special support frame, he opened the box and lifted out a brass telescope with the loving care another man might exercise when handling his firstborn. Lucius lowered it into the frame, then secured it in place with a series of special clasps.

Only then did he glance back at Angela, who stood a little ways away, still trying to screen the candle's wildly flickering flame against the breeze.

"Why, Lucius Daventry." The look on her face could not have conveyed greater contempt if she *had* caught him in some sacrilegious activity. "You brazen humbug."

A sudden gust of wind extinguished the light.

What had possessed her to say such a thing? Angela froze in the dark, cursing her own foolishness.

Just because Lord Daventry appeared innocent of making diabolic sacrifices with the Babbits' missing pigs did not mean he was a man to trifle with. The way his green eyes had blazed in the instant before the candle had flickered out made Angela suspect he wanted to pitch her over the waist-high parapet that ran around the edge of the tower.

She didn't dare flee. If she tried to descend those treacherous winding stairs in the dark, she'd likely tumble all the way to the bottom, breaking her neck.

Firm, deliberate footsteps approached and out of the darkness came Lord Daventry's black-velvet voice. "Humbug? I haven't the slightest notion what you're talking about."

Angela told herself not to answer. Unfortunately, she found it impossible to heed her own warning.

"You know perfectly well what I mean...*Lord Lucifer.*"

"Oh, that." He hesitated a moment. "See here, I didn't start those absurd rumors."

Though she doubted he could see her, Angela still shook her head. "You've done nothing to counter them, either."

"Why should I?" His words whispered on the wind. "People believe as they please no matter what evidence they're given to the contrary. Besides it suited me to have everyone shy away from...this place. I won't be bothered and I won't be—"

The night seemed to swallow his words.

"Won't be what?" Angela asked, though she knew she shouldn't.

He didn't reply at once. Angela wished she could see more than his crisp black silhouette.

"I've indulged your curiosity enough for one night, my dear." His voice sounded cool and poised, with a faint echo of mockery. "Besides, it's probably long past your bedtime. Shall I relight that candle and escort you home?"

Sorely as his invitation tempted her, the familiar yet foreign beauty of the night sky tempted her more. Or could it be the strange lure of the man himself?

She countered his question with one of her own. "Why astronomy?"

"Can you think of a better occupation for a man who must live his life at night?"

Angela could think of one or two. One in particular that set a warm shimmer through her flesh. But for a man of intellect who craved solitude? "I suppose not."

A fragile silence quivered between them, broken only by the sighing of the wind through the leaves and the haunting calls of night birds. Any moment Angela expected Lord Daventry to invite—or order-her to leave. But the longer she tarried there, the less she wanted go.

"Since you're here," he said at last, "and you've climbed all this way, would you care to take a look?"

For the first time since he had appeared at Netherstowe to propose to her, Lord Daventry sounded a trifle uncertain. Uncertain about the wisdom of asking her, Angela wondered, or uncertain whether she'd accept?

For some reason, it felt imperative to reassure him on that count. "Yes, please. I've never looked at the night sky much, even with my own eyes."

"Then you're in for a treat. Come along."

"Ah—would you mind leading me by the hand?" She held hers out. "You know your way around up here and you're probably more accustomed to finding it in the dark. I'd hate to blunder into this apparatus of yours and break something."

"Of…course." His fingers found hers.

Then, in a movement like something from a country dance, he pivoted as he drew her toward him until her hip pressed against his thigh and his free arm crooked around her waist.

Though she could only make out vague shapes and shadows as Lord Daventry guided her toward the telescope, Angela found herself moving with greater confidence than she often did in broad daylight. The firm power and warmth of his touch promised that he would not let her stumble or bump into anything. It was a novel, heady sensation, and one she was sorry to lose when he settled her onto a low wooden bench.

Through the fabric of her bonnet, she could feel his lips brush against her ear. "I hope you won't find it too uncomfortable."

His murmured words sounded almost like an endearment.

From habit, she turned toward the sound of his voice. Her lips grazed the light stubble of whisker on his cheek.

"Not at all," she replied in a breathless whisper.

Lord Daventry hovered behind her, leaning over her to look through the telescope, reaching past her to adjust its position and tilt. Parts of his body pressed into hers and brushed against hers, setting her a-tingle from head to toe.

"There now," he said after one last adjustment. "What do you think of that?"

Not certain what to expect, Angela leaned gingerly toward the eyepiece and peered into it.

"Oh, my," she breathed, overwhelmed by a sense of wonder. "It's…"

"It's Saturn." Lord Daventry sounded as gratified by her reaction as if he'd crafted that celestial jewel with his own hands—a lustrous pearl set in a circlet of gold—then suspended it in the night sky for her to admire.

"I know *what* it is." She'd heard of that distant planet with its strange rings. She had even seen a drawing of it once.

Neither of those could approach the marvel of viewing it for herself. "I was trying to find a word to describe it, but I can't think of one half fine enough."

"I know. I suppose I've looked at it a thousand times, yet it never fails to astonish me whenever I see it again. I always find it more wondrous than I'm capable of remembering."

He seemed on the verge of saying something more, but he stopped himself. Angela wished she could master that skill.

"Would you like to see a falling star?" he asked instead.

"Can I?"

She felt him nod his head as he leaned past her to adjust the angle of the telescope. "With a little patience and a little luck."

"I've never considered myself lucky." Then why did it feel like good fortune to be here, with him? "But I'm told patience is one of my virtues."

He looked up into the star-strewn sky. "Let us hope the heavens reward your patience tonight."

Once more Angela peered into the eyepiece of the telescope. This time she saw a cluster of stars with one especially large and dazzling. If Saturn looked like a celestial pearl, this glittering star must be a flawless diamond.

"That's the constellation Lyra," Lucius Daventry explained, as if he could divine her thoughts.

Angela hoped he could not guess *everything* she was thinking.

"That bright star is Vega."

"Does every star have a name?"

"Heavens, no!" His words slid out on a soft chuckle that sounded charmed by her curiosity rather than contemptuous of her ignorance. "We should have run out of names long ago. It's only the brightest stars that have names—Vega, Ceres, Aldebaran in Scorpio, Rigel and Betelgeuse in Orion."

The encouraging tenor of his answer emboldened her to ask another question. "What do you mean when you say 'in Scorpio' or 'in Orion'?"

"Those are the names the ancients gave to other clusters of stars that make pictures in the sky. Constellations, they're called." When he stopped weighing and guarding every word that left his lips, the baron's deep, resonant voice took on a beguiling melodic quality.

"Lyra, the one you're looking at now, its shape was thought to resemble a harp. Orion is the hunter. Betelgeuse and Bellatrix are his shoulders, and Rigel his raised foot. Three other bright stars shine like gemstones on his belt and a great nebula makes up the hilt of his sword."

Angela found this new subject so fascinating she could not keep herself from interrupting with more questions. "What's a nebula? Can you show me this Orion fellow in your telescope?"

"By and by, my dear. Orion is only visible to us in the winter months. Don't forget your virtue of—"

"Oh! I saw one!" Angela groped for his hand and squeezed it.

She'd been watching where Lucius had bidden her, but not giving it her full attention when a tiny star had suddenly blossomed where none had been before. Then, it had descended, at great speed, trailing a long white plume in its wake to disappear as quickly as it had come.

"Is the star really falling?"

"It *is* really falling," Lucius confirmed, "but it isn't really a star."

He went on to tell her about meteorites and comets and half-a-dozen other marvels she had never suspected were taking place night after night in the dark sky over sleeping Northamptonshire. Each new piece of information intrigued her, spawning fresh questions in the way Lucius had told her a comet's plume bred falling stars.

"You know," she confessed at last, "until tonight, I've always been rather afraid of the night sky."

"Why is that?"

"It's so immense. Limitless. Like the ocean, only worse." She remembered that long, sad, frightening ocean voyage back from India after her father's death, and being taken up on deck one calm night. "It made me feel so tiny, so insignificant. Of no consequence whatsoever."

Somehow, even the little knowledge Lucius

Daventry had shared with her tonight gave her a curious sense of mastery that had blunted her fear. Angela couldn't put it into words, nor could she find a proper way to express her gratitude.

"I've always found comfort in stargazing," Lucius mused aloud. "When one contemplates the vast, exquisite precision of the universe, one can't help but believe in…something."

He ached for that. Angela hear the edge of hunger for it in his voice.

No wonder the stars had seduced him so thoroughly from the daylight world. What could the gossip or petty doings of his neighbors matter to a man who consorted with the ageless and the infinite?

The familiar sense of insignificance threatened to overwhelm Angela again. Not with fear this time, but with a gentle, bewildering sorrow she could not fathom.

"I'm sorry to have taken up so much of your time, tonight, my lord. You haven't gotten a jot of work done, thanks to me and my endless questions."

For the first time since she'd looked into his telescope and beheld the wonder of Saturn, Angela noticed she was cold and tired. A deep yawn overtook her.

"On the contrary, Miss Lacewood." His voice was still magnificent, but once again cool and distant as the stars. "I should be the one to apologize for detaining you here so late."

He began to unfasten the telescope from its

mounting. This time he did not reach around her to do it but moved away, breaking the contact between them.

As he replaced the instrument in its box and wrapped the support in canvas once again, Angela groped about for the candle. As soon as her hand closed over it, she struggled to rise on her cramped, cold legs.

"Here, let me help you!" Lord Daventry reached out to steady her.

She felt a tension in his stance, and in the way he held her, that had been quite absent while they'd stargazed together.

Her body tensed in reply, as if stretched taut by the opposing forces of her inclination and her will. The former bid her to melt in Lucius Daventry's arms and raise her lips to his for a kiss...the likes of which he had expressed a resolute desire to avoid. The memory of her humiliation the previous evening urged Angela to pull away from him before she made another such idiotic blunder.

The two opposite compulsions of intense but equal power threatened to tear her in half. She wished Lord Daventry would take the decision out of her hands, either by letting her go, or by kissing her cross-eyed. But he did neither.

Could it be that the baron was also pulled in two contrary directions? The possibility sent a shiver through Angela.

Even Lord Daventry felt it. "We must get you home at once! You must be chilled to the bone."

He let her go, as Angela had half hoped he

would, then picked up the box holding his telescope and strode toward the small penthouse that sheltered the tower's stair head.

Angela trailed after him, wishing with her *whole* heart that he'd kissed her, instead.

Chapter Eight

He had come so close to kissing her again, and this time he would have had no saving excuse. Confronting his near loss of self-control shook Lucius to the core.

Three days after Angela Lacewood had bearded him in his den, he tossed and turned in his bed, trying to stop thinking about her. He was enjoying a conspicuous lack of success.

He could not escape the preposterous sensation that Miss Lacewood was present in the room, watching him. Only an hour ago he'd woken from the most alarming dream, in which she'd been kneeling beside his bed. With one hand, she'd stroked his body in the most provocative manner, while with the other she had reached up to tear away his mask.

Lucius had returned to consciousness with a violent start, his pulse and breath racing, his body slick with sweat and aching for a woman...though not just any woman.

Angela Lacewood had come close to seducing him that night on the tower roof. And she hadn't even needed to deploy the potent weapon of her beauty. Instead, she'd sprung an ambush, led by her eager interest in his vocation, ably supported by the golden lilt of her voice and the warm zest of her company.

Come to think of it, even the faint scent that hung about her seemed calculated to snare him. It was nothing like the usual fussy, floral odors other women used to captivate men, and to which Lucius had cultivated an aversion. It put him in mind of a bakeshop—vanilla, cinnamon and bread fresh from the oven.

He had believed himself safe, protected by his familiar shield of darkness. Otherwise, he'd never have risked inviting her into his sanctum. That, and the mistaken certainty she would be too timid to take him up on his offer.

Twice she had fooled him, leaving Lucius torn between outrage and admiration, just as he'd been torn that night between desire and discretion.

"Blast it all!" Abandoning his futile struggle to sleep, Lucius rolled out of bed.

This had to stop. In a few short days, Angela Lacewood had turned his life upside down. What state would it be in at the end of three months?

He would have to persuade her to break their engagement immediately. That's all there was to it.

No doubt she'd be relieved to rid herself of him.

Lucius recalled the shudder that had rippled

through her when he'd held her in his arms a fraction too long. It had flatly contradicted her charitable reassurance that she would not mind kissing him again. No doubt Miss Lacewood had meant she could stomach a pretense of lovemaking played out for the amusement of his grandfather.

Grandfather.

Lucius scowled as he thrust his legs into a pair of buckskin breeches.

The old man wouldn't be pleased by this turn of events. But if he believed the decision to end their engagement was Miss Lacewood's, the earl might distance himself from her. Then he and Lucius could enjoy the time they had left together, without the intrusion of a stranger.

A twinge of shame struck Lucius as he donned his shirt, but he ignored it. He was engaged in nothing less than a war for his peace of mind. He could not afford to give quarter. Once dressed, he pulled on his mask and set off to do battle.

Lucius steeled himself against the glare of daylight. But when he opened his bedroom door and stepped out into the wide portrait-decked corridor, he found it agreeably dim for the hour. The recent relentless spell of fine weather must have broken itself at last.

The change boded well.

Catching sight of the earl's valet tottering toward the head of the stairs, he called out, "Carruthers, do you know if my grandfather is by himself in the library?"

If Carruthers felt any surprise at seeing the

young master awake in the middle of the day, his solemn face betrayed none.

Nor did his bland, deferential tone. "By himself? Just so, milord, but not in the library. Last I saw of the master, he was wandering about the orangery."

The orangery? During his childhood, Lucius had enjoyed spending time in that bright indoor garden room, with its glass roof and great banks of windows. Since returning to Helmhurst after the war, he'd seldom ventured there. On an overcast day like this, it might be tolerable.

After a quick word of thanks to Carruthers, Lucius proceeded to the orangery, where he found his grandfather strolling among the ornamental citrus trees and beds of flowers too delicate for the English climate.

Lucius glanced around, pretending to look for Angela. "My lovely fiancée not visiting today?"

The earl fixed him with a long, silent stare before countering with a question of his own, "Would you be here if she were?"

Lucius had no more intention of taking that bait than he would have charged a formed infantry square. Instead he feigned interest in the flowers, stooping to sniff a cluster of blossoms with a deep blush on one side of each petal. They reminded him of Miss Lacewood, in spite of his determination not to let them.

Perhaps the earl grew tired of waiting for an answer. "Angela dropped by just long enough to apologize for having to leave again. Then she went off to the village with the vicar. Some invalid friend of hers has taken a bad turn, I gather. I don't expect her back for dinner."

Hard as Lucius tried to summon up a sense of satisfaction over her absence, he could not.

"Then it'll be just the two of us today." He strove to appear as well pleased with the situation as he should have been. "What do you suggest we undertake to amuse ourselves?"

By slow, stiff-jointed degrees, the earl lowered himself onto a chair upholstered in dark leather. "I'm afraid it simply won't do, my boy. I've advised Angela she had better break this engagement of yours."

Lucius straightened up so fast he almost knocked his head against the branch of a lemon tree that overhung the flowerbed. "You did what?"

The earl shook his head in a deliberate manner that suggested both regret and resolve. "No matter how much I might like to have the dear girl in our family, or how much I think you need a wife like her, I'm too fond of Angela to sit by and watch you treat her badly."

Before Lucius could compose himself to ask what ill treatment Miss Lacewood was supposed to have suffered at his hands, the earl went on. "No. She had much better marry the vicar, I think."

A fierce heat blazed in Lord Daventry's chest, like a large meteor plunging to earth in flames. The more intense the emotion, the greater determination he felt to conceal it.

"Had she, indeed?" He spoke as though he were commenting on some distant acquaintance rather than the young lady to whom he was betrothed. "Has the vicar asked her? When I proposed to Miss Lacewood, she assured me she was free to accept my offer."

She had done nothing of the kind, his conscience protested. When he'd asked if she had any particular admirers, the young lady had first accused him of mocking her, then asked why he thought she might have beaux paying her their addresses. She'd failed to give him a direct answer, something Lucius had often been accused of doing. Not without reason, he had to admit.

He did not enjoy being on the receiving end of such an ambiguous reply.

The earl cast Lucius an uncomfortably discerning look. "I don't believe Mr. Michaeljohn has declared himself. From what I saw of him today, he appears a rather diffident young man in spite of his good looks."

"Handsome fellow, is he?" Lucius tried to sound indifferent, though the meteor inside him blazed hotter than ever.

The earl nodded. "Adonis in a clerical collar."

"Is he?" Lucius paced the floor of decorative brickwork. "Miss Lacewood is quite smitten with him, I suppose?"

"I doubt the dear girl is aware of his feelings. Perhaps the vicar is not fully aware of them himself. Some men are like that, you know."

For the first time in his life, Lucius asked himself why he was so devoted to his grandfather. The earl could be a most exasperating old owl by times.

"So it's your opinion this vicar fellow would treat Miss Lacewood better than I?"

The earl shrugged. "He's in her company now. You, by contrast, have spent the past three days going to ridiculous lengths to avoid her. I believe that speaks volumes, don't you?"

"Avoiding her? What nonsense!" Lucius heard his tone sharpen in spite of his strenuous attempt to curb it. "Did she complain to you of my absence?"

"No, but I could tell she felt your displeasure keenly all the same. Tell me, are you angry because she trespassed on your privacy? Or is it because she discovered the perfectly commonplace truth behind this sinister myth you've allowed to build up around yourself?"

"I am *not* angry with her!" Lucius roared.

At least he shouldn't be. He knew enough about women to realize Angela Lacewood had made no effort to tempt him that night on the tower. Quite the contrary, in fact. He had no right to blame her for his own wayward inclinations.

"If you are not angry with her," grumbled the earl, "you have a poor way of showing it. Your lack of civility the past few days has been inexcusable. I can't think what's got into you. Even when you were a child, you never sulked like this."

Lucius flinched from his grandfather's mild

reproof. He had undertaken this betrothal business in an effort to make the earl's last months as happy as possible, yet it appeared to be having the opposite effect. All because he was trying so desperately to keep Miss Lacewood at arm's length.

Might it work better if he threw himself into this courtship as if he meant it, then worry about extricating his heart later?

If so, some manner of peace offering was clearly in order. But would it be too little, too late?

"For me, Miles?" Angela glanced up from her breakfast at the fancy ribbon-trimmed box her brother held out to her. "Why, thank you, dearest!"

Miles handed her the box, then slipped into his usual place beside her at the table.

Raising the lid, Angela gasped at the sight of her favorite barley candy, a full pound of it at least, wrought in fanciful little shapes.

She plucked out a bright yellow one in the shape of a tiny plump bird and prepared to pop it into her mouth. "You shouldn't have spent your money on a treat for me, though. It must have cost you a pretty penny."

The dear boy must have bought it the previous day, on his way home to Netherstowe from school.

As he reached for his coffee, Miles Lacewood pulled a rueful face. "I'd gladly have spent more than that on you if I'd had it, but I'm afraid I can't take credit. The sweets are a present from

Lord Daventry. I meant to give them to you last night, but in the commotion of stowing my gear, it slipped my mind."

Lord Daventry? Angela's hand froze within inches of her mouth. There was not enough barley candy in the kingdom to sweeten her present feelings toward him!

Looking back on the past few days, she found it difficult to believe her stimulating companion in stargazing could be the same man who had taken such obvious pains to avoid her since then. Even the earl had marked and disapproved of his grandson's behavior, going so far as to advise she should reconsider the engagement.

Angela was sorely tempted.

And Lucius Daventry was sorely mistaken if he believed he could purchase her pardon with a box of her favorite sweets!

Battling her craving for the candy, Angela thrust it back into the box, which she pushed to the far side of the table, hoping it would tempt her less from a distance.

"You mean to say Lord Daventry went to fetch you home? I thought he'd just sent one of his carriages for you."

A serving maid bustled into the dining room just then, setting a heaping plate of breakfast in front of Miles. Clearly Tibby planned to fatten him up before he set out for India.

The young man gave an appreciative sniff. "One thing I shall miss about England is Tibby's cooking!"

He flashed Angela a fond look. "And you, of course. Though I shan't mind quite so much, knowing you're well settled. I wish I could stay around for the wedding, though."

Angela watched her brother dig into his breakfast with obvious relish. She could not recall the last time she'd seen him in such high spirits.

She'd tried to refuse Lord Daventry's offer to purchase Miles a commission, in part because she did not feel her service to him merited such lavish compensation. As well, she'd hated the notion of being obligated to him.

Could she bear her brother's disappointment if she broke her engagement to Lucius prematurely, canceling their bargain?

Eyeing the box of candy, Angela considered her brother's situation and remembered her night of stargazing. Lucius Daventry might not be as diabolical as he sometimes pretended, but the man was a master of temptation, nonetheless.

"At first I couldn't imagine what you saw in the fellow," said Miles, between bites of broiled tomato and sausage. "Apart from the title and fortune, which I know you don't give a fig about. The more I've seen of him, though, the better I like him. I'll wager he was a damn fine officer."

"Do mind your language on the Sabbath, Miles."

"Sorry." Her brother bolted a drink of his coffee. "But you know what I mean. Coolheaded in a crisis. Ready to get the job done, no matter how dangerous or unpleasant."

Angela nodded. Lord Daventry had his share of admirable qualities, she would be the last to deny it. She only wished his cool head didn't extend to his heart. Neither did she enjoy being made to feel like an unpleasant duty he'd undertaken.

The barley candy called to her from its pretty box.

As if he read her thoughts, Miles gave her a gentle nudge. "Go on, have one. You've already eaten your breakfast. It's not as though you'd be spoiling it."

He reached across the table, pulling the sweets closer. "I wouldn't have thought his lordship the kind for buying presents, but it's no secret he's smitten with you."

A tart denial rose to Angela's lips. She snatched a piece of barley candy and stuffed it into her mouth to keep from saying what was on her mind. It wouldn't do to have Miles suspect relations between her and Lucius Daventry were less than what he'd been led to believe.

"He doesn't go on and on, of course, like some chaps," continued Miles. "Still waters running deep and all that. There's something about the way he says your name, though, and the look he gets whenever I talk about you."

Had she heard an echo of that tone? Seen a flicker of that look? The possibility kindled a sensation within Angela that matched the peculiar mellow sweetness of barley sugar.

But what if her brother had only imagined what

he wanted to see and hear in Lord Daventry's impassive speech and expression? What if she had?

Sliding the candy into the pouch of her cheek,
she mumbled, "I must go dress for church. Will
you come to the service with me?"

"Perhaps next week, if you don't mind." Miles
gave an exaggerated yawn. "I'm still rather tired
from all the packing and traveling."

"Very well," replied Angela in a tone of mild
reproach. "I'll say an extra prayer for you."

She glanced out the dining room window, trying to judge whether the light fog might turn to
rain. What she saw almost made her choke on
her barley candy.

Lord Daventry's gig emerged from the fog,
driven by the man, himself.

Without another word to her brother, Angela
bolted up the stairs and began to dress her hair.
A few minutes later, she heard a knock on her
bedroom door.

"Yes, what is it?" she called, as if she didn't
know.

"Lord Daventry, miss," replied Hoskins, the
butler. "He begs the privilege of escorting you to
worship this morning."

"Privilege?" Angela muttered to herself. "The
liar!"

"I beg your pardon, miss?"

It was quite a little walk to Grafton Renforth
from Netherstowe, and the fog did looked as
though it might turn to rain. Besides, she had a
thing or two she wished to say to Lord Daven-

try, out of his dear grandfather's hearing, and her brother's.

"Tell his lordship I'll be along directly."

"Very good, miss."

Angela glanced down at her gown. Like most clothes she'd worn since Clemmie and Cammie had sprouted taller than she, it was a castoff of her cousins'. Would Lord Daventry consider it too brightly colored and immodest in style for churchgoing?

His opinion was of no consequence to her, she reminded herself as she collected her shawl, bonnet and gloves. Besides, his lordship had not darkened a church door in years. He would hardly be an authority on suitable fashion for attending worship.

All these assurances to the contrary, Angela's stomach churned and her knees grew weak as she descended the stairs to meet her escort. A temporary feeling of relief buoyed her when she saw no sign of him in the entry hall. Then she heard muted voices from the dining room.

She peeped in the door to discover Lord Daventry in conversation with her brother.

The instant he caught a glimpse of her, his lordship broke off in mid-sentence, "My dear Miss Lacewood, how charming you look, as always."

He caught both her hands in his and bowed over them. To Angela's surprise, the glance he lofted toward her was not his usual inscrutable look. His green eyes fairly sparkled with admiration, even the one shadowed by his mask.

That look ignited a curious sparkle within her, much to Angela's annoyance. She did not *want* to be elated by Lord Daventry's approval any more than she wanted to be cast down by his displeasure. Both gave him far too much power over her.

"I understand you've come to fetch me to church, my lord." She tried not to betray the rush of pleasure it brought her to hear his beguiling voice again. "To what do I owe the honor?"

"The honor is entirely mine, my dear." The baron bowed even deeper. "Since our engagement has been puffed out to the papers, I thought it might look well if we appeared together to accept the good wishes of your friends."

Of course, he meant to play this all for the benefit of an audience, just as his present show of courtesy was no doubt intended to impress her beaming younger brother.

She glanced toward the mantel clock. "I suppose we oughtn't tarry. The vicar is very punctual about commencing worship."

"An estimable gentleman, this vicar of yours." Though Lord Daventry spoke in the smoothest of tones, Angela could not help wondering if he had some spite against Mr. Michaeljohn.

But that was ridiculous. To her knowledge, the two men had never met.

She and Lord Daventry kept up a cordial performance in front of Miles as they set off for church. A performance somewhat more restrained on her part, somewhat more exaggerated on his.

Once they had driven out of earshot of Netherstowe, she turned toward him. "What *really* made you come here this morning? I didn't win that wager with your grandfather."

"No. But you won a wager with me." He offered her a crooked attempt at a smile, which Angela guessed was far more sincere than his earlier compliments. "Perhaps I should say, I lost a wager against myself."

"W-what wager?"

His gaze held hers and would not let it go. "I gambled that you wouldn't have sufficient nerve to come up to the tower with me when I invited you the other night."

If only he knew what a near run thing that had been!

"But since you did," Lord Daventry continued, "I felt I owed you some manner of winnings."

"I thought the chance to see Saturn would have been payment enough."

She didn't want to forgive him, if, indeed, he was begging her pardon in some roundabout fashion. But the memories of that night came back to her in such vivid detail she was compelled to admit it had been one of the most magical in her life.

Breaking abruptly from their gaze, Lord Daventry shrugged. "A box of sweets and a drive to church hardly compare, do they?"

"The candy was very nice, thank you."

He replied with a brief nod. "I'm glad you enjoyed it."

Hard as he might try to conceal the fact, Angela suspected such gestures did not come easily for him. Not even when disguised as her winnings in a wager. What's more, *her* approval clearly mattered to him.

That was a heady notion for Angela to embrace. "Some of the best I've ever eaten. And a whole pound for myself. I shall have to take care not to sicken myself on it."

How much considerate attention could she accept from Lord Daventry, Angela wondered, before she glutted herself? Or might her taste of his companionship spoil her appetite for other men?

The notion almost made her laugh aloud.

What other men?

How could Angela fail to realize that the handsome vicar was smitten with her?

Mr. Michaeljohn hadn't finished calling his parishioners to worship before Lucius knew it without a doubt. Why, the man could scarcely keep his eyes on his prayer book!

With every adoring glance the vicar directed at Angela, Lucius fancied the lethal hiss of a bullet hurtling past his ear. Every soldier's instinct urged him to take cover and fire back, or to fix lance and charge. But this was one battle for which he possessed neither arms nor ammunition.

His grandfather had not overstated matters

when he'd referred to the young vicar as Adonis in a clerical collar.

Mr. Michaeljohn's golden hair and steadfast brown eyes matched well with those of his favorite parishioner. His height and figure might have shown to better advantage in a Hussar's uniform than in a surplice, but Lucius supposed the ladies of St. Owen's still found much to admire. Certainly none of them would ever flinch from the sight of features so flawless they might have belonged to a classical sculpture.

Were it not for the vicar's obvious partiality toward Angela, Lucius might have been grateful for the fellow's handsome face. It drew the eyes of the congregation away from his own ruined visage, after the first flurry of curious stares.

Those stares returned to him in full force once the service had concluded.

Having spent the past three years trying to avoid such scrutiny, Lucius felt as if he were running a gauntlet of mortar fire. Each look, quickly averted when he met it, each whisper passed behind a raised hand, each pitying shake of the head dealt his pride a direct hit.

Then he felt a firm but gentle grip on his arm. He glanced sidelong at Angela to discover her face turned toward him. Suddenly the church might have been empty for all Lucius cared.

"Well, what did you think?" she asked. "Didn't I tell you the vicar's a fine preacher?"

"A man of many gifts."

"Just so!" She appeared to take his remark at face value. "I know he's anxious to meet you."

"And I him." The way a warrior might wish to take the measure of his adversary.

But that was ridiculous. The handsome vicar was *not* his rival for Angela!

Lucius was still trying to convince himself of that when they reached the church door, where the vicar stood greeting his parishioners.

"Miss Lacewood, I understand congratulations are in order." A minor chord of regret played counterpoint to the tender melody of affection in Mr. Michaeljohn's fine voice.

"Er...yes." Angela tugged Lucius forward. "I don't believe you've met Lord Daventry."

The vicar held out his hand. "I have not had that pleasure, though I enjoyed my brief introduction to the earl, when Miss Lacewood and I called at Helmhurst the other day."

Lucius shook the vicar's hand. "I seldom get about much during the day."

A middle-aged woman behind them must have overheard his remark, for she nudged the man beside her and whispered furiously in his ear, all the while casting black looks at Lucius.

His brow cocked at what he hoped was an arrogant angle, Lucius treated the woman to a menacing stare.

Then Angela spoke up. "Lord Daventry is obliged to sleep during the day, Vicar, because most of his nights are given over to the study of astronomy."

The volume of her voice told Lucius she meant others to hear, as well. "He has the most wonderful vantage of the heavens from an old lookout tower on the grounds of Helmhurst."

Lucius watched the information spread from one group of parishioners to another, like ripples across a pond. Though he would never let anyone suspect, in his heart he mourned the death of *Lord Lucifer*.

"Astronomy?" said the vicar. "Fascinating subject. I would enjoy hearing about your observations, sir."

"Then you shall." Lucius let his gaze rest on Angela in a pose of tender devotion. "Now that I have such an agreeable reason to keep more regular hours, I hope to become better acquainted with you."

"I look forward to it, Lord Daventry. Please accept my congratulations on your betrothal. You're a most fortunate man."

The unintended irony of that statement stung Lucius. Yet, with Angela by his side and everyone convinced she would be his bride, he suddenly felt more fortunate than he had in years.

Her manner toward him had thawed markedly over the course of the morning. Now, as they made their way to the spot where Lucius had hitched the carriage, he steeled himself to inquire where he stood with her.

He glanced around to make sure there was no one close enough to hear. "Grandfather tells me he urged you to throw me over."

Angela kept her face averted from him. "Do you want me to?"

"No!"

The fervor of his reply made Angela start. It surprised Lucius no less.

He lowered his voice as he helped her into the gig. "But if that is what you feel you must do, I will not withdraw my support for your brother."

While she considered what he'd said, Lucius unhitched the horse, then climbed into the gig beside her. A fleeting glimpse at her face told him she'd made her decision.

"I am prepared to continue, Lord Daventry, if you are prepared to treat me as an ally instead of an enemy."

Lucius hesitated. He had seen firsthand the treachery of so-called allies. At least with an enemy, one always knew where one stood and what one could expect.

"Agreed," he said at last.

"Does that mean I may come watch the stars with you again?"

Lucius nodded. Something elusive but vital had been missing from his work the past few nights. Much as he hated to admit it might have been Angela's infectious sense of wonder, he could not discount the possibility.

Chapter Nine

If Lord Daventry didn't yet regret continuing their bogus engagement, he soon might.

Angela couldn't help thinking so as she watched him sitting opposite her in the darkened interior of his traveling coach. Chaperoned by a disapproving Tibby, they were taking Miles to London. There the young man would collect the gear he'd ordered and the uniforms for which he'd been fitted on a previous trip to the city. Then he would board a ship bound for India, to take up his commission.

Ever since they'd set out from Grafton Renforth early that morning, her brother had been pestering the baron with question after question about regimental life. Hours later, he had still not exhausted the topic, though Angela was becoming heartily bored with it.

"It's going to seem pretty rum, giving orders to enlisted chaps old enough to be my father."

"You'll do well to leave most of the ordering to your sergeant," Lord Daventry advised. "Chances are he's forgotten more about soldiering than you'll ever learn. Let him know you're in charge, but do your best to back him up, especially in front of the men. A capable sergeant has been the making of many a young officer."

Miles nodded eagerly. "I see what you're driving at. What about my fellow junior officers?"

Lord Daventry looked tired. Angela knew he was accustomed to sleeping during the day.

Though she enjoyed the sound of the baron's beguiling voice, she nudged her brother's foot. "Lord Daventry has been very patient to answer all your questions. I think you ought to give the poor man a rest, don't you?"

Before Miles could answer, Lucius Daventry shook his head. "I don't mind, truly. It helps pass the time. I only wish someone with a little experience had told me a thing or two about soldiering before I went off to fight."

Across the compact space of the carriage, he fixed her with his potent gaze, though he addressed his advice to her brother.

"Listen more than you talk around the officer's mess. Keep up your end in any enterprise, even if it's only a cricket match. That way you'll get a reputation for dependability. Treat your superiors with the respect you'd like to receive from the men in your command, but speak your mind if you have something to say."

Good advice, all of it, for a young officer about to embark on his career. Angela hoped

Miles would heed it. She couldn't help wondering, though, if Lord Daventry's natural restraint had been further ingrained by his experiences in the cavalry. Such virtues in military life might well prove impediments when it came to affairs of the heart.

Perhaps she should give Miles the benefit of a little *sisterly* advice on that subject, before he went away.

Her brother gazed at Lord Daventry with transparent hero worship. "I've been dreaming of this ever since I can remember. Now that it's come, I can scarcely contain myself. I do wish I'd been able to postpone my departure until after your wedding, though, so I could walk my sister down the aisle!"

In Angela's mind there rose a vivid image of herself gowned in silk and lace with a wreath of orange blossoms adorning her bonnet, walking down the aisle of St. Owen's on her brother's arm. The notion of Lord Daventry waiting for her at the foot of the alter did not alarm her as it once might have.

"My sister will make a beautiful bride," declared Miles. "Won't she, Lord Daventry?"

"Indeed, she will," replied the baron in a velvety murmur that sent a warm sparkle sweeping through Angela.

That sparkle intensified to a prickling blush when she found herself imagining wedding vows spoken by that voice.

"Miles, you mustn't say such things!" She pretended to be embarrassed by their flattery. "Besides, you don't want to linger in England until Uncle Bulwick returns. Who knows what he might do to prevent you going to India if he took it into his head. Sometimes it's easier to secure pardon after the fact than permission before."

"Humph!" Tibby squirmed in the seat beside Angela. "You're the one who'll bear the brunt of his lordship's displeasure, since Master Miles will be on the other side of the world."

She directed a sharp look at Lord Daventry, as if to say he was the one who deserved to suffer their uncle's ill humor.

Before Angela could protest, Tibby grumbled, "How much farther is it to London, anyhow? What a long journey it makes when a body can't even look out the window to see where we are."

Angela chided herself for entertaining a similar thought. "You insisted on accompanying us, Tibby. I'd have been quite content to bring Violet or Jane."

Tibby muttered something barely audible about it not being seemly for a chaperon to be even greener than her mistress. It was clear she believed Lord Daventry capable of debauching both Angela and a young maidservant during their sojourn in the wicked city.

If only Tibby knew how little the baron wanted her, in that way!

Prompted by Tibby's complaint, Lord Daventry consulted his pocket watch. "We should be stopping for tea within the hour."

That said, he leaned back in his seat and closed his eyes, perhaps to escape Tibby's glowering looks or Miles's bothersome questions.

What he could not escape was Angela's gaze. While his piercing green eyes were closed, she felt safe to stare at him as long and as avidly as she desired, without worrying how he might interpret her interest. Angela wasn't certain *she* knew how to interpret her interest.

She was no longer afraid of Lord Daventry… at least not in the way she'd once been. After he'd shunned her for venturing too close to him on their first night of stargazing, a different kind of wariness had beset her. For the safety of her heart, she knew she should keep her emotional distance from him.

His generosity to her brother and his attentiveness to her did not make that easy. No matter how frequently she warned herself that his pose as a solicitous fiancé was nothing more than a necessary new mask he'd adopted.

If Lucius had needed any proof that he'd done right to hide himself away in the countryside, his visits to London on Miles Lacewood's behalf provided it in ample measure.

Back in Grafton Renforth, the locals were becoming accustomed to the sight of his mask. Every time he ventured out with Miss Lacewood, fewer and fewer people paid him any heed.

In London, he was a definite object of curiosity.

They spent the day, between their arrival in town and Miles's departure, calling around to the various tailors and boot makers, collecting what they'd previously ordered of his tropical kit. At each establishment they entered, Lucius steeled himself against the stares, the carefully averted looks, and the whispers that followed him.

Was it his imagination, or did he draw more of this offensive curiosity when Angela Lacewood was by his side, presenting a striking contrast between her divine beauty and his own sinister appearance?

By the time they arrived back at the Clarendon laden with parcels, Lucius felt as though his head had been stuck in a vise that was being squeezed tighter by the minute.

"Shall we change clothes and meet for dinner in an hour?" asked Angela, as they stood in the corridor watching a parade of hotel porters fetch Miles's gear. "I can't say I'm impressed with London otherwise, but the food here is marvelous."

"Too rich for my digestion." Mrs. Tibbs wrinkled her nose. "All them French sauces. Besides, I want to get Master Miles's uniforms properly packed, and that'll be a good evening's work."

Marching into the young man's hotel room, she called over her shoulder, "Have a pot of tea and a plate of cold meat sent up for me, if you please. And no sauces!"

For a moment, Lucius felt the pain in his head ease as he and the Lacewoods exchanged exasperated glances. Then it returned, worse than ever.

"I regret I must decline, as well." The clatter of cutlery and the bright light of the hotel dining room would be more than he could stand. Not to mention more stares.

He turned to Miss Lacewood. "You and your brother should enjoy one last private dinner before he goes away—just family."

"But you *are* part of our family," Miles protested, "or soon will be. Come on. I've got at least a dozen more questions I still need to ask you."

Miss Lacewood glared at her brother. "Don't plague his lordship anymore! Can't you see you've exhausted him already?"

Her tender sympathy galled Lucius. Against his better judgment, he heard himself suggest, "We could dine in my room, if you'd rather?"

"A marvelous idea!" cried Miles.

His sister hesitated. "Are you sure? We wouldn't be intruding?"

Though his head throbbed like the very devil, Lucius forced himself to shake it...slowly. "Not at all. As Miles says, I'll be part of your family soon."

"Very well, then." She didn't look quite convinced. "Send for us when you're ready."

Was he mad? Lucius wondered as he entered his own room and rang for a servant to take his dinner order. What he needed tonight was darkness, privacy and quiet. A cold cloth on his forehead and perhaps a glass of brandy to ease the pain.

The brandy might be a good idea in any case,

he decided, pouring himself a generous medicinal dose. By the time he'd dressed for dinner and the first course had been laid out on a small table by the window, he'd begun to experience some relief.

To his surprise, his headache continued to abate once the Lacewoods arrived. As he listened to them reminisce about their early years in India, he found himself slowly but irresistibly drawn into their magic circle.

Their early lives had been no easier than his— less, in fact. Orphaned at a young age, dispatched to a cold, distant land to be raised on the grudging charity of relatives. Yet their experiences did not appear to have embittered them. Lucius suspected Angela had done much to protect and support her younger brother over the years.

Now, as the three of them sat eating, drinking and talking the hours away, Angela's warm brown eyes glowed with pride and affection for the boy. And if her soft smile held a faint trace of wistfulness or worry, she succeeded in hiding it from him.

"I must get to bed," she said at last, "or Tibby's bound to come looking for me. Then there'll be the devil to pay."

Lucius rose from his chair, somewhat unsteadily, for he'd consumed a quantity of wine with the meal, on top of his brandy. As he escorted Angela to the door, he struggled to keep his eyes averted from his own bed, in case he should imagine her in it.

"Are you coming, Miles?" She glanced back

over her shoulder. "It'll be an early morning to-morrow."

Miles yawned. "I won't be much longer."

"See that you don't. Lord Daventry needs his rest, too, you know. We'll have a long ride back home after we see you off."

The young man placed his hand over his heart. "On my honor, I won't keep your husband-to-be up carousing till all hours."

Angela caught Lucius's eye. "Don't let him impose upon you. Thank you for inviting us tonight. This was so much more cosy than the hotel dining room."

Lucius held her gaze. "The pleasure was mine, entirely."

From the table, Miles called, "My back is turned. If you kiss each other good-night, I shan't be a whit the wiser."

Should they? With a meaningful glance and a lift of his brow, Lucius asked Angela.

He knew he probably shouldn't, for in his present state he wasn't sure he could stop. Not even with her brother sitting only a few feet away.

Angela bit her lip in an unsuccessful effort to subdue a shamefaced grin. Her gaze skittered away from Lucius as she backed toward the door, shaking her head.

Was she remembering what he'd said the first evening he'd delivered her back to Netherstowe? Nonsense about hoping it would never again be necessary for them to kiss?

The depth of his disappointment took Lucius by surprise. He struggled to conceal it as he opened the door for her. "Sleep well, my dear. I'll see you in the morning."

"Good night," Angela whispered as she slipped past him.

Lucius watched as she made her way down the corridor to the room she shared with Mrs. Tibbs.

Back at the table, Miles hoisted an almost empty bottle of wine. "Shall we share what's left?"

The faintest breath of a sigh escaped Lucius as he closed the door. "Go ahead and finish it."

While he resumed his place at the table, Miles poured the last of the wine into his glass, then drained it in one draft.

"Ah! I expect it'll be a great while before I sample that fine a vintage again."

"Having second thoughts about going?"

The boy shook his head. "Not really. I stayed behind to ask you something."

"Oh?"

"It's Angela." Miles Lacewood planted his elbow on the table, then cupped his chin in the palm of his hand. "She has such a tender heart, you know—easily hurt, easily put upon. All our lives she's looked out for me. Now, finally, when I've reached an age where I might start looking out for her, here I am, going off half-a-world away."

Leaning back in his chair, Lucius nodded absently. He recalled something Angela had said on the day he'd proposed to her. About being fonder of his grandfather than of anyone else, except her brother. Soon she'd be losing them both from her life, poor girl.

Miles Lacewood heaved the exaggerated sigh of one who'd had a trifle too much to drink. "You *will* look out for her, won't you, Lord Daventry? I thought you and she would make an odd pair when I first heard you'd become engaged, but now I see the sense of it. A girl like Angela needs a man who's strong, even a bit ruthless if need be, to protect her."

The boy's words ambushed Lucius. It had never occurred to him that he might have something to offer Angela Lacewood besides a fortune and a title that meant nothing to her.

"Rest easy, my boy. I'll see that no harm comes to your sister." The very thought of anyone threatening Angela roused all his old soldiering instincts.

"Of course, you will." Miles surged up from the table. "Daft of me to ask, really." He gave a fuddled chuckle. "It's plain to see you're as mad about her as she is about you."

Fortunately, he did not seem to require a reply, for Lucius could not have provided one.

His mind churned in a manner that warned him he'd get little sleep that night. He wasn't certain which part of Miles Lacewood's well-intended words alarmed him more. That Angela might fancy him in a romantic way? That he might entertain such feelings for her?

Or that whatever feelings he had for the young lady might show?

"Poor man, you don't look as if you slept a wink last night!" Angela barely resisted the urge to reach up and caress Lord Daventry's lean cheek.

She cast a reproachful glance at her brother. "You promised me you weren't going to keep him up until all hours."

A small army of hotel porters issued from Miles's room, ferrying his uniform cases and other gear down to the carriage.

"I'm innocent, I swear," Miles protested with a jaunty grin. "I didn't stay more than ten minutes after you left."

"It's true." Lord Daventry nodded as he smothered a yawn. "In my cavalry days, I used to be able to sleep outdoors in the pouring rain. Now I'm spoiled. Can't get a decent rest except back at Helmhurst in my own bed. I hope you both fared better."

"Like a top." Miles bounced on the balls of his feet, clearly eager to begin his new life.

"I wish I had." Angela pretended to concentrate on donning her gloves. "I don't sleep well away from home, either."

That had only been part of the problem, of course. Which was why she didn't want Lord Daventry to catch a close look at her face. With his too-perceptive gaze, he might guess that their awkward parting last night had prompted her restlessness.

The last of the porters marched out of Miles's hotel room.

Tibby stalked down the corridor after them. "I suppose we'd best get this over with."

"It's going to be a long drive back to Northamptonshire," Lord Daventry muttered under his breath as he consulted his pocket watch.

He, Miles and Angela followed Tibby and the porters down the Clarendon's wide staircase.

"Don't mind Tibby," Angela begged him. "She's just worried about Miles and me. People have different ways of showing their feelings, you know."

Tibby's included fussing over the physical comfort of those she loved and fretting over anything she judged a threat to them. The earl channeled his into wry wit, sometimes flattering, sometimes critical. What about Lord Daventry?

The man seemed determined to hide his feelings, if he could not suppress them altogether. Was it possible his feelings might change without anyone being aware of it?

When they emerged from the Clarendon a few minutes later, Angela wrinkled her nose at the malodorous London fog. "What a gloomy day!"

With her beloved brother about to sail out of her life, she didn't need anything to further depress her spirits.

"A gloomy day for you is an ideal one for me,"

Lord Daventry reminded her as he helped her into the carriage. Was it her fancy, or did his hand tarry on hers? "If you like, we can draw back the curtains, to see where we're going. As much as one can see in weather like this."

The heavily laden coach rolled through the streets of Greenwich, toward the East India Dock, where Miles's ship waited. Now that Angela had seen London, she could not fathom why her cousins went on about it so, or why Tibby considered her slighted for never having been brought to town by the Bulwicks.

She was pleased for her brother that he would not have to toil away in the city, in some uncongenial situation procured by their uncle. And yet...

It took every crumb of fortitude she possessed to keep a cheerful smile on her face when it came time to bid Miles goodbye. Watching Tibby blink back tears didn't help.

"Be sure to go to church, regular. And don't be ruining your digestion with a lot of foreign food." The cook thrust a small tin box into the young man's hands. "Here are a few biscuits. Don't eat too many in case you get seasick."

"I will...I mean, I won't." Miles stooped to kiss her on the cheek. "Thank you, Tibby. Take care of yourself."

When Lord Daventry's turn came, he dropped a small handful of guineas into Miles's breast pocket. "Try not to lose it all at cards before you get to India."

Tucking Tibby's biscuit box under his arm,

Miles shook hands with the baron. "Thank you… for everything, sir. Your sound advice, most of all. I only hope I can be the kind of officer you were."

He turned to his sister. "Have a splendid wedding, old girl. You'll have to be an especially good wife to Lord Daventry to repay him for everything he's done for me!"

Angela threw her arms around her brother's neck and hugged him tight. If she tried to speak, she'd only burst into tears.

A piercing whistle sliced through the fog. Miles mashed his lips against her cheek, then pulled away from her and dashed up the gangplank.The tears she had managed to hold in check until now began to fall. Angela turned away from the ship. She didn't want Miles to see her crying if he happened to glance back.

The next thing she knew, she felt herself gathered against Lord Daventry's broad chest, held securely in his strong arms.

She tried to resist the sense of safety and solace that enveloped her, knowing it was only an illusion. But she needed it so much, just then. And it felt so genuine.

The question she had asked herself back at the Clarendon returned to perplex her. Was it possible Lord Daventry's feelings might change, without anyone being aware of it?

Not even himself?

Chapter Ten

❡

"I don't know when I've seen a man so altered for the better in such a short time." The earl's murmured words echoed Angela's own thoughts.

The two of them sat at a small writing table at one end of his library, addressing invitations to the ball. At the other end, Lord Daventry and the vicar were bent over a chessboard.

"Perhaps not *altered,*" the earl corrected himself, taking care that his grandson should not overhear. "Restored to what he once was. You've had a better influence on him than I dared hope, my dear child."

Angela kept her head bowed over her writing, so the earl's shrewd gaze would not divine her true thoughts on the matter. She knew very well it was neither her influence nor for her benefit that Lord Daventry had made such an effort to be sociable recently.

And it had been an effort. Angela was under no illusions about that.

She had seen the stares and overheard some of the whispers that first morning at St. Owens. Though Lucius Daventry had concealed his feelings as deftly as ever, Angela had sensed the depth of his aversion to being such a spectacle. How often in her younger years had she felt the same way, when some blunder of hers had provoked disapproving looks and tongue-clucking?

After that morning, she would not have blamed Lord Daventry if he'd retreated back into his shell of fierce privacy, armed to sting anyone who ventured too close.

But he hadn't, and for that she admired him.

Instead, by small but significant stages, Lord Daventry had begun to involve himself in the little world of Grafton Renforth. He now attended church regularly, and had even put in a brief appearance at a farewell party for Miles.

The earl glanced across the room at his grandson and Mr. Michaeljohn. "He seems to have taken a great fancy to your vicar, which surprises me, I must say."

Angela looked up for a moment to see the two men hovering over the chessboard, one so dark and one so fair they put her in mind of the black and white kings in their game.

"They're of an age," she reminded the earl. "They share a number of interests. I don't see why they shouldn't be friends."

That was not quite the truth, though. For all Mr. Michaeljohn had become a frequent guest at Helmhurst, Angela was not convinced Lord

Daventry enjoyed the vicar's earnest company. Perhaps he was looking ahead to the day his grandfather might need the comfort of a clergyman.

"Are you feeling ill, my dear?" asked the earl. "You look rather pale all of a sudden."

"Just a little tired after our trip to London." She manufactured a smile to reassure him.

In fact, over the past weeks she'd succeeded in pretending that the earl's health had improved. That wishful hope made it possible for her to visit Helmhurst day after day without betraying any sign of worry or grief. It allowed her to share the earl's eager plans for the ball in a way that seemed to heighten his enjoyment.

Such rose-colored fancies were fragile at best.

Now and then, a sharp thorn of truth would puncture her flimsy illusions. A hollow cough from the earl, or a shadow of pain crossing his face. A casual reference to the future of which she feared he would not be a part.

Then, shards of spun glass would gouge her heart, as they did now.

"Tired, my dear?" The earl glanced toward the tall pedestal clock nearby. "No wonder. Look at the time. The rest of these invitations can wait until tomorrow."

"Lucius, my boy," he called, "you must fetch Angela home at once. I fear I've exhausted her with all my preparations for the ball. I'm as bothersome as a child with a new plaything."

"Not in the least," Angela protested. "You

know I'm enjoying myself quite as much as you are. Pray, don't interrupt your game, gentlemen."

The vicar shook his head. "I can concede defeat with a clear conscience. It's only a matter of time until Lord Daventry has me in checkmate. I was certain I had him tonight. My position looked so promising until a few moves ago."

"You're a worthy opponent, Vicar." Lord Daventry moved one of his men, then removed a white piece from the board. "And a fine tactician. Check."

"I fear I'm no match for a strategist of your caliber." Mr. Michaeljohn contemplated his weakened position with a dispirited shake of his head, before advancing one of his remaining pieces. "Netherstowe is on my way back to the vicarage. As my forfeit of the game, I'll be glad to drive Miss Lacewood home."

Angela tried to ignore her twinge of disappointment. The vicar was a dear fellow—kind, diligent, obliging and very handsome in his way. Yet, compared to Lord Daventry, she found his company rather bland, without the baron's wry wit or far-ranging intellect to lend it zest.

"I protest, Mr. Michaeljohn." Lord Daventry captured another of the vicar's men. "Check. Had I been aware of the *penalty* for losing, I might have thrown the match in your favor."

He turned and leveled his gaze at Angela, who could not escape the sensation that he'd reached clear across the room to slide the backs of his fingers down her bare neck. Even knowing it was a performance to gratify his grandfather, she found herself powerless to resist the dark thrill Lord Daventry's intimate look sent coursing through her.

"I believe you'll agree," he continued in a husky tone that made Angela wish she had a fan to cool her flushed face, "that the honor of escorting Miss Lacewood is a prize that should go to the winner."

"Um, yes." The vicar made a tentative move, then took it back. "You are right, of course."

He thrust a different piece forward. "Check!"

Lord Daventry withdrew his gaze from Angela with a convincing pretense of regret that kindled a genuine one in her. For a moment he surveyed the board. Then he picked up a piece between his forefinger and middle finger, Angela thought it might be a knight.

"Check." He placed it back upon the board with restrained finality. "And mate."

He held out his hand. "Thank you for a challenging match, Mr. Michaeljohn."

"My pleasure," replied the vicar, gracious in defeat. "Now, if you'll excuse me, I must be getting home."

After shaking hands with Lord Daventry, he made his way to the far end of the room, where Angela was addressing one last invitation. "Since his lordship has won the honor of seeing you back to Netherstowe, Miss Lacewood, shall I look in on Mr. and Mrs. Shaw for you?"

Though she was certain he hadn't meant it to, the vicar's offer made Angela fairly squirm with guilt. She'd been so preoccupied with hoping Lord Daventry might invite her stargazing again, she'd forgotten poor Mrs. Shaw.

"I'd be ever so grateful if you would, Vicar. I can't think what's gotten into Mr. Shaw lately. He's the most pleasant of men…when he's sober."

"Shaw the blacksmith?" Lord Daventry stroked his chin and the color of his eyes seemed to darken until they appeared almost black. "Wasn't he a gunner in the war?"

Angela nodded. "I believe he and Mrs. Shaw's first husband served together. Most of the time he's quite temperate in his habits. But once or twice a year he starts drinking more than is good for him. Then Mr. Shaw becomes most *unpleasant*…to his wife in particular. I worry for her and for the child when he gets in that state."

"An unfortunate situation, to be sure." The vicar looked troubled, even somewhat puzzled, by such behavior. "If I find Mr. Shaw sober, I'll endeavour to encourage him. If he appears the worse for drink, perhaps I can persuade Mrs. Shaw to take sanctuary at the vicarage."

"That would be most kind of you." Angela chided herself for having compared the vicar unfavorably with Lord Daventry. "I hope it will bring Mr. Shaw to his senses."

The earl clucked his tongue. "Really, my dear, I'm not at all sure I approve of you involving yourself in such an unsavory situation."

"Nor I," Lord Daventry growled.

Such comments put Angela in mind of her

aunt's scoffing disapproval. Indeed, they offended her more, since she'd come to care for the good opinion of Lord Daventry and his grandfather in a way she'd ceased to value those of her relations.

"What state would our world be in if everyone felt as you do?" Trembling with emotion, she rose from her place at the writing table. "If people of goodwill never involved themselves in *unsavory situations?*"

She ignored both the earl's look of mild shock and Lord Daventry's dark glower. "What if England had never involved herself in that unsavory situation on the Continent?"

Such reckless outspokenness appeared to rob both gentlemen of speech. Her usual prudence swept away on a flood tide of indignation, Angela glared at them. What right had they to gainsay her sympathy, from which they had both benefited?

"I feel sorry for Mrs. Shaw and for her husband...for the little one most of all. I could not sleep at nights to think of that family in such distress if I failed to render what small assistance I am able."

Her conscience whispered that she was not being fair, that she was making Lord Daventry and his grandfather the target of her long-festering grievance against the Bulwicks. But the two men were responsible for stirring up other intense emotions to which she dared not give voice. A little righteous anger would not hurt either of them.

Before her wrought-up feelings spilled over into forbidden channels, she swept toward the library door. "Mr. Michaeljohn, I believe I will take you up on your kind offer of a drive. We can look in on Mr. and Mrs. Shaw on our way."

"But, surely..." The vicar pointed to the chessboard. "Lord Daventry...the match?"

Summoning the last embers of her indignation, Angela fixed his lordship with a glare that challenged him to oppose her. "Lord Daventry will have plenty of opportunities in future to collect on his *winnings*."

With that she tried to execute a crisp pivot on the toe of her slipper, but her foot caught the edge of the carpet, and she nearly went sprawling to the floor. At the last instant, she righted herself and flounced from the room while Mr. Michaeljohn hurried down the gallery after her.

Her foolish pique with the earl and Lord Daventry had burned itself to ashes. Now Angela was far more vexed with herself. Instead of enjoying a few enchanted hours of stargazing with the baron, she could look forward to the pleasure of confronting an obnoxious drunkard.

This was what came of cutting off her nose to spite her face.

As the retreating footsteps of Angela and Mr. Michaeljohn grew ever more faint, the earl rubbed the bridge of his nose. "I haven't been told off like that in a very long time."

He paused for a moment, perhaps to ponder his reaction. Then his wrinkled countenance blossomed into an unexpected grin. "It's rather refreshing, don't you agree?"

Lucius continued to glare at the library door. "So's a bucket of ice water over the head, depending on how you look at it."

He felt as if he'd just received such a cold dousing, and *refreshing* was not among the words he would use to describe the experience.

He'd been hoping to persuade Angela to make a detour on their way to Netherstowe. Perhaps up to the tower for an hour or two huddled over his telescope? The annual meteor shower in Scorpio was proving much more spectacular than usual this year.

While contemplating it the night before, Lucius had been inspired to the romantic nonsense of making a wish on one of those falling stars.

Just now, he had seen the evidence of his sentimental folly. Clearly Angela would rather mediate some domestic dispute between the blacksmith and his wife than spend the evening with him. No amount of wishing on his part was likely to alter that.

More to the point, perhaps, she appeared eager to keep company with the handsome and virtuous Mr. Michaeljohn. On the basis of a fortnight's critical acquaintance, Lucius had to admit the vicar was a worthy fellow, with a character as flawless as his features.

Lucius wasn't certain which he envied more.

The earl replaced the stopper on the inkwell and glanced over the stack of invitations Angela had finished. "She was right, of course, which is always vexing. I shouldn't be surprised if someone warned her against becoming involved with an unsavory character like you, my boy, or a fussy old invalid like me. We ought to thank our lucky stars Angela persists in thinking the best of everyone."

Lucky stars? Lucius shook his head at the notion. What made people fancy those great flaming balls of gas, millions of miles away, had any control over human destiny? Was it the friendly way they hovered in the night sky, twinkling like the fond eyes of a mother peering into the cradle of her sleeping infant?

Well, that was a whimsical illusion. Rather like the illusion that Angela had begun to care for him.

His grandfather's words had brought Lucius to his senses. Angela cared for everyone—drunken blacksmiths and their wives, ailing noblemen, disfigured war veterans—just as the stars cast their gentle radiance over saint and sinner alike. He mustn't deceive himself into believing he had, or ever could, claim a special place in her heart.

"I still don't like it, though," said the earl as he returned to his favorite armchair. He cast a glance over the vicar's defeat arrayed on the chessboard. "Angela getting in the middle of something nasty. England paid a great price for meddling in General Bonaparte's plans for conquest."

His grandfather's remark set thoughts shifting in Lord Daventry's mind. He had an urgent sense that there were several disparate pieces of information he possessed, which would create a meaningful pattern if only he could marshal them all together.

The earl pressed his fingertips together and rested his chin against them. "Feel free to dismiss me as an old busybody, my boy, but can we talk about what happened to you at Waterloo?"

"Waterloo—that's it!" All the facts fell into place.

"Thank you, Grandfather." Lucius headed for the door. "We will talk about it, I promise you, but at the moment I have a pressing matter I must see to."

The earl waved him on his way with a look that seemed to understand…perhaps better than Lucius did himself.

Mr. Michaeljohn's modest carriage had not reached the main road when it met a pony trotting up the lane to Helmhurst.

"That you, Vicar?" called the rider.

In the deepening twilight, Angela thought he looked like Mr. Barnes, the miller.

"Yes." Mr. Michaeljohn reined in his carriage horse. "Is something wrong?"

"It's the wife, Vicar. Just birthed twins."

Even as she exclaimed her congratulations, Angela realized that Mr. Barnes would hardly have come to Helmhurst in search of the vicar if all was well with his wife and their new offspring.

"Wee things, the pair of 'em," said the miller, confirming Angela's fears. "The wife is worried

they won't live. She's anxious to have 'em christened. Can you come, Vicar?"

"Of course. I'll just drop Miss Lacewood at
Netherstowe on my way."

As the miller turned his stocky mount and rode
back toward the village, Mr. Michaeljohn glanced
at Angela.

"Perhaps you'd rather go back to Helmhurst,
and let Lord Daventry fetch you home after all?
I'm truly sorry if I sparked a disagreement between the two of you this evening. Much as I
admire your charitable nature, I can sympathize
with his lordship's wish to protect you."

Protect her? The notion brought a lump to Angela's throat, but she dismissed it before it could
take root in her heart. There could be any number of reasons Lord Daventry might frown on her
association with the Shaws. She doubted a desire
to protect her was among them.

"I don't want to keep you from christening
those babies, Vicar. Just let me off at the Shaws'.
It's so close to Netherstowe, I can pay a quick
call, then walk home."

"Are you certain?" The vicar jogged the reins
and his horse continued down the lane at a smart
pace. "What if you find Mr. Shaw the worse for
drink?"

"Then I'll invite Mrs. Shaw to bring her little
one and spend the night at Netherstowe."

Angela strove to sound more confident than
she felt. Aunt Hester would be livid at the thought
of her giving shelter to *strays* in the family's ab-

sence. Perhaps she could persuade the servants to look the other way, just once.

"I fear Lord Daventry would not approve." The vicar could scarcely have sounded in greater awe of the Almighty, himself.

His anxiety stirred the embers of Angela's irritation with Lucius. "If his lordship disapproved of reading the scriptures on Sunday, would you refrain from doing that, too? I fear he's having an unwholesome influence upon you, Vicar."

"I protest, Miss Lacewood. It's just that—"

"Please," Angela interrupted him, "I would never forgive myself if I delayed you reaching those poor infants. Not to mention the comfort it may give their mother to have them properly christened."

"Well…if you're resolved…"

In the same situation, Lord Daventry would not have been swayed by her protests or excuses, Angela knew. Though the last thing she wanted was for the Vicar to stand firm, the fact that he wavered somehow diminished him in her eyes. Contrary and unfair though it was, she could not deny the feeling.

"I am resolved entirely," she replied. "I expect I've been worried about nothing. Mr. Shaw may be as sober as a justice, or so full of drink that he'll be sound asleep, and no threat to anyone."

"I hope you're right." Though he sounded dubious, the vicar gave a firm pull on the reins to slow his horse as they approached the Shaws' cottage.

Angela did not want to give him an opportunity to change his mind. While the carriage wheels were still rolling, though very slowly, she hiked up her skirts and jumped out.

"I'll be fine, Vicar." She waved him goodbye. "Thank you for the drive, and do give my best regards to Mrs. Barnes."

Was it only her fancy, or did she hear raised voices from within the blacksmith's cottage? Not wanting the vicar to hear, Angela gave his mare a light smack on the rump. The horse obliged by moving off at a brisk trot.

Angela inhaled a deep breath to fortify her courage, then she marched to the Shaws' door and knocked. The door flew open with such force it made her start.

"Who's there?" The surly challenge burst forth on a gust of gin fumes.

"It's Angela Lacewood, Mr. Shaw," she answered with forced brightness. "I'd like to speak with your wife, if I may."

"Why ye callin' at this hour?" demanded the blacksmith, his unshaven jaw thrust forward.

"Is it an inconvenient time?" Angela glanced past Mr. Shaw at his wife, whose face looked very pale and whose eyes showed too much white. "I do apologize. The vicar was driving me home from Helmhurst and I saw lights on, so I thought—"

"What d'ye want with our Lizzie, then?"

"Well…" Angela grasped for the first excuse that came to mind. "The earl is hosting a masquerade the week after next, you see. And I know your wife is a lovely seamstress, so I was hoping she might—"

"D'ye think I can't take care of me own wife? That she has to take in sewin'?"

The blacksmith took a menacing step toward Angela. Though Mr. Shaw stood an inch or two shorter than she, his darkened hands looked large and powerful, as did his forearms. The thought of how painful a blow he could inflict made Angela want to turn and run home to Netherstowe. The same thought kept her rooted to the spot, for Lizzie Shaw's sake. As long as she kept Mr. Shaw busy at the door, the man was no threat to his wife.

"Of course not." Angela willed Mrs. Shaw to scoop her little one from his truckle bed and steal out the back door while her husband was occupied. "Your wife would be doing me a great favor, as a matter of fact. I don't often get new clothes, so I have no acquaintance with any dressmakers."

Angela would have suffered torture before she'd have admitted such a thing to anyone else in Grafton Renforth, but she was desperate to hold the blacksmith's attention. His wife appeared to have heard her mute urging, for the woman tiptoed over to her young son's bed and lifted the sleeping child to her shoulder.

"I'm sure you're very prosperous," Angela rattled on, "but the earl has offered to pay for my gown and every little bit helps, doesn't it, when one is raising a family?"

Perhaps Angela's voice had become too loud

and shrill from fear. Or perhaps, in her haste, Mrs. Shaw handled the child less gently than she might have.

Whatever roused the child, he rubbed his eyes and asked, "Where we go, Mama?"

In the instant before Mr. Shaw spun about to confront his wife, Angela saw his eyes widen and his nostrils flare in the way she had once seen a bad-tempered bull do.

"Answer the boy, Lizzie! Where are ye takin' him?"

Mrs. Shaw's terrified gaze flitted from her husband to Angela. "I...I..."

"My, what a handsome little fellow!" Angela cried. "I expect he needed to use the chamber pot, didn't he, Mrs. Shaw? One hates to risk wet linen."

The blacksmith appeared not to heed her explanation but found his own in the frightened, furtive look on his wife's face.

"Damn ye, Lizzie!" He started toward her.

"Please, Mr. Shaw!" Angela latched on to his arm. "Don't do anything you'll regret!"

For an instant, relief flooded her as he spun back around. Then she saw the rage in his eyes, as well as something she had missed before...a black abyss of pain.

"Ye connived at this, din' ye?" He shook off her grip and raised his arm.

Torn between fear and pity, Angela braced herself for a blow that would send her reeling. As she closed her eyes, the queerest notion flitted through her mind. Might Lord Daventry have a spare mask he could lend her?

If the blacksmith struck her in the face, she would surely need one.

Chapter Eleven

When he saw the blacksmith raise one massive hand against Angela, Lucius wondered if his mask had caught fire. Then he realized that he was feeling a manifestation of his own rage. If he'd had time to think about it, the intensity might have frightened him.

But he only had time to act, with a swiftness that seemed to outstrip even thought. The next thing he knew, Lucius had the blacksmith's fist pinned to the door.

"Lay so much as a finger on her, Gunner Shaw," he growled, "and I'll make you regret it for as long as you live."

The well-honed edge of his threat seemed to penetrate the blacksmith's gin-soaked brain. "No, Lord Lucifer…Col. Daventry…sir!"

"And if you bring harm to your wife," Lucius added in a grave but less menacing tone, "you will not need me to make you regret it."

All the rage seemed to leech out of the powerful, stocky man. "I know…sir."

Lucius released the blacksmith's arm. "Let's
walk."

He shot a glance at Angela. Vexation and
relief fought a bloody skirmish within him. "Stay
here till I get back."

She replied with a wooden nod. Once the
blacksmith had staggered out of the her way,
Angela dashed inside the cottage to Mrs. Shaw.

For a moment Lucius stood in the dooryard,
shaking his head over the blacksmith, who fairly
radiated misery. Then he began to walk at a slow
pace that even a drunkard might manage. He was
rewarded by the sound of ponderous footfalls behind him.

"It's Waterloo, isn't it?" He scarcely needed
to ask, for he'd felt the ominous approach of that
anniversary himself, like the silent, disquieting
advance of an eclipse.

"Hell of a day, that," grunted the blacksmith.

"Hell." The word wafted out of Lucius on a
heavy sigh. After a long pause, he asked, "Told
your wife about it?"

"Nah. Don't want to, neither."

"I know."

Perhaps it would do him good to speak of it. No
doubt it would be painful at first, like lancing a
boil. But that might be preferable to letting the old
poison continue to fester, as he had been doing.

They wandered toward Shaw's forge, a short
way from the cottage. In the pale silver light of

the full moon, Lucius could make out a crude wooden bench beside the door. He lowered himself onto it, and after a slight hesitation the blacksmith sank down beside him.

The two men sat in silence for a time, listening to the chirp of frogs from a nearby bit of marsh. Lucius found himself wondering if that few acres of farmland on the road to Brussels looked and sounded this peaceful tonight. Or was the ground too steeped in violence, pain and blood ever to rest easy again?

"Does the drink help?" he asked, genuinely curious.

"A bit." The blacksmith shrugged. "Don't feel quite s'much like I'm goin' to explode."

Lucius nodded. He'd been tempted to get roaring drunk, himself. Especially in those early days when his wounds were fresh and raw. But in the end he'd feared the loss of self-control even more than he'd dreaded his demons. By and by he'd found his own means of escape, winging off to the stars.

"Wounded?" It was a daft question, Lucius acknowledged even as the word left his mouth. Weren't they all, even the ones who'd come away still whole in body?

"Nah, not then. Couple o' times in Spain, wi' old Nosey."

Lucius smiled to himself in the darkness. He hadn't heard the duke called that in a long time.

Beside him, the blacksmith kept talking, half

to himself. "My mate, Joe Liddle, got hacked to pieces by a French horseman."

An ugly noise followed the words, and Lucius knew the man must be vomiting, as he wanted to do.

For he'd taken part in a wild cavalry charge on the French artillery at Waterloo, and he had hacked one or two of their gunners to pieces. It was the last thing he remembered until he'd woken in hell, surrounded by dead and dying from both sides, with broken ribs and a smashed face.

A queasy sensation gripped Angela's stomach when she heard footsteps and muted voices approaching the Shaws' cottage an hour or so later. It wasn't fear, though. At least not in the usual sense.

She knew the blacksmith would never dare harm her after Lord Daventry's dire warning. And from the tone of the two men's voices, she doubted Mr. Shaw would pose a threat to anyone that night.

A good thing, too. From what Mrs. Shaw had confessed to her, and what Angela herself had guessed, the blacksmith and his wife had suffered enough already.

The cottage door opened and Mr. Shaw shuffled in, his head hung. Lord Daventry walked tall and erect behind him.

The blacksmith glanced up at Angela with red, swollen eyes and a look of such abject misery on his whisker-stubbled face that any fear she had felt of him melted away.

Lord Daventry bowed toward Mrs. Shaw. "Put your husband to bed, ma'am. I think he'll behave himself after this. If not, I want you to send me word, whatever the hour, and I'll come."

Angela had never heard the man speak in such a gentle, solicitous tone. It could not have been easy for him, coming here tonight. For so many reasons.

What had compelled him?

Gingerly, Mrs. Shaw took her husband's arm. "I will, milord. Thank you for coming tonight." She shifted her glance to Angela. "And you, miss. It was very brave of you."

Angela tried to summon a smile in reply as Lord Daventry beckoned her to leave. She didn't feel very brave confronting the prospect of a stinging rebuke from him. No matter how much she deserved it.

Out in the moon-dappled dooryard, Lord Daventry grasped the reins of the horse he'd left tethered there. "I suppose I should have brought the gig, but I was rather in a hurry. Do you mind walking back to Netherstowe?"

The better for him to lecture her on the subjects of reason and responsibility, no doubt. A scolding like that was bound to lose some of its authority if delivered over one's shoulder, to a person clinging to one's waist, on the back of a moving horse.

She considered protesting that she was capable of walking home by herself, but decided that would only make matters worse. "Not at all."

After a few moments she added, "I didn't even hear you ride up. I suppose my heart must have been pounding louder than the hoofbeats. Thank you for coming to my rescue. It would have served me right if you hadn't."

"Yes...well," he muttered, "I mean to have the vicar's head for this."

"Please don't. He got called away to the village. I assured him I'd be fine on my own. I thought I would be."

They walked in silence for a while, and with each step Angela waited for the ax to fall. When Lord Daventry cleared his throat, she braced herself for a verbal blow that would hurt more than any the blacksmith's huge hand could have inflicted.

"It was brave, what you did."

Were her ears working properly? Angela wondered.

"And I don't only mean standing up to Mr. Shaw," Lord Daventry continued. "It takes a special kind of courage to involve one's self in people's lives the way you do."

He didn't sound angry. He didn't even sound icy and controlled in an effort to contain his anger. His fine voice chimed with a deep, sincere note of approval.

Perhaps even...admiration.

So why were tears spilling from her eyes? And

why did her breath come out in an almost hysterical tangle of laughter and sobs?

"Angela?" He dropped the horse's reins and reached for her. "What's wrong?"

What was wrong? Angela asked herself the same question, only to shrink from the answer her heart gave.

It was wrong she should feel so safe and cherished in Lucius Daventry's arms when that was only a dangerous illusion. It was wrong that she could risk a beating at the hands of a violent drunkard, but not dare reveal her growing feelings for the man who now held her in his embrace.

"I was…certain you'd be…angry." She managed to gulp the innocent half-truth between bouts of sniffling.

"What makes you think I'm not?" he demanded with such an exaggerated pretence of severity it made her chuckle through her tears.

"You haven't threatened to make me regret it if I ignore your warnings in future," she quipped, sensing safety in jest.

A deep, cleansing laugh shuddered through Lord Daventry's chest. "Somehow, I don't think you respond well to threats, my dear Angela."

She could tell he meant it for a compliment, and a rare one at that. But she could not bring herself to trust this change in his manner. It felt like a trap, inviting her close with appealing bait, only to snap shut when she ventured too near.

Much as she wanted to linger in his arms, she

pulled back ever so slightly. Lord Daventry released her at once.

Angela fumbled for something to say that might smooth the awkward moment. "This business with Mr. and Mrs. Shaw, it's about the war, isn't it, and Mrs. Shaw's first husband?"

"Yes." Lord Daventry retrieved his horse's reins and began to walk again. "Shaw and the other man were on the same artillery crew. The friend asked Shaw to take care of his wife if anything happened to him, which it did unfortunately. That sort of thing happens quite often among the enlisted men."

"I see." That tallied with what she had learned from Mrs. Shaw. "But why does he take to the drink and get so angry?"

"Why *now,* you mean?" Lord Daventry stopped and lifted his face to the night sky. "I ciphered that answer shortly after you left with the vicar. It's why I came after you. I knew only another veteran of Waterloo could talk sense to Shaw tonight."

"Waterloo, of course." Angela chided herself for not realizing. About this time last year there had been trouble with the blacksmith, too. "I still don't understand what makes him so angry with his wife."

"The man's angry with himself," Lord Daventry corrected her. "He wouldn't be the first to feel guilt for surviving when so many of his friends did not."

Was he talking about Mr. Shaw, or himself? Angela wondered.

"He might have committed some minor error that day." Lord Daventry mused in a voice so burdened with regret Angela could scarcely bear to listen. "Failed to follow an order quickly enough, perhaps, or heeded a stupid one when he should have turned a deaf ear."

In the warm, safe quiet of that country evening, Angela tried to imagine the awful clamor of battle she knew must be echoing in his thoughts. But it was useless. She had never heard more than a handful of guns fired at once during hunting season. How could she hope to understand what men like Mr. Shaw and Lord Daventry had experienced that day, or how it had affected them?

She'd never seen a freshly maimed body, either, Angela reminded herself. Yet she knew something about wounded hearts. "You mean, he might feel as if it was…all his fault, and that he doesn't deserve any happiness because of that?"

No wonder she'd felt such unaccountable sympathy toward Mr. Shaw, when she should have been frightened or indignant. She had never watched comrades die or anything like that. But from her youngest years she had been made to feel a burden and a bother to her mother's family. Was that why she'd been beset by gnawing doubts about her worthiness for any good in life?

"Foolish isn't it?" Lord Daventry gave a low mocking chuckle. "But then, men are foolish creatures."

She watched him standing there, bathed in the cool, phantom light of the moon and stars that were his true passion. In that moment, Angela felt herself drawn to Lucius Daventry in a different, deeper way than she had before.

Not just as a fascination with the forbidden, or the stirring of a forlorn fancy from her girlhood. Not even the compelling appeal of a strong protector. It was a complicated mixture of all those, and more that she could not yet fathom.

How could he guess what demons drove poor Mr. Shaw, she wondered, unless he had felt the barbs of their pitchforks himself?

Was it possible these same moon and stars had shed their light on that field of carnage three years ago?

Lucius could hardly believe it, and yet…

"When I first woke up after the battle, I thought I'd died and gone to hell."

The pain. The revolting symphony of moaning, whimpering and keening that brought no earthly relief. The suffocating stench of blood and gunpowder.

"Yet everything looked so quiet and peaceful overhead. I kept staring up at it with my good eye, wishing some angel would swoop down and fetch me away. By and by, I fancied one had."

"How awful!" cried the angel.

Damn! Lucius crashed back to earth again. He hadn't realized his thoughts were coming out in words.

And he hadn't intended to tell Angela any of this, no matter how much he sensed it might ease him. He wanted to protect her from the cruel ugliness of what had happened to him, in the same way he'd protected her from the blacksmith's hurtling fist.

Not just for her own sake, either, or for the promise he'd made to her brother. He cherished her innocence and her goodness. Just being close to her, hearing her voice, breathing the same air, had brought him a measure of healing that had so long eluded him.

The last thing he wanted was to taint her with the poison that still festered inside him.

She edged closer to him until Lucius could smell her comforting bakeshop fragrance. "No wonder you fell in love with the stars. It was more than just an interest you could pursue during the night hours wasn't it?"

Lucius nodded. "They still have the power to take me away from who I am, and what I've become."

He could think of one other endeavor that might provide a blissful means of escape. One best indulged in the seductive concealment of night.

His body responded to that notion and to Angela's nearness. What would he give to see her, just once, naked as a goddess, kissed by the rosy glow of daybreak or twilight, her golden curls loose in a wanton cascade over her shoulders and her breasts? Then to waken her from maidenhood with the worship of his most skilful lovemaking, and finally to lose himself in her warm, welcoming flesh? What *would* he give?

His title? Without a question.

His fortune? Readily.

His soul? Perhaps even that.

Her hand slipped into his. If he turned just a little, he could skim it against the lap of his trousers, to show how little it took from her to rouse him.

But that might frighten her away, as even the faintest stirring of his ardor had done on other occasions. Tonight he could not bear to part with her a moment sooner than he must.

"I don't think you've become anything so terrible." Her voice sounded almost timid, as though she expected her words to invite a rebuke from him. "I never find myself anxious to escape your company."

Her words pierced him like a shaft of pure, shimmering gold. At first, he did not dare reply for fear his self-control would desert him entirely.

Perhaps his silence invited her to say more than a response would have. "You, and Mr. Shaw, and all the other men who fought, you gave yourselves, your hearts and souls, to be wounded as badly as your bodies, if not more. The men who died, perhaps they were the fortunate ones."

Often in the past three years he had thought so, too. But not tonight. The past three years suddenly seemed a small price to pay for moments like this one. Even if they could never be anything more. Even if they couldn't last.

He had better return home before the bewitchment of moonlight made him do something he would rue for a long time to come.

"Do you always see the good in everyone?" He started to walk again, her hand clutched in his. "Even when people can't recognize it in themselves?"

She hesitated before replying. "Not...always."

"But often?"

As they rounded a bend in the lane, the lights of Netherstowe came into view. Would one of the servants be waiting up for her return? His friend, the butler, perhaps? Or that glowering old scold of a Tibbs woman, to whom Angela was so perversely devoted?

"I...suppose so," she admitted. "Is that such a bad thing?"

"Hazardous." Lucius found himself clinging more tightly to her hand. "Tonight, for instance."

"So it's safer to assume the worst about people?" Though she posed the question in a tone of gentle curiosity, Lucius recognized a challenge to who he was and how he lived.

He shrugged. "It saves time."

The horse had been following quietly behind them. Now it blew out its breath in what sounded like an exasperated sigh.

Angela gave a silvery peal of laughter. "What a cynical old brute you are, Lucius Daventry!"

From her exquisite lips, it sounded almost like a compliment.

"Yet you find something to approve, even in a cynical old brute?"

"Much."

That one whispered word made his heart miss a beat. Desperately as he wanted to ask what, Lucius found he could not work up the nerve.

Fortunately, Angela did not leave him in suspense. "You have the courage to look at the world with no illusions. I sometimes wonder if I don't deceive myself into seeing people and circumstances in a hopeful light because I'm afraid to face them as they truly are."

He would rather do without the praise, Lucius realized, if it meant she must condemn herself.

"I don't believe for a minute that you lack courage, my dear. It took a great deal of pluck to discover the truth about Lord Lucifer, and to stand up to Mr. Shaw tonight. And it takes courage to put on a carefree face for my grandfather, day after day, when I know you must be dreading what's to come."

"As you do?"

"As I do." Of late he had found himself shrinking from it more and more. Not only because it meant losing his grandfather, but because it would mean losing Angela, too. "At least I'm not obliged to appear cheerful. Grandfather would become suspicious if I altered my usual manner."

He had been checking the length of his stride in an effort to delay their parting, but now they were within a few yards of Netherstowe's front door. Lucius thought he could make out the shadow of

Mrs. Tibbs keeping her grim vigil in one of the second-floor windows.

He toyed with the notion of giving Angela a wicked, lingering kiss good-night, just to shock the old cat.

Partly to shock the old cat.

But could he trust himself to stop once he gave his pent-up passion free rein? Lucius feared not.

Angela had become too great a threat to his self-control.

"You are naturally lighthearted. I brood." He must remind himself…and her, perhaps, why this make-believe courtship of theirs could never be more than that.

"You are trusting. I am wary. You are merciful. I am ruthless. You show your heart for all to see. I keep my feelings secret from everyone— even myself, sometimes."

The list of contraries went on and on, some of which he hardly needed to point out. His disfigurement, for instance, as opposed to her flawless beauty.

How enchanting she looked at that moment, softly illuminated by the muted candlelight spilling from the windows. Like that heavenly jewel, Saturn—each time more beautiful than he remembered.

Angela's bonnet had fallen back onto the nape of her neck, and the evening dew had teased her hair into the most delicious golden tendrils. Her eyes had never looked so luminous, glowing with admiration, even affection, for the man she believed him to be.

That noble ideal did not exist any more than Lord Lucifer had. Less, indeed.

Lucius lifted her hand to his lips in a hasty farewell and made one last effort to dispel her illusions. Lest they begin to seduce him, too. "You and I are as different as day and night."

A strange look came over her face, one nothing like what Lucius had anticipated.

"Day and night!" Her eyes sparkled brighter than Sirius on a crisp winter night, and her lips parted in a smile of breathtaking brilliance. "What a marvelous idea! That's exactly what we shall be!"

Chapter Twelve

Like day and night.

The words played a sweet, haunting melody through Angela's thoughts as she twirled around the sitting room, showing off Lizzie Shaw's exquisite handiwork to Tibby, Hoskins and the rest of the servants.

"Ye look like a princess, miss, or a duchess!" squealed Violet, the parlor maid.

For the first time in her life, Angela felt like a princess. At least, the way she *imagined* a princess might feel. Though perhaps the blithe, buoyant sensation that bubbled through her veins was superior to anything a true princess might experience. A lady born to the crown might take her exalted station and privileges for granted.

For Angela, tonight would be a fairy tale come true.

Mr. Hoskins beamed his approval of the silk and lace confection that billowed around her in shades of gold and blue. "A countess, you mean,

Violet. Our Miss Angela will be Countess of Welland, one day."

Though she knew he'd said it to please her, the butler's words flattened a few of Angela's bubbles. Tonight's masquerade ball at Helmhurst would be like a scene from a fairy tale. But she must not expect it to end *happily ever after* with the scullery maid in the arms of her prince…or her baron.

"If you ask me," said Tibby, her arms folded across her flat chest and her tiny eyes narrowed to tight slits. "She's going to catch cold in that flimsy excuse for a bodice. Whatever was Mrs. Shaw thinking?"

"Cold?" Angela could scarcely believe her ears. "Why, Tibby, it's past midsummer night. If I wore anything heavier, I'd roast."

The barb at the heart of Tibby's rebuke she could not dismiss quite so easily. Her costume as Lady of the Day did leave a rather provocative expanse of shoulder and bosom on display. Not that Angela cared about showing herself off to most of the earls' guests.

As long as Lucius approved.

Ever since the night he'd rescued her from Mr. Shaw, she had begun to sense in him a growing awareness of her as a woman.

Just last week, when Lucius had helped her on with her cloak, she'd felt a barely restrained tremor as his hands lingered on her shoulders. Often when he'd sat poised behind her atop the tower, introducing her to some new marvel of the heavens, she had heard his breath quicken or catch in his throat. Even the way he looked at her these days betrayed a curious fascination, as though she were the first woman he'd ever seen.

"Is my mask on straight?" she asked, grateful for the protection it provided her too-candid features. Just thinking about the subtle but significant attentions Lucius had paid her of late set a fevered blush glowing in her cheeks.

Violet cocked her head to one side. "It looks fine to me, miss. My, but it's cunning. Is it made of real gold?"

Before Angela could reply that it was only gilded papier-mâché, Tibby sniffed. "Pack of nonsense, if you ask me. Who ever heard of holding a ball outdoors? All the guests masked like highwaymen? Heaven knows what riffraff could sneak in!"

Perhaps the butler had put up with more of this sort of grumbling from Tibby over the past two weeks than had reached Angela's ears, for he shot the cook a pointed glance. "I don't recall anyone asking you, Mrs. Tibbs."

Tibby's eyes bulged wider than Angela had ever seen them, and she appeared to swell in size, like a cat getting ready to fight. Angela feared domestic warfare might erupt at that very moment on the sitting room carpet.

She rushed to come between the cook and the butler, who'd been on such amiable terms before her engagement to Lord Daventry. "Don't be cross, Tibby, please! You don't want to spoil my lovely evening, do you?"

"I don't want to spoil anything, my pet!" Tibby clutched Angela's hands. "I just don't think it's proper for a young lady to be celebrating an engagement her nearest relations know nothing about."

Angela sighed. "Tibby, we've been over and over this. You know Lord Daventry and I won't set a date for our wedding until Aunt and Uncle and the girls return from Europe."

She'd repeated this fiction so many times it now tripped off her tongue as if she believed it with all her heart.

Or wanted to.

"Do you truly suppose Lord and Lady Bulwick will object to my marrying a man of title and fortune?"

Tibby's pointy little face took on such a grieved look, Angela could not stay vexed with her. "There's more to a happy marriage than rank and money, pet. You've lived in this house long enough to know that, surely?"

Of course she had, and it was partly for that reason Angela had never hankered after marriage as most young women seemed to. But lately she'd been recalling more and more moments from her early life. They had given her tantalizing glimpses of a different sort of marriage.

"Oh, Tibby, there's ever so much more to his lordship than those things. Mr. Hoskins knows

it, and so do I. Now will you please stop fretting
and be happy for me?"

The cook muttered something under her
breath. Angela thought she heard a reference to
her soft heart...and the butler's soft head.

"Come see, miss!" cried Violet from the window. "Was his lordship sending someone to fetch
you over to the big house?"

Eager for the distraction, Angela flew to the
window. She'd hoped Lucius might come to collect her himself, in the familiar little gig drawn
by the black horse. That way they could savor a
few precious, private moments together before
being swallowed up in the crush of strangers at
Helmhurst.

She could barely contain a sigh when she saw,
instead, a magnificent closed coach coming up
the lane, pulled by a fine pair of matched bays,
and driven by the earl's head coachman in full
powdered wig and livery. A pair of footmen, simi-
larly attired, rode on the outside perches.

"My word," murmured the butler, who stood
behind Angela, staring out the window. "If that's
the rig I reckon it is, it's only been used a time
or two since the earl and his countess rode in the
great procession for the old king's coronation."

From Hoskins's reverent tone, Angela guessed
she was meant to be impressed by the honor. In
truth, though, she would rather have driven to
Helmhurst in a dogcart accompanied by Lord
Daventry, than sent for in the grandest coach.

"It's probably more fashionable to keep them

waiting." Angela struggled to subdue her disappointment as she adjusted her mask one last time, and headed out of the sitting room. "But that would be cutting off my nose to spite my face, wouldn't it?"

She let Hoskins march on ahead of her to throw open the doors. Then she swept after him, praying she would not trip on the hem of her skirt.

The stately carriage had just come to a halt in front of the entrance when Angela stepped outside. One of the footmen leaped from his perch to open the carriage door for her.

At least she thought it was for her until a familiar figure emerged from the coach and strode up the steps to meet her. As she caught sight of him, her heart seemed to inflate until Angela wondered how her chest could contain it.

She had grown accustomed to Lord Daventry's taste in black clothing, but for his costume as Lord of the Night, he had taken it beyond boots, trousers, coat and waistcoat, to a curious-looking black shirt and cravat, as well. A full black cloak billowed out behind him, a perfect match for her gold one. Here and there about his attire, cut glass buttons were sewn in clusters to resemble the constellations.

Taken with the rest of his garb, the close-fitted black mask Lucius wore over his whole upper face did give him the air of a highwayman. Tonight Angela found it more stimulating than sinister.

A few steps short of her, he froze. "I came

to fetch you to the ball, Miss Lacewood. Now I wonder if I dare."

Was something wrong with her gown, Angela wondered? Did he find the cut too immodest, as Tibby had? Then why did his voice sound amused…even admiring?

"It is not polite for a host to flaunt his good fortune under his guests' noses, after all. I fear I shall be the envy of every gentleman present."

"You mustn't tease me like that!" Angela put her hand to her bosom, hoping to settle her wildly fluttering heart. "You gave me an awful fright, thinking I couldn't come to the ball."

Lucius chuckled. "Never fear, my dear. I'm neither so brave nor so foolhardy that I would risk my grandfather's wrath by returning to Helmhurst without you."

As he took her hand and led her toward the carriage, he whispered, "No matter how tempted I might be to keep you all to myself."

The oddest sensation rippled through Angela just then, as potent as it was bewildering. Approaching the carriage, she glanced up to see the evening star beginning to glitter just above the trees on the eastern horizon. Lucius had told her it was not a star at all, but a planet.

Venus—named for the Roman goddess of love.

Suddenly it appeared to Angela as though the warm evening air shimmered with stardust magic. And *happily ever after* felt as if it might just be within her reach.

* * *

He didn't deserve her, in more ways than he could name. Lucius had discovered more of those ways each day of the past month.

But should that stop him from making a determined bid for her? he wondered, as he heard himself spout the kind of lavish compliments he had once disdained. To his surprise, they tasted very sweet on his tongue.

True, he might fail, and Lucius Daventry could not abide failure. Tonight it occurred to him that the most unbearable failure of all might be if he failed to make the attempt.

Angela remained unaccountably quiet as they settled opposite each other in the carriage and it pulled away from Netherstowe. Her silence made Lucius uncomfortable. Of late, she had become more and more talkative in his company. He'd grown to enjoy her conversation and her sly but gentle wit. Had his greeting offended or frightened her into silence?

Lucius wished he could coax her into removing her mask. Then he might get a proper sense of her reaction to his belated, perhaps futile, attempt at wooing her. Did she ever experience a similar frustration on his account? he wondered. Not only with the mask he wore, but with the cool facade behind which he so often hid his true feelings?

He started when Angela suddenly snapped open her fan and began to wave it in front of her face, making it impossible to guess anything of her expression.

"A warm evening," she said. "Marvelous weather for the ball, though. Had many guests arrived by the time you left?"

"Rather a lot, as it happens." Lucius couldn't decide whether he approved of that. Tonight he wanted to share Angela with as few other people as possible. "I'm surprised so many were willing to make the journey. Curiosity must have got the better of them."

Her fan stopped in mid-flutter. "Curiosity?"

Lucius nodded. "To gloat over the poor mangled recluse who used to be the 'handsomest beau in England.'"

"I'm certain that is *not* how people think of you."

"Now, my dear." He wagged his forefinger at her. "You are thinking the best of everyone again."

"Of course, I am." She tapped his finger with her fan in a gesture of innocent flirtation that set a will-o'-the-wisp of hope wafting in his heart. "And you are supposing the worst."

Angela's eyes sparkled like tawny gems set in her golden mask. "Can we not compromise? I will concede that a few bird-wits may come to gloat or to satisfy their curiosity, if you will grant that at least as many kind souls may come to see how you're getting on and to wish you well."

"That will only account for a small number," he reminded her. "What about all the rest?"

She responded in a flash. "Why, they're the vast majority who don't give twopence about you either way. They only want to eat, drink, dance and flirt."

Charming girl! What a perfect idiot he'd been the past three years to ignore such a treasure under his nose. "Now *they* sound like a sensible crowd. Shall we throw our lot in with them for tonight?"

"In every particular?" asked Angela. She had retracted her fan. Now she opened it again, not with a quick snap, but spreading it leisurely, one gilded panel at a time.

Lucius shrugged. "Why not?" It had been a long while since he'd used the seductive power of his voice upon a woman. If he used it on Angela tonight, in the darkened garden, perhaps she could imagine him as he'd once been and begin to fall in love.

"I'm hungry," he murmured. Though not for anything he was likely to find on the buffet. "Aren't you?"

"I can't decide if I'm too nervous to eat," Angela confessed, "or so nervous I'm likely to nibble every sweet thing in sight."

"I know what you mean." Lucius could see a number of sweet things he wanted to nibble, beginning with the delicate curve of her neck. "But you have no need to be nervous, truly. You're sure to create a favorable sensation. Besides, a glass or two of champagne will calm your nerves."

Her lips twisted in an impish grin. "I seem to recall a drive you and I took along this road a while ago, at which time you warned me I should avoid champagne unless I wished to make a fool of myself."

Remembering the things he'd said to her that evening, Lucius felt a proper fool himself. He recalled some prophetic nonsense about her reforming his reputation, and turning his life inside out. Fortunately for him, Angela had gone ahead and done both, despite his warnings to the contrary. Even for his grandfather's sake, how had she ever put up with him?

"Don't misquote me now." He leaned forward and caught her free hand in his. "I said you should avoid champagne unless you wished to commit *an indiscretion*."

"When you say it like that, it sounds positively... tempting." Her whisper fell like a tender kiss on some place in his heart that had been asleep so long he'd almost given it up for dead. Now it stirred again.

"It does, doesn't it? So much so, I might be tempted to join you. I believe I've had rather too much discretion in my life until tonight." Lucius leaned forward, as if he intended to kiss her hand. At the last second he tilted his face to graze his cheek against the backs of her fingers.

"Gracious, I can't believe we're here already!" Angela's fan fluttered...or did it tremble?

He lifted his head with the greatest reluctance and offered her a reassuring smile. "Then we are agreed on our program for the evening—eating, drinking, dancing and flirting?"

"In that order?" Her fingers whispered against his as she withdrew them from his grasp.

Lucius made his voice a velvet caress, just for her. "In whatever order you desire, my dear."

The carriage came to a smooth stop. Footmen scrambled from their places to open the door. Lucius half expected a flourish of trumpets to greet their arrival.

He emerged from the carriage first. Was it his oversensitive imagination, or did heads turn and the chatter of the guests suddenly grow quiet? Let them look, he insisted to himself. Let them talk. He would soon give them something worth talking about.

Turning toward the carriage, he extended his hand to help Angela alight. As she emerged, soft gasps of admiration ran through the crowd.

A liberating sensation of relief flooded through Lucius, that he was no longer the target of curiosity. It was followed by a fierce swell of pride in Angela. And gratitude that she'd diverted the attention of the crowd from him, as well as insuring that no sensible man present would dare to pity him.

Quite the contrary in fact.

Everyone was staring at her. The whole dazzling aristocratic assembly. Beneath her skirts, Angela's knees began to tremble.

Her costume *was* too immodest. If she opened her mouth, she was sure to say something stupid and countrified. If she took a step, she was liable to trip over her own feet. For an instant, Angela yearned to throw herself back into the protective cocoon of the carriage and wail for the driver to fetch her back home before she disgraced Lord Daventry and herself.

Then Lucius took her hand, and she remembered how he had grazed her fingers against his cheek only moments ago. What did all the stares in the world matter, as long as he held her in his compelling green gaze? What did any opinion in the world signify, as long as he believed her beautiful and made her believe it, too?

As if he sensed her apprehension, Lucius tucked her hand securely in the crook of his arm. If she stumbled now, he would steady her. That heartening certainty filled Angela with a heady sensation she had never fully experienced until that moment.

It tingled through her veins. Anchored her rapid, fluttering pulse until it beat steady and strong. Straightened her spine and ignited her smile. All as if by some powerful sorcery. For the first time in her life, Angela tasted the magic potion of confidence, and found it delicious.

"So you have come to join the festivities, after all." Over the breathless hush of his guests, the earl's fine voice rang out, more robust than Angela had heard it in a great while. "Though I hardly blame you for wanting to keep your charming fiancée to yourself for as long as possible."

The crowd parted for Lucius and Angela to make their way toward his grandfather. The earl

sat on a raised dais that gave him a superb view of
the festivities. He wore a turban and the brightly
colored silk robes of a Far East potentate.

On either side of him sat two ladies of his own
generation—one slender and delicate in appearance, the other stout and regal. Both were splen-
didly attired, though not in costume.

The earl beckoned Lucius and Angela closer as
the hired musicians struck up a tune and guests
flocked to the improvised dance floor on the terrace. "Lucius, Angela, I must introduce you to
two dear friends of long-neglected acquaintance.
The Dowager Marchioness of Warmouth and the
Dowager Duchess of Alderton. Ladies, my grandson, Lord Daventry, and his fiancée, Miss Lacewood."

Angela managed a reasonably graceful curtsy
to the women, who pronounced themselves
charmed, though they did not look it.

"Lacewood?" muttered the stout, regal lady,
peering at Angela through her lorgnette. "Who
are your people, child?"

Before Angela could stammer that she had
no family of any consequence, Lucius spoke. "If
it makes any difference, Miss Lacewood is the
niece of our neighbor, Lord Bulwick."

The tiny woman glanced around the earl at her
larger friend. The two of them shook their heads.
"Never heard of him."

Angela's cheeks flamed. If her uncle was beneath the notice of these titled creatures, how

much lower must his penniless orphaned niece reside?

One hand still tucked in the crook of Lord Daventry's arm, she felt his muscles tense with coiled, dangerous power. She cast him a sidelong glance only to shrink from the grim set of his features and the unholy blaze of his eyes. Could all that barely contained rage have mustered in her defense?

He began to speak, his words striking sharp and swift. "Why, you malicious—"

Lord Lucifer seemed to take possession of him, pronouncing a dread curse.

Angela tugged on his arm. "Please, don't."

The earl gave a dry chuckle as he turned to the dowager marchioness. "My dear Louisa, when you were Miss Lacewood's age you must have wished no one had ever heard of *your* uncle."

The stout dowager duchess laughed until her whole round face was nearly as red as the spots of paint on her cheeks, while the dowager marchioness grew more pale than her powder.

"It is a great pleasure to meet you, of course, Miss Lacewood," she declared, in a tone that sounded perfectly sincere. "Any woman capable of drawing out this pair of recluses to host a ball is worthy of closer acquaintance."

"I can vouch for the worth of Miss Lacewood's acquaintance." The earl planted his hands on the arms of his chair and pushed himself to his feet. "Will you do me the honor of the next dance, Louisa? Are you still as light on your feet as ever?"

Though she protested that she hadn't taken the floor in years, the dowager marchioness rose and clutched the earl's arm readily enough.

Lord Daventry turned to Angela. Apparently, his grandfather's diversion had allowed him to reassert the self-control he'd come dangerously close to losing.

He nodded toward the terrace dance floor. "Shall we join them? Or would you prefer a little refreshment first?"

Angela glanced toward the dancers. The movement of their brightly colored costumes created ever-shifting patterns as the sky darkened overhead and the tiny lanterns in the trees twinkled like earthbound stars.

"A dance, I think. Then a drink to refresh ourselves."

"As you command, my lady."

They took their places and had not long to wait before the musicians began to play a rather sedate country dance. For the first few bars, Angela gave her full concentration to the steps, anxious not to embarrass Lord Daventry.

Lead down. Cast back. Circle four-hands. Reverse.

But gradually the touch of his hand and the warmth of his gaze drew her out of herself, until she had eyes and ears for him alone.

How well he looked! Her Lord of the Night, so tall and spare, his movements so lithe and assured. He held her spellbound in his gaze and wrapped her in the dark velvet of his voice.

True she had once feared him as she had feared the limitless enigma of the night sky. But Lucius had revealed its hidden charms to her. In doing so, he'd allowed her to glimpse his own hidden charms and hidden wounds.

Both drew her and bound her to him.

Before the night was out, Angela vowed to herself, she would make Lord Daventry forget his resolve not to kiss her again.

Chapter Thirteen

Had he once hoped it would never be necessary for him to kiss Angela again?

As she glided over the terrace at his side, Lucius resolved to eat his foolish words, even if his pride choked on them.

"You claimed you did not dance well." He leaned close to whisper the words in her ear as they moved off the terrace after several very pleasant dances. "What other mistaken ideas do you have about yourself, my dear?"

"I said I hadn't much practice," she corrected him. "I believe I might enjoy dancing, perhaps even become good at it, if I had more opportunities. And a congenial partner."

Something about her answer troubled him faintly. Since he could not decide what, Lucius dismissed it from his thoughts.

"Would you care for a drink to refresh ourselves? We must not neglect our program for the evening. Remember, dancing was only part of it."

A little wine, another dance or two, perhaps something sweet from the buffet. Each and all served up with a generous dollop of flirtation. It had been so long since Lucius had allowed himself to admire a woman openly he'd almost forgotten how much he enjoyed it.

If he had ever enjoyed it as much as he did tonight… with her.

Angela sniffed the air. "Something smells very good. I was too nervous to eat all day. Now I find myself sharp set."

He understood, better than she might guess, how a long-suppressed appetite, suddenly awakened, could intensify to an unbearable pitch.

He leaned toward Angela, as if he meant to whisper in her ear again. Instead he drew a deep, lingering breath, inhaling as much of her subtle spicy-sweet fragrance as his lungs would hold. A muted gasp escaped her lips, but she did not pull back from him. Did he detect the delicate musk of desire mingled with her innocent bakeshop sweetness?

It created an irresistible bouquet.

"By all means, let us eat," he purred. "My hunger has been growing for some time. It has reached ravenous proportions."

Lucius drew back from her with a powerful reluctance that taxed his self-control.

As he led her toward the heaping buffet table, a few sharp little doubts worried at the edge of his awareness. Lucius refused to pay them any mind. Once they'd been hulking mastiffs, barring

Angela from his heart with their deep menacing growls. But with each passing day, and himself scarcely aware of the change, they had withered and shrunk until now they were the size of runt lapdogs, their shrill warning barks more an annoyance than a deterrent.

Taking a plate, he surveyed the bountiful spread. "That French pastry cook Grandfather engaged has certainly earned his pay. Which of these delicacies can I tempt you with?"

The tip of Angela's tongue peeped from between her lips and made a rapid circuit of them. "Gracious, I hardly know where to begin. Except at Christmas, Tibby never bakes anything more elaborate than plum pudding or gingerbread."

After a moment's deliberation she pointed to a platter of small boat-shaped pastries. Each bore a crimson cargo of glazed berries, only slightly less succulent than her lips.

"One of those, please. No, wait! Make it two. And a few of those iced cakes with the glazed violets on top, one of them wouldn't make a proper mouthful."

They proceeded to plunder the refreshment table until the plate Lucius held threatened to spill its contents.

"Another of these?" He pointed to a pyramid of soft pastry nuggets filled with flavored cream.

Her shameless appetite for sweets was one of the many things that enchanted him about Angela. He had denied himself the sweet things of life for too long. Lately Lucius had begun to ask himself why, and find himself less than satisfied with the answers he received.

"I daren't." Angela shook her head, flashing him a grin that looked a trifle guilty. "And you mustn't tempt me any further."

"Oh, but I must," he murmured as he shepherded her through the throng of reveling guests to a small table on the farthest edge of the lawn. "It's such an amusing pastime…temptation."

He deposited the heaping plate of sweets on the table, then held a chair for her.

Music wafted from the terrace, as delicate and delicious as the pastries. The tiny lanterns laced through the tree branches spread a golden glaze over the whole scene. It heightened the vivid colors of the costumes against the soft, dark backdrop of the summer night.

Lucius set his chair closer to Angela's and sank onto it. He plucked a golden brown ball of pastry from the plate and lifted it to her lips. "Can I coax you to eat out of my hand?"

She picked out an identical pastry and offered it to him. "Only if you will eat out of mine, as well."

Talk of temptation! It flared within Lucius, searing his flesh from the inside out.

"I will." He parted his lips for a taste of the pastry. "I believe I already have some practice at it."

He bit through the delicate shell that tasted of butter to the cool, moist sweetness of cream inside. When it gushed out over his tongue, Lucius could not stifle a groan of pleasure.

Until tonight, he'd been rather indifferent to food as long as he got filling meals at regular intervals. Never had he relished it with all his senses and found it so enjoyable.

He almost groaned again when Angela dipped her head to nibble the pastry from his hand. Her tongue swiped against his fingers, then her lips closed over them to retrieve the last drop of cream that might linger there.

Could she guess the provocative effect her actions had upon him? Lucius doubted it. Yet, somehow, her naive, playful sensuality roused him more intensely than any deliberate attempt at seduction.

Since the day he'd proposed to her, Angela had seduced him back to life, little by little. One new sight at a time. One sound, one scent, one taste, one texture. All distilled to their purest, sweetest essence through her.

Now he longed to return the gift she'd bestowed on him, by showing her all the delicious sensations a skilled and ardent lover could stir in her body.

True, he'd believed the horrors of the battlefield had scarred his heart beyond the capacity for love. Either to give or to inspire it. In spite of his devilish looks and reclusive ways, Angela had made him believe she could care for him.

And what man who possessed a heart, no matter how damaged, could fail to care for a woman like her?

He licked the cream off *her* fingers, one at a time, to give Angela an enticing foretaste of how he longed to fondle the peaks of her breasts with his tongue. Perhaps the fervor of his intentions communicated themselves to her body, for even in this shadow-wrapped corner he could see her nipples jut out beneath the light fabric of her gown.

Lust bounded through him. He was hard-pressed to restrain it.

With deliberate care, he looked over the plate of dainties and selected one of the iced cakes topped with a candied violet.

He offered it to Angela. "I can't help feel that anything so toothsome must be a wicked indulgence."

"Quite the contrary." The gentle music of her voice beguiled Lucius from his cynical folly. "I'm certain it must be a special blessing."

She ate the cake from his hand, savoring each tiny bite with such singular delight that Lucius fancied he could taste it on his own tongue.

What had he done to deserve a blessing like Angela in his life? Lucius wasn't sure he could bear to give that question a truthful answer.

"This is all too rich for me," Angela declared after they had eaten a few more of the pastries, turnabout.

Lifting one of the boat-shaped berry tarts from the plate, she held it between her and Lucius. "This one looks so good I'm dying for a taste.

I don't believe I can eat it all, though, or I may sicken myself. Shall we share?"

Though he wondered how such a trifle could tax her appetite, Lucius heard himself agree. He bent forward to take a bite at the same moment Angela did. The wild, sweet tang of strawberries, raspberries and red currants flooded his mouth, but Lucius knew it would be flavorless compared to the taste of her kiss.

He was right.

Though he almost choked trying to swallow the berries and pastry to free his mouth, the object of his haste proved well worth it. He captured Angela's lips with his. Not only did they yield to his tender siege, but parted in welcome.

Sweeter than berries, richer than cream, as intoxicating as champagne, her kiss set his heart pounding in time to the music, and whetted his already keen appetite for more of her.

Once he mastered his runaway passion, Lucius resolved to put his lips and tongue to the second best use he could imagine for them. He would explain to Angela what an intense and unexpected reversal his feelings for her had taken. Then he would court her in earnest.

Would it be possible, he wondered in a delirious rush, for his grandfather to give the bride away and also stand as his groomsman? The way his grandfather looked tonight, Lucius was convinced the doctors must be wrong, and the old fellow would live to be a hundred.

"I say, is that Daventry back there?" asked a male voice from a little distance away.

Another voice, somewhat slurred, chimed in. "You really oughtn't skulk off to the fringes of your own fete, old fellow."

"No matter how pretty the girl," added a third man, in a suggestive tone that immediately raised Lord Daventry's ire.

He pulled away from Angela with a guilty start and glared toward the garishly dressed trio. Pendleton, Vaughan and Smythe—had he once been desperate enough for friends to take up with these three?

"Who in their right mind invited you lot?" he demanded.

"Now, now," mumbled Bertie Smythe, always the first of the three to get falling-down drunk on any occasion. "Is that any way to greet old chums you haven't clapped eyes on in five years?"

Had it been only five years? To Lucius it felt like several lifetimes ago—back in the indolent, carefree days when he'd been called the handsomest beau in England.

"We weren't precisely *invited*," Toby Pendleton admitted. "Aunt Warmouth insisted I accompany her, so I fetched these two along for moral support."

Under his breath Lucius muttered, "When did any of you acquire morals?"

Clarence Vaughan sidled closer, his eyes fixed on Angela. "We simply had to come when we heard you'd been snared in the parson's mouse-

trap, Daventry. I assume this divine creature is
your betrothed?"

He'd hardly be kissing her if she weren't, would
he?

"This is my fiancée, Miss Angela Lacewood.
My dear, may I present, the Honorable Messrs.
Vaughan, Pendleton and Smythe, old acquain-
tances of mine."

"A pleasure to meet you, gentlemen." Angela
sounded sincere, though perhaps a little embarrassed at having been caught in a kiss. "Thank
you for coming this evening to help us celebrate
our engagement."

Vaughan bowed with exaggerated courtesy.
"The pleasure is entirely ours, Miss Lacewood.
Pray, will you do me the honor of a dance for the
sake of my longstanding friendship with Lord
Daventry."

"I...suppose that would be all right." She
glanced toward Lucius. "Wouldn't it, my dear?"

Lucius shrugged his assent. It was that or grab
Vaughan by the cravat and beat the smarmy grin
off his face. It alarmed him to find his self-control taxed over such a trifle. He fought to keep
his composure as he watched Vaughan escort Angela toward the terrace, lavishing her with flattery every step of the way.

"You're looking fit enough, old fellow," said
Pendleton, dropping into the chair Angela had
vacated and helping himself from their plate of
sweets. "I'd heard the Frenchies had given you a
nasty going-over. Left you an invalid or some rot."

Smythe bellowed at a passing waiter for a drink as he pulled up a chair.

"I was luckier than most, I suppose." Lucius kept his eyes fixed on Vaughan and Angela as they wove in and out among the other dancers. What were they talking about? "I came out of it alive. Kept all my limbs."

There were times he wished he'd lost a leg, instead. That would have been a far easier defect to conceal.

Smythe bolted his drink. "I thought you were mad to molder away out in the country like this. But, by heaven, if that Miss Lacewood of yours is a fair sample of the young ladies a chap can find out here, I may have to retire to some nice rural district."

"You're wise to keep her away from London." Pendleton popped another pastry into his mouth. "Unless you fancy fighting lots of duels. Why, she'd draw men like bees to a rose."

Lucius found himself nodding in time to the music, and in agreement with Toby Pendleton's offensive opinion.

If Angela had been given the opportunities she deserved to find a proper husband, she could have attracted eligible suitors with ease. Once attracted by her beauty, any right-thinking man would soon fall under the spell of her cheerful wit, her generous heart and her gentle courage.

Just as he had done over these past few weeks, in spite of his resolve to keep her at arm's length.

If he wooed Angela now, Lucius had every confidence he could win her. But could he hold her?

General Bonaparte had made a rapid conquest of Europe, yet the overconfident emperor had lost it all again before he'd had the chance to savor his victory. In the end, he'd been left with nothing—imprisoned on a desolate bit of rock in the middle of the Atlantic.

Unable to stand the sight of Angela on the arm of another man, particularly as notorious a rake as Clarence Vaughan, Lucius rose from the table. Without a word of parting to the others, he strode off into the night.

He'd been living an austere, solitary existence before Angela had entered his life. Yet he'd been content enough with it, in his way. Did he dare risk a conquest he could not hope to hold? For if he lost her, Lucius doubted he would ever know contentment or peace again.

No wonder Lucius had been content with stargazing in the country, Angela decided as her interminable dance with Mr. Vaughan concluded—if this was the sort of company he'd kept before the war.

"Can I implore you for one more turn, Miss Lacewood?" Her partner made a deep bow. "You are quite the most graceful dancer I've squired in ages."

This man was quite the most blatant liar she'd encountered in ages. He'd rattled her so with his insincere admiration of her *beauty* that she'd ended up treading on his toes several times, the last not altogether by accident.

"Perhaps later, Mr. Vaughan, thank you. At the moment I have something particular I would like to say to Lord Daventry, if you'll excuse me." Without waiting for an answer, she snatched her hand out of his grasp and hurried away before he could detain her.

After fending off dance invitations from two other men, she finally reached their table. Messrs. Pendleton and Smythe had made themselves at home there, eating all the remaining cakes and pastries. Lucius was nowhere in sight.

What was the man playing at?

He'd begun the evening gallant and attentive, gradually progressing to a playful seduction that had set delicious, baffling sensations rippling through her. Like a craving for the sweetest confection imaginable—one to which only he could introduce her.

Then, with the sudden appearance of his *old friends,* Lucius had turned quite indifferent toward her. He'd let that odious Vaughan fellow drag her off to dance without a murmur of protest. Now he'd deserted her entirely.

"Did either of you gentlemen mark which way Lord Daventry went?"

Mr. Smythe scratched his head and looked around, as if he'd just become aware of his friend's absence.

Mr. Pendleton made a vague gesture into the

darkness. "Gone off and left you, has he? The blighter! Why don't you come dance with me, then, to make him jealous?"

If she'd thought for a moment such a plan had a chance of succeeding, Angela might have taken Mr. Pendleton up on his offer, childish as it sounded.

Instead she gave him the excuse she'd practiced often in the past few minutes. "Later, perhaps, once I've spoken with Lord Daventry."

"Ah, Daventry." Mr. Pendleton pulled a sulky face. "Wish I'd half a crown for every time some young lovely has turned me down in favor of him. Smythie, fetch more drinks, will you?"

A glass of champagne sounded like a fine idea to Angela, just then. But not if it meant lingering in the company of these two.

Lifting her skirts to keep from tripping, she ventured out into the darkness, wondering where Lucius could have gone.

And why.

Had he been overwhelmed by the crush of guests and stolen away to his tower to commune with the stars? Had meeting his old friends made him long for the life he'd once led? Was he having second thoughts about flirting with her—fearing she would take it all much more seriously than he'd meant it?A heaviness welled up from deep inside of her, crowding her lungs and her heart. She *had* taken his flirting for more than Lucius must have meant it. Because her feelings for him had undergone such a dramatic shift, she'd made herself believe his had, too. Examined in a harsh rational light, the motive for his conduct this evening could have been one of many that had nothing to do with love.

Suddenly the whole notion of this ball seemed like folly.

She had made her appearance. The champagne was now flowing freely enough that she could probably steal away home without anyone noticing.

Angela tore off her mask and let it fall to the ground. It had been pleasant enough to hide behind for a short while. Now she found it stiff and stifling, and the narrow eye slits restricted her vision. Choking back a sob, she lifted the hem of her skirt higher and dashed toward the familiar path that would lead her home.

Her flight picked up urgent speed with each step until she slammed into something large and solid. Something warm, which wrapped around her to keep her from falling...yet tempted her to take a much more dangerous kind of fall.

"Is that you, Angela?" Lord Daventry's voice wrapped around her, as warm and secure as his arms, in spite of her determination to resist. "Where do you think you're going?"

"Home." Though she yearned to linger in his arms, Angela made herself pull out of his embrace. "Where people don't pretend I'm anything more than an obligation to them."

"What do you mean?" His words took on hard

edges. "Has someone insulted you? Vaughan didn't take any liberties with you, did he?"

Lucius sounded so furious on her behalf, as though he'd wreak violent vengeance on anyone who distressed her.

"Why do you care?" she demanded. "You let that awful man cart me off to the dance floor without saying a word."

"I didn't hear you protest." Lucius caught her by the wrist. "Show a little backbone after this, why don't you? If you don't want a man's attentions, tell him so. Don't always wait for someone else to step in and rescue you."

Perhaps what he said was true, but why did he make it sound like some sort of accusation? *He* had no right to be angry with *her*.

"Let go of me, Lord Daventry! Is that backbone enough for you? I thought Mr. Vaughan was your friend. I didn't want to appear impolite by refusing him."

"I beg your pardon, my dear." He released her wrist so abruptly Angela almost toppled over. "One must always strive to be polite and charitable, I suppose. Even when it means pretending to enjoy uncongenial company."

Damn him! She would far rather endure the rare sting of his anger than suffer the icy indifference behind which he so often hid his feelings.

"So, you admit it then?" Angela despised the tight, plaintive sound of her own voice. But if she waited until her own emotions were under better control before she confronted Lucius, she might turn coward and never do it.

"Don't be cryptic," he snapped. Clearly the sheath of ice over his emotions was thin and brittle. "Admit what?"

Could she say it without bursting into silly tears? "That you…seduced me, tonight, with all your talk of indiscretion and temptation. You made me believe you felt something for me… perhaps something you didn't want to feel."

"Is that what you would like?" His words hovered on the night air, almost overpowered by the distant clamor of music, conversation and laughter. "To make me feel things I don't want to feel?"

How Angela wished they could just forget the last half hour and go back to their sweet, airy flirtation! Yet, she could not deny the dangerous undercurrent of true intimacy that seemed to hum between them at this moment.

"Why not?" She almost choked on her own bitterness. "You've done it to me. And tonight wasn't the first time. Is it so ridiculous to hope you might have come to care for me, too?"

The instant those words left her lips, she would have done anything to recall them. She sounded like a pathetic little beggar with her bowl out, soliciting a few meager coins of his affection. What right did she have, then, to disdain what he had offered her out of charity?

"Not ridiculous." He caught her hand again, but gently this time. "Only unfair…to you."

He drew her toward him, as if to embrace her.

Instead, he spun her slowly under his arm, until she came to rest with her back toward him, his cheek pressed into her hair.

"The day I came to Netherstowe with my proposal, I told you I intend never to marry. Now let me tell you why."

Angela tried to concentrate on what Lucius was saying instead of on the way he held her and the intense sensations it produced. One powerful arm encircled her waist, the other spanned her shoulders. If only they would each fall a few inches lower, as her body ached for them to do.

"It would not be fair for me to take a wife," whispered Lucius, "when I already have a mistress who claims so much of my attention."

"Mistress?" Angela tensed, powerless against the hot surge of jealousy that swept through her. "What mistress?"

Lucius tilted her chin up toward the star-strewn sky. "That one. She is cold and rather demanding, I fear. But very beautiful and absolutely faithful. Whenever I come to her, I always find her waiting with open arms."

Put like that, what chance did she stand of winning him?

Then, from somewhere inside her came the answer, couched in her friend the earl's wry, muted voice. *Why, none at all, of course, if you don't try.*

Suddenly she understood where soldiers found courage in the face of certain doom. There was something strangely liberating about having no hope and nothing to lose.

Twirling about in Lord Daventry's arms, she pressed her warm, pliant body against his, daring him to resist her.

Angela's sudden shift caught Lucius off balance. Standing behind her, he'd been in control. Of her, and of himself.

"Your mistress?" she cried as her arms went around his neck. "That's the most ridiculous thing I've ever heard! You told me yourself, it's just a great black void, filled with burning balls of gas. It doesn't know who you are. It can never care about you, no matter how you may care about it. I can!"

Her words dug into Lucius like the pincers that had once gouged musket shot from the mangled flesh around his eye. No doubt it had been necessary to save his life. At the time, he would have murdered that army surgeon with his bare hands if he could have worked them free.

The pressure of Angela's sweetly rounded body against his was torture of a different order. So were the promises she could not hope to keep and he dared not risk believing.

"You're fooling yourself, my dear." He mustn't let himself think about how much he wanted her. "You can't possibly care about me. You don't even know who I am, apart from what I choose to let you see."

"I know more that you think, Lucius Daventry."

He could only see a faint outline of her face, as she held it up to him, but he knew where he would find her lips waiting. Sensing the threat she posed, he had made a strategic retreat into the shadows, but she had brought the battle to him. Under the barrage of her embrace and her defiant declaration of her feelings, both his body and his heart threatened humiliating surrender.

She left him with no choice but to marshal a desperate offensive charge.

"You know nothing!" he growled as his arms tightened around her and his mouth closed over hers, hot for plunder.

He forced his tongue on a rough skirmish past the feeble resistance of her lips, while his hands ranged over her body and through her hair to demonstrate how easily he could master her, if he wished. Lucius meant it for a harsh but necessary warning to withdraw from those territories of his heart she had invaded.

After the shock of his first onslaught, he expected her to fend him off, or to break free of his grasp and flee. Even as he continued his conquest, he braced for a counterattack. Her nails across his cheek, perhaps. Even a blow to the lap of his breeches.

He did not expect to feel her fingers tug at his hair or slip beneath his cravat to knead the tight flesh of his neck. He did not expect her mouth to open wider and her tongue to slide against his in a reckless caress of welcome that ambushed his self-control and nearly blew it to kingdom come.

Lucius mustered just enough composure to

push her away, though his forces threatened to mutiny at any moment.

"What the devil are you doing, Angela?" His breath heaved out in ragged gasps and his legs would scarcely support him.

She replied with a soft, breathless volley of laughter that held a faint ring of triumph. "Perhaps you don't know me as well as you think, either, Lord Daventry."

Chapter Fourteen

"I should have hosted a ball ages ago," said the earl as he and Angela waved goodbye to the last of his guests a few mornings later. "I found the whole event most invigorating. Now it's too fine a day to go back inside. Let us wander around to the rose garden and sit there awhile."

"Very well." Angela took the earl's arm and they began to walk. "I'm glad you enjoyed it all so much. It was everything I ever dreamed a ball would be."

Almost everything.

The earl patted her hand where it rested in the crook of his elbow. "A rare jewel deserves a perfect setting in which to shine. I must say, you sparkled admirably that night."

"But not much since?" She cast him a sidelong glance. "Go ahead and say it, for I can tell that's what you're thinking."

"Would I ever insult a lady with such a remark?" The earl shook his head and did his best to look offended. "I expect we all tend to droop a little once the excitement is over."

"Are you feeling poorly?" Angela looked more closely at his face to check his color, and to see if he had lost flesh.

"Don't fuss, child. I'm only a little tired, and that's to be expected at my age, don't you think?"

Perhaps that's all it was, Angela told herself. Contrary to what his physicians had predicted, the earl's health seemed to have improved since she and Lucius had become engaged. Or had she wished it so hard she'd made herself believe it?

They had reached the rose garden by this time. The earl lowered himself onto a bench in the shade of an arched trellis over which thorny green tendrils swarmed. The morning sun had begun to coax the fragrant scarlet flowers to unfurl their petals. A tiny speckled thrush perched on top of the trellis and poured out a summer morning song.

Angela sat down on the bench beside the earl, and for a while they kept quiet company. If only her thoughts and her feelings had matched the tranquility of the garden!

It did no good to go over the events of that night again, for she had done it a hundred times already, each time coming up with a different explanation for Lord Daventry's every word and action. There was only one thing of which she could be certain—she had said and done the worst thing possible at every turn.

Now that she'd felt and tasted his unleashed

passion for a few breathless moments, it galled her to know she might never experience it again. All because she'd done everything she'd been taught and told for years *not* to do. She had confronted him, contradicted him and finally thrown herself at him like some brazen hussy.

What had possessed her?

The earl's voice broke in on her muddled musings. "Don't let him shut you out now that you've managed to pry the door open."

"I—I beg your pardon?" Had she been thinking out loud, or had he read her mind?

"No need to beg mine." The earl turned upon her the placid gaze that always seemed to divine more than she wanted him to. "Perhaps I should beg yours on my grandson's behalf. I don't know what's gotten into him the past few days. Something between the two of you the night of the ball, perhaps?"

Angela couldn't bring herself to answer right away. Then again, the fierce blush that prickled in her cheeks probably spoke for her.

"I just don't understand him! Or myself, either, half the time." She jumped from the bench and began to pace around the garden. "One minute I know how I feel and have reason to presume he feels the same, then the next minute it's all sixes and sevens."

"Why, my dear child." The earl chuckled. "That sounds rather like love, if you ask me. I believe a sense of confusion is part of its charm."

"Well, I don't find it charming." Angela threw

up her hands. "I find it a great bother! Why can't love be safe and certain?"

"Perhaps because life is seldom safe and never certain."

Wise words, though not ones she wanted to hear.

"But I make mistakes enough when everything's straightforward. When it's all muddled like this, I seem to make nothing *but* mistakes."

The earl treated her to a fond look. "Will it help to hear that everyone makes mistakes when they're in love?"

"Not as bad as mine," Angela insisted.

For instance, confiding in his grandfather about their relationship, or lack of one. If Lucius found out, he'd probably exhume Lord Lucifer to put a monstrous curse on her.

"I'll wager my grandson could give you a run for your money on that score."

"Making mistakes, you mean?"

The cool, composed Lord Daventry put a foot wrong? Angela found it hard to credit. Then again, he hadn't been very cool or composed the other night when he'd swept her into his arms.

Perhaps, behind that mask of his, he was as flustered by all of this as she.

"Making mistakes, indeed." The earl glanced back toward the house. "He'll be making a great one if he pushes you away. Bear with him, if you can, my dear, but not too far. I want to see my grandson happy, but not at the expense of your happiness."

"I'll try." Angela whispered as she stared at the rosebush nearest her.

How tightly the bloodred buds clenched, and how fiercely the thorns guarded them. Yet, given time and the sun's patient warmth, they could not resist easing open to dazzle the world with their passionate color and intoxicating perfume.

She had told Lucius that patience was one of her virtues. What would patience avail her, though, if the earl's time ran out?

Three months come and gone, with no sign of his grandfather ailing, much less dying.

Lucius adjusted his telescope toward the constellation Perseus, where meteor activity had begun to intensify.

Profound relief radiated through him, tainted by a nameless unease. He'd hoped a few hours of tranquil stargazing would soothe his nerves, but so far it had failed. His reliable mistress no longer provided the comfort and release she once had.

Mistress? Damn! Lucius braced for his thoughts to return to *that night,* knowing he was powerless to prevent them. As he recalled the days since, he began to wonder if the whole evening had been some sort of bizarre dream. Certainly, that tempestuous midnight skirmish with Angela had plagued his dreams ever since.

For a day or two afterward, they had trod warily around each other, though neither of them had spoken of it. Little by little, the tension had subsided until Lucius became convinced his warning to Angela had discouraged any foolish romantic fancies she might have about him.

And a good thing, too. If her feelings for him could be so easily thwarted, what chance would they have for a life together? Better to lose her now than later, when she had burrowed deeper into his heart. Better to dismiss her from his life than to have her slip away while he tried to hold her.

Not that she was gone from his life…yet. They'd been almost constantly in each other's company since the night of the ball. Keeping up congenial appearances for his grandfather. Playing chess or pall-mall, going to church, dining together, even bantering a little for the old man's amusement.

But when night fell, Angela always managed to find her way home without his assistance. Often courtesy of the vicar, whom Lucius had come to respect and even like, after a fashion. The poor fellow was as hopelessly smitten with Angela as ever, though of late that had ceased to irritate Lucius the way it once had.

Indeed, he and Angela had settled into a pleasant pretense of intimacy without any troublesome substance. Which was just what he wanted. Lucius reminded himself of that whenever a vague dissatisfaction crept up on him, as it did far too often.

He would have been content, more or less, to continue on in their present fashion indefinitely. But with his grandfather looking likely to live forever, and Angela's relatives due back from their Continental tour any day, the engagement would have to end. One way or another.

What was that? The faint, far-off sound of someone calling his name? Not just someone—Angela.

No. It couldn't be. Lucius forced his attention back to the sky, where a meteorite had just begun its blazing descent. His ears must be playing tricks on him again.

The last two nights he'd come to the tower, he had fancied he heard Angela calling him. The first time, he'd almost broken his neck dashing down those narrow, winding stairs. If he couldn't control his traitorous imagination, at least he could ignore it.

"Lucius!"

Leave me alone, damn you! You don't plague me like this when I'm with you, why must you do it when we're apart?

"Lucius?" It was louder this time, more difficult to dismiss or ignore.

What if something had lured her back here for one last night of stargazing? His heart felt as though it was tumbling about in his chest, fast and wild.

He scrambled over to the parapet and called down, "Angela, is that you?"

No answer. Lucius cursed his foolish eagerness as he headed back to his telescope.

"Of course…it's me." The words wafted up on the night air—faint, breathless and angry. "Who else would it be…at this hour. Come down at once…your grandfather's taken ill!"

His tumbling heart seemed to plunge over the parapet. "I'm coming!"

Lucius rushed down the tower stairs in pitch-darkness, two and three at a time, narrowly escaping disaster more than once. He found Angela waiting for him just outside, her breath coming in great heaves. Without thinking what he was doing, he caught her hand in his and set off toward Helmhurst.

"Is it very bad?" he made himself ask.

"Very. His heart…I think. They sent for me…and the doctor. I sent someone…to fetch the vicar."

"Why didn't someone come and fetch *me?*"

The answer hit him before Angela managed to gasp out the words. "Servants…too frightened… Lord Lucifer."

Damn! When he raked his fingers through his hair, Lucius realized he had forgotten to replace his mask. He let go of Angela's hand just long enough to rummage in his pocket and put it back on.

No sooner had he reached for her again than she stumbled. Lucius caught her in his arms.

"I…can't keep up."

He could feel her chest heaving.

"Go on," she gasped. "I'll come…soon as I… catch my breath."

"We'll go together," Lucius insisted. Whatever

he would face back at the house, he wanted her with him. "A minute or two won't matter, surely."

Angela had the good sense not to waste his time or her breath arguing.

As he held her there, his eyes fixed on the distant lights of Helmhurst, Lucius realized they were standing on the very spot where they had quarreled and kissed on the night of the ball.

All the words he'd held back since then crowded on his tongue, demanding to be spoken. "There's something I need to tell you that I should have said long before this. I acted like a damn fool the night of the ball. I had no right to speak to you or…treat you the way I did."

"No, you didn't." It was not a reproach, just an unsparing statement of fact.

"I'm sorry." Until that moment, he hadn't realized how much.

"So am I." Her arm went around his neck and she pressed her cheek to his for the briefest instant.

Just long enough to restore something within him that Lucius hadn't realized he'd been missing.

Then Angela jumped to her feet and pulled him up after her. "I've caught my breath. Let's go."

After their headlong rush from the tower, the stillness at Helmhurst felt oppressive to Angela. She wanted to turn and run back out into the night. To pretend this wasn't happening, just the way she'd pretended all summer that it wouldn't happen.

But the earl needed her. So did Lord Daventry, whether he knew it or not.

They met the physician, just leaving the earl's bedchamber.

He must have read the question on their faces, for he shook his head. "He's conscious and resting. I gave him a draft to make him comfortable, though I don't believe he's in any great pain, now."

Perhaps he saw a desperate light of hope in their eyes, for he added, "I don't expect him to last the night, I'm afraid. Then again, the old rascal has proved me wrong before."

Angela drew a deep breath that came back out with the frayed edge of a stifled sob. It felt as though every tear she'd held at bay with her pretending all summer had settled in her bosom, saturating her heart.

Then Lucius reached for her hand and gave her fingers a gentle, heartening squeeze. "You needn't come in if you'd rather not. Grandfather will understand."

She looked into his eyes, willing her voice not to quaver. "I want to."

"In that case…" He eased the door open and held it for her. "Thank you."

Angela gathered her courage and stepped over the threshold.

A single low-burning candle sent long shadows flickering about the large, airy chamber. The vast dimensions of his four-poster bed made the earl

look shrunken. Against the sun-bleached white
of the bed linens, his skin appeared a sallow gray.

The earl's eyes were closed, and everything
about him was so still that Angela wondered if
he had already slipped away. But when Lucius
fetched a chair for her by his grandfather's bedside, the earl opened his eyes and smiled at them
both.

"Ran him to ground, did you?" he whispered
to Angela, with a subtle nod toward his grandson.

The earl's breath sounded shallow and raspy.
His voice, which she'd never heard raised, was
softer than ever, like the rustle of silk slippers
over a rich Persian carpet.

Angela nodded and tried to smile. "He can't
hide from me for long."

"Hear that, my boy? Angela says you cannot
hide from her. I think you had better not bother
in future."

Lucius pulled up a chair for himself on the
opposite side of the bed. "That would be rather
futile, wouldn't it? I say, are you in any pain? Is
there anything we can do for you?"

"Just keep me company. Though perhaps you
could come sit beside Angela so I don't have to
keep turning my head."

"Of course, Grandfather." Lucius brought his
chair around the foot of the bed and placed it beside Angela's. "How thoughtless of me."

"That's better." The earl's pale-blue gaze rested
on them both, like a benediction.

Then he closed his eyes again and a warm, melancholy silence settled over the room.

Angela leaned toward Lucius, offering her hand. For the first time in weeks, she did not hesitate to ask herself why or wonder how he might react.

A moment of sweet clarity had enveloped her hopeless confusion. Regardless of how he felt about her, she *knew* what she felt for him was love.

He glanced over at her, then slowly raised his hand to thread his fingers through hers. She remembered the sensation of his hands on her body, but without a blush. The earl would not mind her warming his room with such memories.

As if her thoughts had called to him, the earl stirred again. "A tedious business, this dying. I would like to have delayed it, at least until after your wedding. But there are some things of which even an earl cannot have the ordering."

A single tear slipped from one of Angela's eyes and drifted down her cheek. "If I had the ordering of it, I would keep you around for a very long time."

"You always did know how to flatter an old man, my dear. But I've been around for more than my share of years. Though not, heaven knows, 'by reason of strength.' Thanks to the two of you, these last months have been my most enjoyable in a great while."

Lucius turned his gaze on Angela. It was as if he had removed some inner barrier, allowing

her to glimpse his truest, deepest feelings for the
first time. Unlike hers, his eyes were dry, yet
they held such a vast expanse of parched grief
that she ached to ease it with the warm rain of
her own tears.

"Besides," said the earl. "In the end, those we
love don't go as far away as we might think."

Slowly and with obvious effort, he dragged
one hand up the coverlet, until it rested over his
heart. He tapped gently with his fingers. "I'll
be there, for both of you. Listen now and again.
You'll hear me."

Lucius breathed a long, faltering sigh.

Untwining her fingers from his, Angela rose
and leaned over the bed to brush her lips against
the earl's worn, hollow cheek. "I love you, Grandfather."

"Goodbye, dear child." His eyes slid shut.

Angela melted back into her chair, fresh tears
following the first one. As she struggled to contain them, Lucius bent over his grandfather and
the two men whispered their private words of
parting.

After what seemed like a very long time, Lucius sat down again. "I believe he's gone."

A harsh sob tore from Angela's chest.

Everything the earl had said had been true, and
comforting in its way. He had lived a long but in-
creasingly restricted life. And she would always
carry his memory in her heart.

At the moment, though, her feelings harkened
back to her childhood out on that vast, empty

ocean, beneath a vast, empty sky. Sailing away from the life she'd always known into an uncertain future. A little frightened, and very much bereft.

Beside her, Lucius pulled a handkerchief from his breast pocket. For an instant, Angela thought he meant to hand it to her. Instead, with a touch no heavier than a whisper, he began to dry her tears. He looked as though he would have liked to shed a few of his own.

If only he could.

Angela glanced at the bed, where the earl lay with one hand still held to his breast. "I miss him already."

Lucius let the handkerchief fall away from her face. "So do I."

He held his arms open to her. It seemed the most natural thing in the world that she should reach for him to give comfort. And, in giving, to find some for her own sorrowing heart.

How long they clung together, Angela was not sure. Long enough for her to feel perfectly at home. Long enough to sate herself on the scent of him. Long enough to glean every morsel of solace she could from that chaste embrace.

And begin to yearn for something more.

She had buried her head against his shoulder and shed a few more quiet tears against the broadcloth of his coat. Now she turned her face inward to contemplate the white column of his linen-wrapped neck and the firm, straight contours of his profile.

The black mask Angela had once thought so sinister looking, she'd since grown to tolerate until she now found it potently attractive. The way she found everything about him attractive, from the toes of his riding boots to the thick mane of dark hair on the crown of his head. Not to mention his rich, sable voice.

He didn't love her. Nor might he ever. Now a powerful conviction formed within her, at odds with her usual self-doubt, that he could love her, given the opportunity. But her time was running out.

A few days' grace while they laid the earl to rest and settled his affairs. Then Lucius would expect her to fulfil her part of their bargain by breaking the engagement.

The night of the ball, she had pursued him, with disastrous results. Since then, she had bided her time, to no avail. If she would be obliged to give him up anyway, Angela wanted as much from him as he would give her. Better one moment of fierce passion to remember him by than weeks of polite pretense.

By slow, tender degrees, she burrowed deeper into his embrace, nuzzling her cheek against his neck linen. Was it only her wishful fancy, or did his arms tighten around her and his head tilt a fraction until her hair whispered against his lean cheek?

Some might have considered it tasteless, or disrespectful to carry on this way in a death room, with the earl's body scarcely cold. Angela knew nothing would have delighted him more, or speeded his soul on swift wings to a contented rest. No doubt Lucius knew it, too.

In a succession of subtle movements that seemed to mirror each other, their heads canted until their lips were perfectly positioned to kiss. The brief space between them quivered with desire and wariness, yearning and hesitation, tenderness and questions.

With all those wrought-up, contradictory feelings, they approached, drew back, advanced again and finally met in a manner so delicate and tentative that it might have been the very first kiss ever, for either of them.

Sweet, nourishing, comforting. Angela wanted it to go on forever. She could hardly bring herself to breathe in case it might stop.

The deft, rhythmic movement of his lips against hers turned her blood to pastry cream— rich, thick and sweet. Then he coaxed her lips farther apart and slid his tongue between them, to acquaint himself with her on a most intimate level, and to savor that familiarity.

Even as he nourished her appetite for him, Lucius piqued it to an exquisite voracity, until all his kisses in the world would no longer serve to satisfy her. She wanted more of him, as close as he could get…and closer. Close enough to fill the aching void in her heart. Close enough for her to fill an answering emptiness she sensed in him.

To give and to take. To receive and to be accepted.

Tonight. Now.

A mannerly tap on the door exploded the intimate hush of the chamber, hurling Lucius and Angela apart with an abruptness that felt wounding.

"What is it?" Lucius called, his voice harsh and tight.

The door eased open and the familiar face of the vicar peered in. His golden hair stuck up in places, and his eyes still had the glazed look of sleep about them. His whole handsome face radiated a sincere wish to bring consolation.

And Angela wanted to box his shapely, well-set ears until they rang like the trumpets at St. Peter's gate!

"I came as quickly as I could," he whispered, peering toward the bed. "Is his lordship resting?"

Lucius rose from his seat, brushing past Angela as he walked toward the door. Every fiber of her being yearned to reach for him, cling to him, but she managed to restrain herself.

"I'm afraid there's nothing you can do for him now, Vicar, except say a prayer to speed his soul on its way to some good place."

The vicar's lips pressed tight in a rueful expression, and he expelled a faint sigh. "I'm sorry I couldn't have come sooner to be with him at the last, though as long as you and Miss Lacewood were here, I doubt he felt the lack of my company."

"It was over quickly," said Lucius. "He seemed at peace and content to go."

"I am sorry for your loss, Lord Daventry." The

vicar reached for his hand. "I know how close the two of you were and what pleasure he took in your company."

Lucius ushered Mr. Michaeljohn in, and the vicar proceeded to read from his prayer book. While the familiar words brought Angela some solace, they heartened her less than the sensation of Lord Daventry's hand clasping hers. Now and then, during the prayers, she opened her eyes to steal a glimpse of Lucius. Once she caught him watching her, and they held that gaze.

Finally the vicar closed his prayer book. "It will have been a long and wearing night for you both. You should get some sleep. There'll be plenty to keep you occupied in the next few days. I'd be pleased to fetch you home, Miss Lacewood."

If urges were truly as wicked as deeds, then Angela knew she'd committed a grave sin against the vicar. Poor man! It wasn't his fault. How could he know she would hate anything that threatened to take her from Lucius just now?

By all standards of proper conduct, she should thank Mr. Michaeljohn for the offer and go with him. There was nothing to keep her at Helmhurst, now, except her own desperate inclination.

Glancing at Lucius, she saw something in his gaze that reminded her of the masquerade ball, when that importunate Mr. Vaughan had carried her away for a dance. Lucius had not intervened on her behalf then.

Grow a backbone, he'd told her afterward.

"Thank you, Vicar. But I'd prefer to remain here, if Lord Daventry has no objection."

"None." His reply came so readily and with such conviction, Angela knew she'd made the right choice. "If Grandfather could, I'm certain he would insist you spend the night."

"I understand." Mr. Michaeljohn rose. "I know how close you and the earl had become, Miss Lacewood. Should I stop at Netherstowe to give them the news and let them know you'll be remaining here?"

"That would be most kind of you, Vicar."

They followed him to the door. There, Lord Daventry, now the new earl, gave orders for the valet, Mr. Carruthers, to sit with his grandfather's body. He also asked if there was a nearby guest room where Angela could sleep for what was left of the night.

"I pray you'll both be able to sleep," said the vicar as he took his leave. "I shall be back tomorrow to render what help I can with the arrangements."

"Thank you, Nathan," said Lucius, using the vicar's Christian name for the first time Angela had heard. "You've been a good friend."

"Strange," Angela mused aloud after the vicar had departed.

Lucius met her questioning gaze. "What?"

"The way you spoke to Mr. Michaeljohn, just now. As if *you* had reason to be sorry for *him*."

"You're tired." Lucius started down the hall, tugging her along. "Let's find you a bed."

Oh, Angela wanted a bed.

Not because she was tired. But because she was starving.

What would Lucius say when she asked him to stay with her? And what would he do?

Chapter Fifteen

"Please don't go." Angela whispered her entreaty into the darkness.

A golden thread with no more substance than a sunbeam, it wrapped around Lucius. Around his hands and his feet. Around his shoulders and his chest. Around his loins and his thighs with a particular, delicious tension.

That she could hold him and kiss him the way she had, after the way he'd treated her on the night of the ball, and ever since, drowned his doubts and thawed his desire.

Around and around him that gilded cobweb spun, snaring his heart for good measure. A hundred times. A million. Multiplying the barely existent force of a single strand into a bond too strong for Lucius to break…even if he'd wanted to.

"Are you certain this is what you want?" Did she understand what his staying would mean and where it was sure to lead? "You're not just doing this as a last kindness to my grandfather? Or because you feel sorry for me?"

"I *do* feel sorry for you," she said. "I feel sorry for myself. I'd do almost anything to oblige your grandfather and I know he'd approve."

The weight of her generous intentions threatened to bring Lucius to his knees. Though his body was ripe and raw with longing for her, he could not accept what she offered out of charity or obligation.

He was about to turn away from her with a sigh, when she pressed herself against him. "I don't want you to stay for those reasons or any others that make sense to me. I want you to stay because I can't bear to be parted from you."

Her lips whispered against his. "Even *this* is too far apart to suit me. Can you show me how to get closer?"

Looking back, Lucius knew this was what he had wanted from the moment he'd first set eyes on Angela Lacewood, in the drawing room at Netherstowe. The brightness of her beauty had dazzled him that day. Every day since, its luster had deepened as he'd discovered that her face and figure were only the beginning of her true beauty.

And yet, with every fine quality he'd recognized in her, every tiny flaw that only added to her charm, the harder a part of him had struggled to resist her. At the moment, he could not recall why. Nor did he make any effort to remember.

"Well?" Angela prompted him. Her hand slipped from its perch on his shoulder, down over his chest until it rested against his galloping heart. "Can you?"

He lifted his own hand to cover hers. "I can."

At least, he hoped he could summon enough of the lover's skills he'd purposely tried to forget to bring the two of them close in the way Angela wanted, with nothing to spoil their joining.

Lucius knew she must be a maiden. Unlike some from his old set of companions, he had no practice bedding an innocent young woman for her first time. He feared Angela might find the experience distasteful, even painful.

Though his body ached with desire for her, Lucius drew a breath and parted his lips to ask again if she was certain this was what she wanted. And if she had any idea of all it entailed.

Before he could coax the words out, Angela stretched herself up on tiptoe and covered his mouth with hers, drowning all his doubts in the clear, delicious depths of her kiss. There, he found all the answers to his questions, reassurance for his misgivings, and ardent urging he scarcely needed to proceed.

As their kiss became more and more intense, Lucius felt the starched linen of his cravat grow tight around his throat. The layers of shirt, vest and coat distanced his flesh from Angela's touch and hampered his attempts to hold her as he wished. His boots pinched and his breeches bound him unbearably!

Never in his life had he felt so clumsy as he struggled to free himself from his clothes while continuing to hold and kiss Angela. Fortunately, she seemed to understand his dilemma, for she began to tug at his neck linen with one hand, while pushing the sleeves of his coat off his arms with the other.

When it dropped to the floor at last, Lucius rewarded himself by pulling Angela closer. Gliding one hand down over the gentle curve of her backside, he hoisted her into his arms and strode toward the bed. It was nearer than he had judged.

His leg caught against it in midstep, sending them sprawling together onto the mattress in an impatient tangle of limbs. Angela gave a winded gasp as his head landed against the lush cushion of her bosom. The gasp changed into a deep, tantalizing purr when Lucius stroked his cheek against the smooth muslin bodice of her dress and felt the peak of her breast thrust out, beseeching his attention.

Lucius did not disappoint her.

One hand slid beneath her, his fingers grappling with a row of tiny buttons down the back of her dress. In the meantime, he continued to rub his cheek against the delightful bounty held captive by her gown and shift. When he judged that he had worked enough of the buttons free, he hooked his chin over the neckline of her bodice and began to push it down. His lips trailed fiery kisses over the rounded tops of her breasts, a foretaste of what she could expect when he had liberated them completely.

Angela squirmed beneath him, the better to

aid his efforts. Her breath came hot and fast against his hair, now and then catching in her throat. They were the sounds of a woman taking pleasure in his touch and hungry for more. They spurred Lucius to fulfil her every unspoken, unguessed need.

The night wrapped them in its liberating, forgiving embrace. In the star-kissed darkness, Lucius could forget he was a far cry from the handsomest beau in England. He could forget the intimidating power of Angela's beauty. They could just be two faceless lovers, drawn together by shared grief. And mutual yearning too long denied.

Angela's bodice fetched up on something and would no longer yield to the downward force of his chin. Her taut, tempting nipples remained barely out of his reach. Hooking his fingers into the open back of her gown, Lucius caught the front of it in his teeth and gave one vigorous tug, wrenching her bodice down the last few inches.

The warm, feminine musk of her flesh enveloped him, and he wished he had two mouths, so he could favor both her breasts at once. Since that was not possible, he gave each his sensual care in turn, fondling the other with his hand to appease it between times. His tongue flicked over the firm, sweet nub, savoring it like a rare delicacy, then drawing it between his lips for a luscious, lingering suckle.

Angela arched toward him. A soft cry escaped

from her, in which Lucius heard exquisite pleasure mingled with an urgent plea for something more.

Something he was desperately eager to share with her.

He continued to savor her breasts as she played her fingers through his hair and stroked his face. All the while her body tensed beneath him in restless anticipation.

His hand parted from her bosom, reluctantly at first. But as it slid down her body in a sinuous caress, it grew more eager. First, it drifted inward at the cinched curve of her waist, something the otherwise admirable fashions of the day did little to flatter. Then it veered out again over the pleasing fullness of her hip and down her thigh.

Lucius fumbled to catch the hem of her gown in his fingers. Then his hand stole beneath and retraced its delicious journey from a more intimate vantage. Her light muslin skirt bunched over his wrist and up his arm as he relished the smooth texture of her stockings. His breath stuck in his throat when his fingertips encountered bare skin, warm and responsive.

Higher and higher he quested, to the luscious cleft between her thighs. Angela quivered beneath his touch, clutching at his shoulders in a manner that roused him almost as much as he had roused her. The proof of her need, slick and sultry, anointed his fingertips.

No question, she was as eager and ready for him as a woman could be for a man. Though his body demanded immediate satisfaction, his heart whispered for Lucius to slow down—savor each sensation and make certain Angela did, too. Since this first mating of hers did not promise the kind of pleasure he longed to give her, Lucius resolved to suspend his own needs long enough to indulge her in the sweet foretaste of rapture.

Only once or twice before, when Lucius had kissed her and held her, had Angela glimpsed the kind of pleasure he could bring her. Now her body warmed like a freshly toasted crumpet, oozing butter and jam. Consuming an entire buffet of sinfully rich pastries could not compare to the delight of being consumed by him.

And yet, the very attentions that sated her with pleasure also whetted her hunger to a pitch so sharp it was almost painful. Could such a ravenous appetite ever hope to gain full satisfaction? At the moment, she could not imagine such a thing, though she longed for it almost beyond bearing.

As Lucius ventured closer and closer to the fissure between her legs, she parted them, inviting him closer to the pulsing center of her need. His fingertips made a tentative foray that set her quivering and keening.

Then he wrenched his hand from under her skirts and lifted his mouth from her breast. Lucius rose from the bed, his breath coming in harsh gasps.

"Don't stop!" If she'd known what to do, Angela might have wrestled him back onto the bed and hurled herself on top of him in an urgent bid for relief.

"I have no intention of stopping," he whispered, "unless you tell me to. And then it would likely tear me apart."

She could hear him fumbling to remove his boots. Then a rending noise as he grappled with his neck linen. Only the anticipation of feeling his bare skin against hers curbed Angela's impatience—at the same time, kindling it hotter.

When she tried to sit up and tear off her own garments, Lucius pushed her back down with a gentle hand on her bared shoulder.

What began as a gesture of restraint rapidly shifted to a caress. "Leave that to me, my angel."

"Very well," she conceded in a husky murmur. "But do hurry!"

"No." His answer sounded at odds with the frenzied rush of his undressing.

Angela tried to picture him in her mind as he shed each garment. Only the faintest silvery starlight through the window penetrated the room's deep darkness. At that moment, she would have given anything for a few feeble rays of dawn to illuminate Lucius in his naked, masculine beauty.

But all she could make out was a vague shadow as he climbed back onto the bed and advanced on her with sinuous, predatory grace. She braced herself for the blissful torment of his touch. It was better than she remembered, even from a few moments ago.

Lucius poised over her, lowering his lips to the point on her shoulder where his hand had rested.

"I've wanted to do this," he breathed, "from the first moment I set eyes upon you."

With those words to inflame her, he began to kiss and nuzzle her shoulder and neck, while the warm flesh and soft hair of his bare chest rubbed lightly against her breasts.

When he had succeeded in coaxing her to a fresh peak of need, Lucius drew back again and ordered, "Roll over, now."

He silenced her inarticulate whimper of protest with a deep, lingering kiss.

"Your clothes." His lips moved against hers as he drew back. "I promised to help you out of them, remember? You must trust that I know what I'm doing, and that I'll make your pleasure worth the wait."

Put that way, how could she deny him? And why would she want to?

Still it was with some reluctance that Angela tumbled onto her belly. Then Lucius began to nibble on her neck and shoulders once again while he unfastened the rest of her buttons. She sensed him kneeling over her, one leg planted between hers, a rigid shaft of hot flesh pressed lightly against her backside.

She had lived in the countryside long enough to know how animals mated. Now she guessed how a man and a woman must fit together in the act of love. Was that what she craved with such in-

tensity? To take the hardest, most masculine part
of him into the softest, most feminine part of her?

The notion frightened and thrilled her, just as
Lucius Daventry had from the moment he'd first
caught her in his arms and whispered to her with
that beguiling voice. Since then she had learned
to trust him. First with her safety, now with her
body and with her heart.

If he said he would bring her pleasure, she believed him.

Once he had the back of her gown completely
open, Lucius moved his attention downward, pulling off her slippers and tossing them to the floor,
where the sound of their landing was muted by
the thick carpet. Then he reached up under her
gown again and gave her backside a delicious
kneading caress before commencing to roll down
her stockings.

Each time his hands reached halfway up her
thigh, Angela could not prevent herself from
straining toward his fingertips and the sweet
touch she knew would set her aquiver. After what
seemed like a taut eternity, Lucius reached up and
began to peel off her gown and shift, until at last
she lay completely bare to his touch.

Not waiting for his invitation, she rolled onto
her back again and began to run her hands over
his taut, smooth flesh with restless curiosity.

"Now?" she asked as her hand strayed down
the firm flat of his belly for a wary, intimate
caress.

Her reward was a raspy growl in which she heard an echo of her own pleasure and wanting.

"Soon," Lucius promised, appeasing her with a hungry, possessive kiss that eventually left her lips to blaze a fevered trail down her throat and over her breasts.

Lower and lower he foraged with his ravenous mouth, feeding his desire and hers. Until a flick of his tongue made her cry out in surprise…and a kind of wanton bliss too sweet for words.

Lucius gave an indulgent chuckle. "I thought you might enjoy this, my dearest. And I so want to bring you joy."

What about him? she wanted to ask. How did this bring him enjoyment, or escape? Or the comfort she had hoped they would share?

But before she could form the words, his tongue lapped over her again and again, emptying her mind of all but pure sensation. A mystical, delirious shattering beyond anything she had imagined.

Her body heaved beneath him in the grip of ecstasy so potent Lucius could feel its echo ripple through him. He knew beyond any doubt that to enter her, as no man had before, would be a joining of more than their bodies.

Stretching himself out beside her on the bed, he held Angela and crooned her name as she returned to herself from the wild flight on which he'd just catapulted her.

"Oh, my darling," she sighed when she had recovered enough to speak, "I had no idea it could be like that."

Lucius pressed a kiss to her brow in reply.

A deep sense of contentment wrapped around his heart, unlike any he'd felt in a very long time. Angela had offered him her trust and her virginity in earnest of her heart. She'd responded to his lovemaking with naive passion that had stirred and touched him in a way no other woman ever had.

He wanted her so much.

Not just for the next hour, or the next night, but for all the hours and nights that had stretched before him, solitary and forlorn. She would fill and hallow them with her presence, her laughter, her kindness.

"You made me feel the most astonishing things." Angela reached up, tracing the outline of his lips with her forefinger. "I don't mean to sound ungrateful, but you did promise we could get as close as possible. I believe we have a way to go, yet."

He kissed her fingertip. "So we do, if you still wish it."

"Of course I wish it! Why would I not?"

"I'm afraid the best of it is over for you," he confessed. "What comes next will not be so agreeable, but only this first time. After that, I hope it will bring you the kind of pleasure you felt just now."

"What about you?" She smoothed a lock of hair

back from his brow. "Will it bring you pleasure when we...come together."

"Oh yes." He didn't dare dwell on the notion for too long in his present roused state, or he might plunge over the edge and render himself incapable of anything more.

"Very well, then." Though Lucius could not see her smile in the darkness, he could feel it. "Let's not waste any more time, shall we?"

"You'd rather not wait until our wedding night?" They must marry now. Lucius wanted it as much as he wanted her.

"No." Angela gave a soft, seductive chuckle. "I want to be able to enjoy it...on our wedding night." She seemed to savor those words as she had the pastries at the ball.

"Then I am yours to bid," Lucius whispered, as he nudged her legs apart and prepared to enter her.

Their love play had readied the way for him, he discovered as he eased himself into the snug, sultry portal.

She flinched and bit back a cry when he pierced her maidenhead. But by the time he had buried himself within her and truly brought them as close as a man and woman could be, the tension had melted from her body again.

Was it because he'd been so long without a woman that he found every sensation heightened? Or was it because this was the woman he meant to worship while he had breath in his body and beyond. The woman his wise, obstinate grandfather had known would make him whole.

For once Lucius did not have to restrain himself from taking his pleasure until he had brought the lady hers. Which was fortunate, for the sound, scent, touch and taste of Angela taxed his control to the limit. Besides, he doubted she would enjoy the usual motion and tempo of mating at the moment.

He moved within her gently, almost gingerly, yet each subtle stroke sent an intense surge of pleasure coursing through him until he could no longer contain it.

Lost in the frenzy that overwhelmed him, he thrashed on top of Angela, growling out her name. Exultant, yet vaguely frightened that she had the power to unleash such potent rapture.

When it had spent itself, Lucius settled on the bed beside her, cradling her in his arms. He felt light enough to float up to the moon with her. When sleep stole over him, Lucius dreamed they had done just that. And danced the rest of the night away in the Sea of Tranquility.

A blissful while later, waking stole over him with the stealth of a changing dreamscape. He felt his heart beating in a delicious, lazy rhythm, keeping perfect time with Angela's. A few strands of her hair clung to his cheek. Her breasts nestled against his chest with such intimate ease Lucius wondered how he had ever abided waking without her in his arms.

Slowly his eyes drifted open.

The faint rosy half light of daybreak spilled in the window and over Angela. The sight of her, loose limbed and naked, took his breath away. Every time he saw her, she looked more beautiful than he remembered from the time before. In the dawning hours of the morning, she looked more beautiful than he could imagine.

Some slight movement or hushed sound of wonder from him must have awakened her, for her lips curved in a smile of lazy contentment as she slowly opened her eyes.

Then Angela flinched back from him, her features contorted into a grimace of aversion.

His mask? His face!

Some time during their lovemaking, perhaps in the throes of his release, the mask must have slipped off. In the first few misty moments of waking, he'd been too preoccupied with happiness to miss it.

Now a giant, invisible fist of iron took Lucius Daventry by the throat. The urge to retch warred with the urge to weep, but he refused to surrender to either. For the look of horror on Angela's face had muted to one of gentle pity.

He would have none of that.

Turning the wounded side of his face away from her, he leaped from the bed, rifling through the pile of garments on the floor in search of his breeches.

"Please come back to bed, Lucius," Angela urged him. "I didn't mean to stare at you like that. Only, it took me so by surprise just after waking up."

The self-control Lucius had discarded in a foolish moment of weakness returned with a vengeance.

"So it would, of course." He spoke with wry dispassion, as if he were referring to a rotting animal carcass or some loathsome variety of vermin rather than the wreckage of his own flesh. "My apologies for distressing you."

Keeping his back turned to her, Lucius thrust his legs into his breeches, then fumbled with the buttons to secure them.

Damn buttons! Damn Grandfather and his damned sentimental notions! And most of all, damn his own stupidity for deceiving himself that he could be more to Angela Lacewood than just another recipient of her charity!

"Don't be angry with me, my darling, please." She laid a gentle hand on his arm.

He spun around to face her again. Though he could tell she struggled to hide her distaste, Angela once again winced at the sight of him.

"I'm not angry," he lied. "Not with you, at any rate. But, in our grief last night, I fear we made an unfortunate mistake."

"I don't believe that." She made no effort to cover herself apart from the cascade of golden curls spilling over her shoulder and hiding one breast. "Nothing that made me feel so wonderful could have been a mistake."

How tempting it was to believe her, just because he wanted her so badly. But Angela deserved better.

Lucius forced out a harsh laugh. "Any man who knows what he's about with a woman can make you feel like that, my dear."

"I don't believe it."

Neither did he, entirely. But that didn't matter. It was true enough to serve his purpose, which was to get him out of this room and away from Angela, while he still had command of himself and conscience enough to do for her what she was too tenderhearted to do for herself.

He made himself shrug and say, "You'll find out someday," though the implication that she might find fulfillment in the arms of another man burned like a mouthful of lye.

"Goodbye, Angela." He headed for the door, leaving his boots and other garments behind him to retrieve later when she'd gone. "I suppose I shall see you at Grandfather's funeral."

"I'm sorry, Lucius!" Nothing she might have said could have bolstered his resolve more.

He turned the door handle and let himself out into the hushed, darkened corridor. Behind him echoed the words that Angela had used to draw him to her the night before.

In the harsh light of day, their power to hold him spellbound was broken. Still they dogged his footsteps as he hurried away.

"Please don't go."

Chapter Sixteen

After all that had happened at Helmhurst the night of the earl's death, Angela had thought her life couldn't get any worse.

Then the Bulwicks arrived home on the eve of the funeral, having been summoned by hysterical letters from Tibby which had finally reached them.

Clemmie and Cammie appeared none too pleased at having their tour shortened, while their parents were clearly outraged over all that had been going on at Netherstowe in their absence. And without their oversight.

Lord Bulwick had scarcely been in the house five minutes when he fixed Angela with a grim stare and demanded, "What's this I hear about your brother buying a commission and trotting off to India without so much as a by-your-leave from the family who raised him like a son?"

A few months ago, her uncle's glowering look, all fierce gray eyebrows and ruddy jowls, would have set Angela sputtering, dropping cutlery and tripping over footstools. But she had faced down a far more dangerous character since then. Besides, compared to losing her dear friend, the earl, and her troubles with Lucius, nothing else seemed of much consequence.

"I would rather Miles had stayed in England, too, Uncle." Angela managed to keep her tone respectful, but she could not recapture her old meekness. Nor did she wish to. "Since his heart was set on going, I resigned myself to it for the sake of his happiness."

The Bulwicks were gathered around her like some committee of inquisition, in the drawing room where Lucius had proposed to her. Though their tour had not lasted nearly long enough to suit her, it seemed as though a great deal of time had passed since that spring afternoon.

"The boy could have waited to consult with me at least." Lord Bulwick flung himself into a chair.

Out in the corridor, servants scurried back and forth, ferrying luggage in from the traveling coaches, with occasional exchanges of excited whispers as those who'd accompanied the family were welcomed home by those who'd remained behind. From below stairs came the aroma of frying sausages as Tibby scrambled to prepare a late supper.

It served Tibby right, for her meddling, Angela thought, no matter how well-intentioned.

She inhaled a deep breath to steady her voice. "An opportunity arose for my brother, so he felt obliged to take it. I believe he was anxious to relieve you of the responsibility for finding him a place."

"What's done is done, Lord Bulwick." Aunt Hester wilted into her favorite armchair, fanning herself.

With the earl's passing, the summer's streak of fine weather had broken. The skies had wept rain ever since, at times only a few soft tears, at others great stormy sobs. Now the rain fell in a steady patter on the leaves outside the open window. But not a breath of air stirred to ease the heavy heat inside Netherstowe.

Despite her discomfort, Lady Bulwick treated her niece to a fond, if rather forced, smile. The most affectionate look she'd ever bestowed on Angela.

"Is it true that you've gotten yourself engaged to Lord Daventry, my dear? Pray, how did that come about? If I'd thought the man might be lured into matrimony, I'd have sent Clemmie over to visit the earl at every opportunity."

From her place on the settee, where she languished beside her sister, Clemmie wrinkled her pert little nose. "Me, wed Lord Lucifer? You can't mean it, Mama!"

She and Cammie shuddered in unison. "Stuck out in the country? Never going to London or Brighton, or even Bath? Why, I'd sooner join a convent! At least then, I wouldn't have to suffer the attentions of that repulsive creature."

"Lord Daventry is not repulsive!" As the words

left Angela's mouth, a weight of guilt landed on her heart.

She must have made Lucius *feel* repulsive when she'd recoiled at her first sight of him without his mask. Remembering the pale seams of scars, the shot-pocked flesh and the shattered line of his brow, she still quailed. His appearance might not have distressed her so much but for the enormous contrast of his injuries with the chiseled perfection of the rest of his face.

For the first time since Angela had joined the Bulwick household as a child, Aunt Hester took her part in a disagreement with one of her cousins.

"Angela's right, Clemmie, you little goose. No man with his lordship's title and fortune can be thought disagreeable in any way. I only wish you and your sister had half your cousin's sense to encourage such an advantageous match, instead of flirting with penniless Italian music masters and the like."

The girls' pretty mouths puckered into identical pouts as they glared at their cousin.

Angela could scarcely believe her ears. How long and how hopelessly she'd struggled to win her aunt's affection, only to see it bestowed too late, for actions in which she took no pride?

"Have you and his lordship set a date for the wedding yet, my dear?" Aunt Hester's fan fluttered a little faster.

"Not without consulting her family, surely?" Lord Bulwick rumbled before Angela could reply.

"Not officially, perhaps." Lady Bulwick spoke sharply as she shot her husband a venomous look. "But all courting couples talk about when they'd like to be married."

Lucius had claimed that any man could make a woman feel the way he'd made Angela feel. Now, contemplating her aunt and uncle, she doubted it more than ever. She could not imagine Aunt Hester lifted to transports of delight, least of all by her bacon-faced bully of a husband.

Did Lady Bulwick ever guess what she'd missed? Angela wondered. Was it possible she'd resented her sister's children less because they were a burden on her household than because they were the product of a love match, a reminder of what she had denied herself?

"Lord Daventry and I haven't made plans of any kind." After what had happened between them the other night, they would have to marry, wouldn't they? Once Lucius got over being vexed at her...if he ever did. "Nothing can be decided while he's in mourning for his grandfather."

All the family sat up straighter.

Lord Bulwick looked even more indignant. "The earl's dead? When did this all take place, and why wasn't I informed at once?"

An angry retort rose to Angela's lips, but Aunt Hester interrupted before she could land herself in trouble.

"So Daventry is to be the new earl and our Angela will be his countess!" The news seemed to act on her like a tonic. "Think, Lord Bulwick,

what noblemen of the first rank they will be able
to put in the way of *our* girls!"

"I will not have Cousin Angela matchmaking on my behalf, Mama!" cried Clemmie, while
Cammie nodded her head in vigorous agreement.
"She'll only throw old men at me. And…and crip-
ples, and all her usual strays."

"Mind your tongue, Clemence!" snapped Lady
Bulwick. "The day may come when you'll be
grateful for your cousin's patronage."

Their bickering made Angela's stomach churn
and her head throb. It was all she could do to keep
from jamming her hands over her ears and running from the room. Instead, she turned to Lord
Bulwick and answered his question.

"The earl took very ill, suddenly, the other
night. He's to be buried tomorrow. Now if you'll
excuse me, I must retire."

"Of course, my dear." Aunt Hester jumped
from her chair and put her arm around Angela.
"You must be quite undone, poor girl. I know you
and the earl were great friends. Oh, and I brought
you back such a lovely treat from Austria. They
make the most charming confections there. I remembered what a sweet tooth you have."

"They weren't meant for her!" Cammie wailed,
but fell silent at a glare from her mother.

It didn't matter. Angela had known the sweets
could not have been purchased for her. "Thank
you, Aunt Hester, that was very kind of you."

Her aunt would not be dissuaded from escorting Angela to her room, all the while ply-

ing her with questions about Lord Daventry and their engagement, to which she scarcely knew the answers herself. By the time she'd been left in peace, with a fancy-looking box of sinfully rich Austrian bonbons, Angela feared her head would explode.

She pried open the box and popped a sweet into her mouth, savoring its buttery flavor. While it tasted lovely, it did not provide the expected sensation of comfort. Why, she could probably consume the whole box and get nothing from it but an acute case of indigestion.

What would she say to Lucius tomorrow, when they met at his grandfather's funeral? Would he allow her to offer him the comfort she knew he must need? Or had she spoiled any chance of that, the way she'd fumbled all her previous opportunities to penetrate the bristling defences he'd erected around his heart?

If he couldn't love her, she did not want to impose herself upon him, no matter what had happened between them that night at Helmhurst. She could not abide having Lucius believe she'd trapped him into marriage for the sake of his exalted title or vast fortune, the way her aunt had made it sound. Before she would let that happen, Angela resolved to withdraw completely from his life.

That might be the easiest course, in any case. She certainly wasn't cut out to be a countess. For as long as she could remember, she'd made do with what she'd been given, while trying to cultivate a proper spirit of gratitude. Nothing in her life had equipped her to fight for what she wanted.

Then again, she'd never wanted anything or anyone as badly as she wanted Lucius Daventry.

How could he face Angela today? Lucius asked himself as he grimaced into the shaving mirror on the morning of his grandfather's funeral. How could he face her, knowing how badly he wanted her? And how soon whatever had been between them must end.

He didn't blame the poor girl for her perfectly natural reaction to what she'd seen the other morning. It must have been a fearful shock, to believe she was being loved by Prince Charming in the dark, only to waken with the Beast in her bed. How could he expect her *not* to avert her eyes from a sight he had seldom been able to tolerate in the past three years?

Now Lucius made himself confront his disfigurement, to steel himself for what he must do today—ask Angela to break their engagement. He had always been a practical man, yet somehow he'd let himself be seduced by Angela's fancy. He'd been drawn to the idealized reflection of himself that he'd seen whenever he looked into her eyes.

Now and then, she'd persuaded him to believe in it. The nights they'd spend stargazing. The night of the ball. The night he'd made love to her. Always the friendly, concealing darkness had allowed him to become something he was not. The ruthless radiance of day always exposed the grotesque truth.

How could he ask Angela to live with a sight he could scarcely stand? How could he ask her to exile herself from the daylight, of which she was so much a creature, to join him in the foreign, frightening realm of the night?

He couldn't, of course. But when he thought of how alone he would be, without even the gently acerbic company of his grandfather, Lucius longed to impose on her tender sympathy. In weak moments, he tried to convince himself he could love her enough to compensate for the burdens of being married to him.

But in his practical heart, he knew that was the most dangerous *make-believe* of all.

Lucius emerged from Helmhurst a while later with a black ribbon tied to his sleeve and a black crepe weeper secured around his hatband.

The day was ideal for its purpose, with no cheery summer sunshine to mock his mourning. Instead, the countryside was swathed in a thick, silvery-gray mist that spared his sensitive eye. Obscuring vision and muffling sound, it carried the aroma of high summer sweetness—perfectly ripe, soon to decay.

His first glimpse of Angela came when his carriage pulled up in front of the church. Thankfully, she had her back toward him, which gave Lucius a little time to rally his composure.

When he noticed the man and three women

standing around her, he could hardly refrain from grinding his teeth. Why could the Bulwicks not have delayed their homecoming until his grandfather was decently in his grave?

At least the earl was beyond their power to annoy. Lucius doubted he could claim the same for Angela. The way they crowded in on her, all appearing to talk at once, all with disagreeable expressions on their faces, put him in mind of how a clutch of fowl would peck at a weakling chick in their midst.

His coach had not come to a complete stop when Lucius surged forth and strode toward the Bulwick family. If they were distressing Angela, there would be hell to pay. And he was just the man to present the bill.

"Excuse me, Miss Lacewood. Is there some difficulty?"

She started when she heard his voice. Lucius thought he detected an instant of hesitation before she turned toward him. Did she think he would shed his mask just because she'd seen what was behind it? Or did she fear that she would always picture his face as she had seen it the other morning?

Beneath her black, veiled bonnet, Angela's face appeared pinched and pale as she turned toward him. Her eyes were swollen with dark smudges beneath them that told of tears she'd shed on his grandfather's account...and perhaps a few on his as well. The notion bolstered his resolve to part from her. She needed a husband who could make her smile and laugh, not one who made her cry or cringe at the sight of him.

Before Angela could do more than cast Lucius a beseeching glance, Lord Bulwick thrust out his ample chest. "Well, well, Daventry…or should I say *your lordship?* You've kept yourself occupied with my family this summer. Shipped my nephew off to India. Got yourself engaged to my niece. Fancy finding suitors for my daughters while you're about it?"

Obnoxious fellow! How had Angela ever tolerated living under his roof?

As Lucius strove to phrase an answer that would not lead to bloodshed in the churchyard, Lady Bulwick gave a laugh that sounded like a cat scrambling over the keyboard of a badly tuned pianoforte. "You mustn't mind my husband, your lordship! We are vastly grateful for your patronage of young Miles, and quite delighted that you've set your matrimonial sights on our own dear Angela! Why, we should be obliged if you did help Clemence and Camilla find suitable husbands, by and by, shouldn't we, girls?"

The daughters, both rather pretty but excessively slender, stared at Lucius as if he was likely to bite them at any moment. He had an unholy urge to lunge at them and shout *Boo!* just to see how they might react.

Their ambitious mother clearly had her heart set on his marrying Angela. What sort of hell was she apt to make of her niece's life when Angela broke the engagement?

Since he could think of no courteous way to answer Lord and Lady Bulwick without choking on his own hypocrisy, Lucius steered the conversation back to the matter at hand. "Perhaps we should go inside. I believe the vicar is anxious to begin promptly."

"Very true, your lordship," agreed Lady Bulwick, herding her family toward the church. "Before you came, we were discussing where Angela should sit. As your betrothed, and a dear friend of the earl in her own right, I think it would be only fitting if—"

"They are *not* formally betrothed!" Lord Bulwick appeared intent on renewing the quarrel Lucius had interrupted. "My consent has neither been asked nor given."

"He asked the girl and she accepted." Lady Bulwick glared at her husband. "That is what matters, surely?"

Angela looked as if her one sound nerve might be about to snap. Lucius was the first to admit he'd be no prize as a husband. But he could hardly blame Angela if she valued him as an escape from her present situation.

"Would you care to take your place with me, Miss Lacewood?" If she did, it would only be to escape her odious relations, or because she felt sorry for him. Besides, it would only postpone their parting, not stop it. "I know my grandfather would have wanted you by my side today."

"Thank you, Lord Daventry...I mean, your lordship." As she reached for his arm, a soft beacon of hope glowed in her eyes, which Lucius knew he dared not trust. "You're very kind."

"I'm nothing of the sort," he muttered out the side of his mouth as they strode away from the Bulwicks. "But you will persist in thinking the best of people, and I suppose there's no curing you of it."

"No." Her grip on his arm tightened. "There isn't."

She must mean the gesture for reassurance, and perhaps a kind of apology. Ridiculous, since it was he who should beg her pardon, not the other way around. For the fright he must have given her the other morning, and for bedding her in a moment of weakness.

Now, in another moment of weakness, Lucius allowed himself to be comforted and sustained by her presence. For the next hour, he'd pretend it would not be necessary to banish Angela from his life.

A somber hush lay over those gathered inside the church, and the glow of candles did little to lighten the gloom. With a pang of regret, Lucius marked how few had come to honor the passing of so high a peer of the realm. Perhaps because the earl had outlived so many of his contemporaries, and because he'd kept so much to himself. Lucius wondered if his grandfather might have preferred it this way.

"'I am the resurrection and the life, saith the Lord,'" intoned the vicar as he walked up the aisle ahead of the pallbearers. "'He that believeth in me, though he were dead, yet shall he live.'"

As the earl's fine casket was laid before the altar, the vicar mounted to his lectern.

"'I said I will take heed to my ways: that I offend not in my tongue,'" he read. "'I will keep my mouth as it were with a bridle…'"

Lucius could not help but feel the psalmist was speaking directly to him.

"'…I held my tongue and spake nothing: I kept silent, yea, even from good words; but it was pain and grief. My heart was hot within me, and while I was thus musing the fire kindled…'"

Like contemplating the limitless expanse of the heavens, the words of scripture brought Lucius a remote sort of comfort. Some other man, centuries ago, had known the bridle of self-control that prevented him from speaking even good words… perhaps good words most of all. The psalmist, too, had felt those hoarded endearments catch fire in his heart.

"'…When thou with rebukes doth chasten man for sin,'" read the vicar, "'thou makest his beauty to consume away, like as it were a moth fretting a garment: every man, therefore, is but vanity.'"

If the early passage had comforted Lucius, this one hit him like a blow to some vulnerable spot. Had his beauty been consumed on that battlefield in Belgium to chasten him? For his pride, perhaps? For the ugly, primal exhilaration he'd taken in combat? For failing to restrain his men from their wild, fruitless charge on the French cannon?

Beside him, Angela raised a black-bordered handkerchief to her eyes.

More than anything, Lucius wanted to spare her further distress.

His selfish inclinations urged him to rescue her from Netherstowe, but prudence warned him that such a course would be worse for her in the long run.

Somehow it seemed disloyal to be pondering such matters in the midst of mourning his grandfather. But in a way, Lucius was only continuing the grieving he'd begun four months ago. Besides, his grandfather would have been the last person to discourage him from thinking about Angela under any circumstances.

Though sorely tempted to wed Angela, as his grandfather had desired, Lucius could not forget the earl's rebuke to him that morning in the orangery. *"No matter how much I might like to have the dear girl in our family, or how much I think you need a wife like her, I'm too fond of Angela to sit by while you treat her badly."*

Perhaps it was the memory of that conversation with his grandfather that made Lucius beckon Angela to join him in the orangery, after the last guests had departed from the funeral luncheon.

He feared he might not be able to say what he must in his grandfather's library, where they had spent so many enjoyable hours together during the past months. As well, there was something about being able to talk while they walked that helped him maintain his composure.

After a few awkward moments searching for the right words to begin, or perhaps a last futile attempt to delay the inevitable, Lucius said, "I'd like to...thank you, Angela."

"Thank me?" She darted as wary a glance at him as when he'd first appeared at Netherstowe to propose. "Whatever for?"

"For doing what we set out to do. And doing it well when I know it must have been a great effort for you at times. My grandfather said himself, the last months of his life were some of his happiest. I owe you a great debt on that account, and one I intend to honor."

Lucius inhaled a slow breath of warm air scented with the tang of ripening fruit. "Now I must ask you to honor our agreement."

"I beg your pardon?" She looked mystified. Had she made believe they were to be married for so long and with such intensity that she'd forgotten how it was supposed to end?

"Our agreement," he repeated. "You promised to break the engagement once it had served its purpose. It has, so I am asking you to free us both from any further obligation."

Angela stopped dead. "You want to be rid of me? After what happened between us the other night?"

Never in his life had Lucius chosen his words with greater care. "I do not want an action taken in a vulnerable moment to hold our futures hostage."

"I had hoped we might have a future together."

She spoke the words so softly they had little more substance than a thought.

Except that thoughts were private, and Lucius was determined to keep his that way.

"I don't believe it's advisable."

He tried to make it sound as though he were speaking of something quite ordinary—buying a piece of land, taking a trip abroad—rather than spending the rest of his life with the woman whose happiness he had come to cherish above his own. "It's never a good idea to deviate from one's original plan."

"Why not?" She drew the veil back over her bonnet. "Was making love to me part of your original plan?"

"Of course not!" Not that he hadn't wanted to from the first moment he'd held her in his arms.

She fixed him with her soft brown gaze. "Are you sorry?"

Why must she ask that? To give her a truthful answer would only rouse her pity for him. But to deny what they had shared and how she had touched him felt like sacrilege.

"It...has complicated everything."

"There's nothing very complicated about love." Her hand fluttered up to his face.

Too close to his mask. Lucius flinched. "Not when two people are well-suited, perhaps."

Angela sighed and her hand fell away. "Are we not well suited, you and I? Your grandfather thought so."

"The fact that one old man loved us both and

was loved by us both is no foundation for a life together."

"What about a child to love us both and be loved by us? Would that be enough?"

All the strength seemed to forsake his body. "What are you saying, Angela?"

"Don't play the dunce, Lucius! You must know it's possible I am with child. If that is the case, I will have to insist you do the honorable thing."

Couldn't she understand, he'd been trying to do the honorable thing?

Lucius turned from her so she would not see the hint of moisture in his eyes. Or the depth of fear and relief that battled for possession of his heart.

Chapter Seventeen

So much for her pitiful strategy to play for time, Angela thought as she drove toward Helmhurst in the carriage Lucius had sent for her.

Though she knew he could easily spare the vehicle, it gave her a queasy feeling of guilt to accept such solicitous gestures from him when she knew she wasn't carrying his child. It was beginning to look as though she never would.

She owed Lucius the truth. Today, after the reading of his grandfather's will would be as good a time as any to tell him.

Or as bad.

Ever since the day of the funeral, when she'd suggested that he might have gotten her pregnant, Lucius had been most attentive, in a distant, abstracted fashion. He'd put his small gig at her disposal for her usual round of visits to her friends. In the evenings, he'd frequently called at Netherstowe to rescue her from the company of the Bulwicks.

But in all that time he had never attempted to touch her or kiss her. Nor had he revealed his feelings with any tender words. Surely if he loved her, if their night together had been more than a mistake made in a moment of weakness, he would have said or done something to show her so?

Or had her aunt's mortifying performance on the day of the earl's funeral persuaded him that she wanted him only for his fortune and title? Before she would permit Lucius to believe such a thing, Angela was prepared to give him up, much as it would pain her.

The coach slowed just then, turning into the broad winding lane to Helmhurst. Behind the avenue of towering elms, Angela caught sight of the house where she'd spent some of the happiest moments of her life. Some of the unhappiest, too, but it was the happy ones she chose to dwell on, now that she might see no more of the place. It had become more of a home to her than Netherstowe would be if she resided there for the rest of her life.

The banks of thick dark clouds overhead matched Angela's mood precisely. Though not a single drop of rain had fallen that day, the weather looked ready to break at the slightest provocation.

As the carriage drew nearer the house, Angela noticed Lucius waiting at the entry. What could that mean?

"You took longer that I expected," he explained when he opened the carriage door and helped her out. "I was afraid something might have happened to you."

He did look rather anxious in spite of his usual attempt to disguise his feelings. Angela wished she could rip away that mask of wry indifference he wore, but he protected it as ferociously as he protected the black leather mask that covered his injuries.

A few times, she had glimpsed what lay behind it. Deep-running passions, some as scarred and wounded as the flesh around his left eye. Others with the compelling, potent beauty of the rest of his face. Both called to her.

If only she'd had the deftness to lure him forth without getting tripped up by her own uncertainty and sending him into retreat every time he allowed himself to get close to her.

"I'm sorry to have worried you on my account. My aunt detained me for a few words as I was leaving. I hope I haven't kept everyone waiting."

"You're here safely. That's all that matters."

Was his concern for *her,* Angela wondered, or for the child he still believed she might be carrying? His excessive consideration for her health and safety in recent days was her only clue as to how he regarded the prospect. Whatever his feelings for her, he must want the child.

Except there would be no child.

Though Angela mourned that lost promise, she also felt a sense of relief. At least now she would not have to spend the coming years racked with guilt for entrapping Lucius, or wondering whether he'd wed her only for the child's sake.

"My grandfather's solicitor is here." As Lucius ushered her into the house, he paused to whisper a few words to the footman stationed by the door.

Then he turned back to Angela. "Everyone is collecting in the library to hear the will read."

She nodded, unable to coax a word of reply past the great lump in her throat. Since the earl's death, she had not once entered the room that held so many vivid memories of him. She wasn't sure she could bear to do it now. Or bear to accept some kindly bestowed token of remembrance from him, when she would rather have had just one more hour of his company than any material legacy he might leave her.

But he would want her there. Angela knew it. And he would want to know his last gift pleased her. Some subtle intuition she was wary of trusting told her that Lucius would want and need her there, too.

That dubious conviction emboldened her to take him by the arm though he had not offered it. "We mustn't keep everyone waiting, then."

A heartening thought occurred to her. "This will be your grandfather's last chance to speak to us."

Lucius glanced down at her. She fancied his green eyes glistening softly with sorrow and gratitude.

"Except in our hearts," he corrected her in a

whisper. "Grandfather said he would speak to us from our hearts."

For a moment, Lucius seemed poised on the brink of falling into her arms and weeping out a lifetime of hoarded tears upon her breast. Then, with a fierce effort of will, he shored up his composure and added, in a tone of cool irony, "What whimsical things people say at times like that."

Once, his words might have exasperated her. But now Angela heard beneath them to a grief that could never heal because it was imprisoned, denied expression.

It was to that grief she spoke. "I miss him dreadfully." Desperation made her add, "I miss you."

Something checked his graceful, confident stride. When he turned his gaze upon her, Angela saw a plea in it. *Rescue me!*

She, rescue him? The notion was quite absurd. Or was it?

"Come along now, if you please." A reedy, impatient-sounding voice called to them from the far end of the gallery.

Angela turned to see a small man with tiny spectacles perched on his nose and enormous side-whiskers bushing out from his cheeks. He was standing just outside the library door, holding a gold pocket watch by its chain, as if to proclaim that time wasted was money wasted.

Lucius released a long, shuddering breath and the muscles of his face all seemed to clench tight.

"Let's get this over with." He started for the

library with such a rapid step that Angela almost tripped in her haste to keep up with him.

The familiar restful scent of the library wrapped around her as she entered. She could not help glancing at the earl's favorite chair to see if he might not be sitting there, waiting for her. She dropped into her accustomed seat by the chess table, while Lucius lowered himself into his grandfather's chair, after casting it a doubtful look.

A few of the servants were already assembled, as was the vicar. He flashed Angela a self-conscious smile. Within the next several minutes, the rest of the Helmhurst staff crowded in. All but the most senior congregated around the edge of the room, as if trying to blend into the walls.

When the solicitor seemed satisfied that everyone had arrived, he took his place behind the earl's desk. There, he unfolded a document of many pages with much throat-clearing and rattling of paper.

At last he began to read. "'In the name of God, amen. I, Arthur Augustus Daventry, Earl of Welland, being in uncertain health but sound of judgment, do make and declare this my last will and testament.'"

Angela concentrated her imagination, trying to hear the earl's words in his own mellow, measured tones, rather than the solicitor's annoying nasal tenor.

"'I give, devise and bequeath to my beloved grandson, Lucius Arthur, Baron Daventry, in addition to those properties accruing to the Welland title, all other properties, goods and chattels of my estate, saving the following bequests…'"

There were presents of money to every one of the servants according to their years of tenure at Helmhurst. Many were singled out by name for a particular word of thanks, which seemed to surprise and please them quite as much as the material remembrance. Mr. Carruthers, the earl's valet, commended for his "faithfulness, patience and discretion," received a sum that would allow him a comfortable retirement in the village.

When the solicitor announced that the earl had provided a substantial endowment for St. Owen's, Mr. Michaeljohn looked like a man whose prayers had been answered.

Angela had become so engrossed in watching everyone's reactions to their good fortune that she was caught off guard when she heard her own name read.

"And finally, to my dear young friend, Miss Angela Lacewood, of whom it is my fondest wish that she may one day be mistress of Helmhurst, I do bequeath additionally in her own right the following properties in the village of Grafton Renforth…"

Angela scarcely heard as the solicitor read the details. Instead, her gaze flew to Lucius. Was it possible he might honor his grandfather's *fondest wish,* even when he discovered she was not with child?

A collective gasp and a flurry of whispers told

Angela she had missed something important. "E-excuse me, sir. Would you mind reading that last part again? I fear I cannot have heard correctly."

The solicitor treated her to a patronizing smile. "I can understand why you might think so, Miss Lacewood, but I assure you, there is no mistake. '…as well as the capital sum of *ten thousand* pounds sterling for her exclusive use and maintenance.'"

"Oh, my word." Ten thousand pounds? And property? She had hoped for a piece of jewelry, perhaps. A few books.

But this…? Her breath began to hasten. Though she tried, she could not slow it down.

"Angela?" Lucius vaulted from his chair and knelt beside her, taking her hand. As he watched her eyes widen and her breath come shallow and fast, fear clutched him by the throat.

"Someone open a window!" he thundered. "Fetch smelling salts! The rest of you, clear off!"

A sinister reputation had its benefits, ready obedience being one of them. His servants fled the library as if it were on fire. A welcome draft of fresh air blew in from a hastily opened window.

"Angela, are you ill? Try to breathe more slowly."

She shook her head. "I…can't!"

Lucius felt someone hovering behind him. "Pardon me, but—"

"I said, clear off!"

"You did, of course," answered the vicar. "But I thought I might be of help."

Reaching past Lucius, he took Angela's hands and lifted them to her face. "Cup them around your mouth and nose, Miss Lacewood, and let your breath come as it will. That's right. I know the air will be stale, but don't worry about that."

Lucius opened his mouth to order the meddlesome vicar away. Couldn't he see that Angela would never be able to draw enough air to sustain her runaway breathing?

Perhaps that was the idea, though—to starve it of fuel, like a runaway fire. After a few gasps into her hands, Angela's breathing began to slow until it finally settled into a normal, steady rhythm.

Swallowing his self-reproach, Lucius held out his hand to the vicar. "Thank you for your assistance, my friend. I must remember this little cure of yours."

"Delighted to be of service." Mr. Michaeljohn beamed. "My father had a high-strung aunt whose breath used to get away from her in times of crisis. 'Do cover your mouth and stop acting like a ninny, Louisa,' my grandmother always used to say."

Hearing what he'd just said, he grimaced. "I don't mean to suggest that you are a ninny, Miss Lacewood. Why, anyone would be overcome at the thought of inheriting such a fortune."

Angela's eyes widened at his words. Lucius feared she might lose her breath again.

"Thank you, Vicar. I believe Miss Lacewood can manage now, with a little peace and quiet."

"Of course." The vicar gave a vigorous nod. "Pardon me for running on. I'll see myself out."

When he had gone, Lucius took Angela's hand, still warm from her breath. He resisted the urge to nuzzle his cheek against it, for fear he would not be able to stop at that. "Will you be all right? Can I get you anything? A sip of brandy, perhaps?"

"Heavens, no." Angela shook her head. "Imagine what a worse fool I might make of myself with a bolt of brandy inside me."

"Nonsense! Michaeljohn didn't mean anything by that drivel about his aunt. I'll admit, I was rather taken by surprise, myself. I expected Grandfather to leave you something of more sentimental value. It seems the old fellow was more practical than I gave him credit for."

Angela certainly wouldn't need him to rescue her from a life of toad-eating at Netherstowe after this. A single woman could live in some style on the income generated by ten thousand pounds. Not that she would need to remain unwed. Many the daughter of a peer did not bring so large a dowry.

None of that mattered, Lucius reminded himself, if Angela was carrying his child. He would never entirely forgive himself for entrapping her that way. But he would spend the rest of his life trying to make it up to her…and hoping it would be enough.

"Ten thousand pounds?" Angela whispered to

herself, shaking her head. "Whatever will I do with ten thousand pounds?"

"Almost anything you dream of, I suppose." Lucius steeled himself to raise *the subject*. "Fit out the most magnificent nursery in the kingdom, perhaps?"

Though she clasped his hand in both of hers, Angela refused to meet his questioning gaze. "That does sound a capital idea, though it will have to wait, I'm afraid. It seems I am not with child after all."

Thank God she had averted her eyes, or she might have seen what a blow her news dealt him. By the time she raised a cautious glance to his face, Lucius had mastered his emotions and confronted what he must do.

"How fortunate for you." He pulled his hand out of her grasp, rose to his feet and strode to the hearth. "For us both. I trust, now, you will consent to break the engagement, as we originally agreed."

Behind him, he heard her rise from the chair and follow him. "Is that what you want, Lucius?"

"It is what we agreed."

"That's not what I asked."

He was only trying to do the right thing, for her sake. Did she have to make it more difficult for him?

"I have told you more than once what I wish you to do. Does that suggest some indecision on my part?"

Damn it! She hovered too close to him—tempting and smothering him with that faint aroma of cooking spices. Making him remember how she felt in his arms, and how her kiss tasted.

Through the layers of his coat, waistcoat and shirt, he felt the delicate pressure and warmth of her hand on his back. "I don't know. Does it?"

He spun about, not because he wanted to face her, but because he had to escape the sweet snare of her touch while he could. "What sort of riddle is that?"

A small, soft smile lit her face. Lucius knew it could be his undoing, if he let it.

"Remember the day you came to Netherstowe to ask for my hand?"

As long as I live. Jamming his lips together to imprison those words, Lucius replied with a curt nod.

Angela nodded back at him with an air of indulgent mockery. "That day I accused you of talking in riddles."

That day, he had sensed all this coming. He had no one to blame but himself. He'd had chance after chance to withdraw from this campaign, if not victorious at least not routed. Now Lucius saw only one line of retreat open, and some part of him had turned traitor. It threatened to join forces with Angela and outflank his beleaguered resolve.

Calling up the last of his reserves, he made for the library door, fighting a vicious rear-guard skirmish. "That day, you also told me, in no uncertain terms, you had no wish to marry me."

"I didn't know you then, except by reputation."

Angela kept her distance, perhaps sensing he might flee if she pursued him. "You must admit, it was not one to inspire a prospective bride with much confidence."

"You don't know me, yet!" Lucius reached up to tap his mask. "You only know the face I present to the world."

"That's not true. Perhaps you haven't let me come to know you as well as I'd like to, but I know you far better than you think I do."

Lucius shook his head. "You make believe I am the kind of man you want me to be. Just as you made believe the part of my face behind my mask looks as pleasant as the rest. When you were made to see the truth, it horrified you."

"It took me by surprise. I tried to tell you I was sorry."

"I don't want your pity, Angela!"

"What do you want, then? My love? You have it, I'm afraid, whether you want it or not. Your grandfather told me I didn't need your permission to care for you. 'What a lady does with her heart is her own business,' he said."

Blast his grandfather! Lucius fancied he could hear the words Angela had just spoken in the old man's voice. The forces arrayed against him were growing stronger by the minute, but he must not surrender. If he gave Angela the opportunity to ask what feelings he had for her, he would be lost.

"I want what I've wanted all along." Lucius rapped out the words with a conviction he did not feel. "To be left alone. By you and by everyone else. No one will think the worse of you for throwing over Lord Lucifer. They'll assume you've come to your senses at last."

A flicker of doubt crossed her face, and Lucius hastened to exploit it. "With your new fortune, you can go to London or to Brighton, and find a husband who is all you want him to be."

"What if I don't? What if I find all the men like those friends of yours who came to the ball?"

Her question drew Lucius up short. Angela's fortune would be apt to attract all sorts of unscrupulous fortune hunters. In her naive goodness, she was apt to imagine them all fairy-tale princes, as she had mistakenly fancied him.

Angela shook her head. "In spite of what you may think, I do care for you, and I believe we could be happy together. When I came here today, I was prepared to do what you ask, because I couldn't bear for you to think I had any designs on your fortune. Your grandfather's bequest freed me of that suspicion, I hope."

"I would never have believed it of you, in any case." Lucius cursed the irony that his grandfather's bequest had robbed him of his last decent excuse to wed her.

"Then you are a *better* man than I thought." She drew a slow, deep breath. "If you are so anxious to be rid of me, you will have to be the one to break this engagement, Lucius. I will not."

"B-but we had a bargain!"

"I will gladly pay back every penny you spent to purchase Miles his commission and all his gear." With deliberate steps, she began to advance on Lucius.

He forced himself to hold his ground. "You can't do that!"

"What?" She chuckled at his foolishness. "Can't pay my debts?"

"You can't hold me to a betrothal we both agreed from the start was a pretense."

"Break it, then," she dared him.

"You know I can't!"

To his surprise, she walked past him to the door. "For all your bluster, I don't think you want to."

He could not bring himself to deny it, so Lucius settled for some ominous-sounding grumbles that didn't seem to intimidate her.

"I'm not doing this to vex you, truly." A flicker of her old uncertainty crossed Angela's face. "I tried for years to make my aunt take an interest in me. It seemed the harder I tried, the harder she pushed me away. I swore I'd never do that again."

The old hurt in her voice tore at Lucius. He could not bear to have her question whether she was worthy of his devotion. Still he resisted the urge to take her in his arms and reassure her with every endearment in his vocabulary.

The two circumstances were not the same. Lady Bulwick had not rebuffed her niece to make Angela seek out an aunt more deserving of her affection. He was making a noble sacrifice for the sake of Angela's future happiness. Wasn't he?

Of course, Lucius insisted to himself. Of

course he was. And one day she would thank him for it.

She didn't look thankful at the moment as she gazed at him. "I can't explain it, but I have a feeling it's different with you. If I let you go, I may never get you back. Perhaps, if I'm patient, you'll come to see that my feelings for you aren't the maiden's daydream you believe them to be. And perhaps you'll come to see that your feelings for me are stronger than you think."

Oh, his feelings for her were strong. Lucius had no doubt about that. Strong enough to tear him apart, if he let them.

Angela put her hand to the knob of the library door, then turned to him again.

"When that day comes," she whispered, "I'll be waiting."

She left, then, closing the door softly behind her.

Behind her, she left a man at war with his own heart.

Chapter Eighteen

"This is your fault, you know." Lucius glared at the fine marble stone that had recently been erected over his grandfather's grave in St. Owen's churchyard. "You filled Angela's head with all this sentimental nonsense about me. The poor girl probably has a misguided notion she's granting some last wish of yours by persisting with this engagement."

Light was fading from the early autumn sky that darkened from a rosy lavender in the west, through hues of purple and blue to velvet black off in the east. Not a single cloud threatened to obscure the view Lucius would get through his telescope in a few hours.

The faint breeze had a bracing nip that warned of colder nights to come. It rustled among the leaves with a sound that put Lucius in mind of his grandfather's voice in a gentle rebuke.

Lucius would have none of it. "You were the one who said you didn't want me to wed Angela if it meant compromising her happiness. You were right about that at least. I see it now. But how can I persuade her to give me up?"

How indeed?

Angela had steadfastly refused to go to London, or Brighton, or anywhere else Lucius had suggested. Instead, much to the consternation of Lord and Lady Bulwick, she'd settled down in the village in a snug little cottage on one of the properties the earl had left her.

She still paid regular calls on Helmhurst several evenings a week, which Lucius was helpless to prevent without causing a scandal. At first, he'd refused to admit how much he looked forward to her visits. Recently he'd faced up to it with a mounting sense of desperation.

The girl seemed to have absorbed his grandfather's gentle, unyielding persistence. Slowly but surely she was wearing down Lucius's powerful resolve. If he didn't soon find a way to divert her, Lucius feared he might yield in a moment of weakness, as he had done before.

With equally disastrous results.

"Why did I even come here?" he grumbled to himself, turning away from the grave, "You weren't any help when you were alive, you old meddler."

"Hello?" called the vicar from the church entrance. "Is anyone there?"

"Just I." Lucius strode toward the pale puddle of light that spilled out the open door of St. Owen's. It galled him to admit how hungry he'd become for a little company. "I wanted to see if that monument of my grandfather's was worth the expense. Don't suppose you'd care to come back to Helmhurst for a game of chess?"

"I shall be grateful to accept your hospitality." The vicar sounded pleasantly surprised by the invitation. "I was just heading home to a cold hearth, and feeling rather sorry for myself on that account. My housekeeper was called away for a few days by some illness in the family."

As Mr. Michaeljohn blew out the candle he'd been carrying and shut up the church, Lucius could not resist rallying him a little. "You need to find yourself a wife, Nathan. Then you won't be hostage to the vagaries of housekeepers and their ailing relatives. It shouldn't be much of a chore if you put your mind to it. I'll wager you could have any eligible woman in the parish for the asking."

The vicar fell in step beside Lucius, and the two men set off toward Helmhurst.

"Perhaps you're right," he replied in a rueful tone, as though Lucius had suggested he should become a missionary to some cannibal tribe. "A man in my position needs to be practical about such things, I suppose."

Lucius cursed his own thoughtlessness. "No man can afford to be a slave to romantic fancies, vicar. Marriage is too significant a step for that."

"Easily said." The vicar let out a long, slow sigh. "When the lady you love happens to be suitable in every way."

Suddenly the answer to both their problems dawned on Lucius with exquisite, excruciating clarity.

"The lady *you* love is suitable in every way for you." He forced himself to speak the words, for they were true. "And you for her."

"The lady I love? There must be some misunderstanding. Forgive me. I should have held my tongue."

"No. You were quite right to speak. And there is no misunderstanding. I've known from the moment I met you that you cared for Miss Lacewood."

"I—I don't know what to say." The poor fellow could not deny the truth. "I swear, I have never given the lady any indication of my feelings, nor sought to divert hers from you."

The vicar was a far better man than he. Looking back, Lucius asked himself why he hadn't had the sense and the honor to encourage a match between Angela and Mr. Michaeljohn when his grandfather had first raised the matter. Perhaps it was not too late to do the right thing.

"Of course, you haven't," said Lucius. "But, for all our sakes, it might be a good idea if you did."

The vicar stared at him in horror. "Have you lost your mind, Daventry? I—I mean, your lordship. You *want* me to tell Miss Lacewood how I feel, after how I've struggled to stop feeling that way? You want me to court her, when she's engaged to you? I've never heard anything so preposterous!"

"It's a rather preposterous situation, I'm afraid." With that, Lucius launched into an explanation of how he and Angela had reached their present pass, while the vicar walked along beside him in silence.

The only parts of the story he withheld were the truth of what had happened between him and Angela on the night of his grandfather's death, and the truth of his baffling feelings for her.

"So you see, Vicar," he concluded as the lights of Helmhurst came into view, "Miss Lacewood is determined to marry me whether I want it or not, and I am powerless to prevent her, unless you will come to my aid."

"I would like to oblige you, of course." The vicar shook his head as if mystified. "I would like to oblige myself. But courting a lady who's engaged to another man? It's impossible. Dishonorable. I can't."

"How can it be dishonorable," Lucius asked, "when I want you to do it? Anyone with sense can see that you and Miss Lacewood stand a much better chance of a happy marriage than she and I do. You have the power to prevent us from making each other miserable for the rest of our lives."

Though every word he spoke was true, Lucius could not subdue a foul sense of shame. Was this how the devil worked his wiles? he wondered. Tempting people with persuasive reasoning to do things they secretly desired but knew to be wrong?

* * *

There were days she was sorely tempted to give up on Lucius Daventry, Angela mused as she glanced around her very own garden, and today was one of them.

Not that he'd said or done anything particularly objectionable of late. In truth, he seemed to have grown reconciled to her visits. Though he continued to treat her with the cool courtesy of a newly met acquaintance, now and then some genuine emotion would flare in his eyes or the tone of his voice. It was enough to convince her afresh that he was not as indifferent to her as he pretended to be.

With a shallow basket on her arm, Angela made a circuit of her tiny walled garden, picking marigolds, petunias and asters. Later she would work them into pretty autumn nosegays to cheer some of her friends who were bedridden.

A few months ago, she would have asked nothing more from life than what she had now. Independence. A home of her own. The means to assist friends who needed her help. It seemed the height of ingratitude to want anything more.

But she did want something more, and there was no use pretending otherwise. She wanted Lucius, but not in the awkward, arm's-length fashion of late.

She wanted to stroll with him in a moonlit garden. To nestle in his arms and gaze at the stars. To lie on a bed with him through the black velvet hours of the night, while he beguiled her with his black velvet voice and his black velvet touch.

"Lovely day isn't it, Miss Lacewood?"

The vicar's cheery greeting jarred Angela out of her sweet, wanton reverie. She fumbled her basket of flowers.

"So it is." She pressed a hand to her flushed cheek in a vain effort to cool it. "Out of the wind, it's quite hot."

Mr. Michaeljohn stood at the gate, casting an admiring gaze at the autumn flowers. "May I join you in your garden?"

"Why, of course." As she threw open the gate, Angela stifled the thought that his presence would be an intrusion. "Do come in. How thoughtless of me not to invite you straight away."

He strolled into her garden. Plucking a bright yellow petunia, he held it to his nose. "Odd, isn't it? The autumn flowers are so bright and pretty, but they haven't the sweet smell of spring and summer blossoms."

Rather like the vicar himself.

That uncharitable notion popped into Angela's head before she could prevent it. "I—I suppose you're right. I hadn't given it much thought."

Mr. Michaeljohn was considered a very handsome man, she reminded herself. More importantly, he was a pleasant and good person. As far as she was concerned, however, he lacked something as subtle, yet vital, as the fragrance of a flower.

An uneasy silence settled over the small garden. Had the vicar just happened by? Angela wondered. Or had he come on a particular errand? If the latter, why didn't he speak of it?

"So," he said at last, "you're getting on well in the village?"

"Very well." Angela continued to pick flowers. "Mrs. Tibbs came from Netherstowe to keep house for me."

She'd been surprised by the offer, and not certain whether to accept it, considering Tibby's vocal antagonism to Lucius. In the end, their longstanding attachment had won out over recent friction. Angela had made it clear she would not tolerate any criticism of her fiancé, and so far Tibby had managed to keep her opinions to herself.

"Pardon me for saying so—" the vicar stared at Angela's trim little cottage "—but it seems a trifle odd that you should take a place of your own when you'll soon be mistress of Helmhurst."

The vicar's comment prompted a ripple of anticipation in Angela. Or perhaps it was a quiver of dismay.

Would Lucius relent and take her as his bride? she wondered. Or would he prolong their engagement indefinitely, in a campaign to exhaust her patience?

"It might seem odd to other people, Mr. Michaeljohn, but it makes perfect sense to me. I've lived at Netherstowe, on the charity of Lord and Lady Bulwick since I was a child. When the earl's generous bequest gave me the chance to be independent, I felt I must take it, even for a little while."

The vicar nodded, as though he understood. "So you are resolved to wed his lordship, even though circumstances have changed?"

"What *circumstances* might those be, sir?"

"I...er...had the impression...and do pardon me if I'm wrong in this...that you and Lord Daventry became engaged...to please his grandfather."

There was no need to obscure the truth any longer, yet somehow Angela shrank from confirming the vicar's suspicions. "It *began* that way, I will admit."

Her admission seemed to untie the man's tongue. Words that had come out in a stammering trickle suddenly gushed forth, to Angela's astonishment...and dismay.

"In that case, I must speak, Miss Lacewood, while there is still time. Believe me, I have chided myself frequently for not speaking sooner. If I'd had any warning that Lord Daventry meant to ask for your hand, I would have bestirred myself from my confounded backwardness to make my own feelings known to you."

Feelings? For her?

Angela scarcely noticed the basket of flowers falling from her slack fingers.

"Please, Mr. Michaeljohn, don't say any more, I beg you. You have been such a good friend to me and to his lordship. I should hate for anything to spoil that."

Contrary to her plea, the vicar strode toward her and grasped one of her hands in his.

"Though I would do most anything to oblige you, Miss Lacewood, I fear I cannot keep silent another moment. I have long felt that his lordship does not prize you as he ought. If you only accepted him because of the affection you bore his grandfather, no one would condemn you for changing your mind in light of the changed situation."

His lordship did not prize her? The charge struck Angela a stinging blow.

Though it might have appeared that way to a casual observer, Lucius had made her feel prized. Every unguarded glance, every impulsive embrace, every reluctant confidence had convinced her of the passionate tenderness he tried so hard to conceal at other times. Or had she simply seized on a few empty indiscretions to convince herself of what she longed to believe?

The vicar appeared to take her stunned silence as encouragement to continue.

"My dear Miss Lacewood, in the course of our acquaintance, I have come to have the most sincere admiration and regard for you. The warmth of compassion you show to anyone in need convinces me that you would make a perfect partner in my work. I would never cease to reproach myself if you wed his lordship in the false belief that no other man desired you as a wife."

"Mr. Michaeljohn!" Angela pulled her hand from his grasp and drew back from him. "I thought you were his lordship's friend. What manner of friendship do you call this, courting another man's fiancée behind his back?"

The vicar flinched under her rebuke, his fair face taking on a fierce scarlet cast. "It is precisely that consideration which has kept me silent until now. If I truly believed his lordship cared for you as I do, I would never have broken that silence."

Angela's hopes crashed to the ground with her fallen flowers. "Has Lucius told you he does not love me?"

The vicar's brow furrowed and a troubled look came over his handsome face. Clearly he regretted distressing her with the truth.

"I have eyes," he murmured at last, paraphrasing a passage of scripture, "and I see with them."

She wanted to hate him for what he had just said, and for presuming to entertain romantic feelings for her when she had none for him. But how could she blame the poor man, considering her own unreturned feelings for Lucius?

"Be that as it may." She struggled to keep her words and her tone temperate. "I have no wish to encourage any romantic attentions from you, sir. It would be uncharitable of me to let you believe otherwise."

"Perhaps my sudden declaration has surprised you," he suggested hopefully. "You may need to reflect on what I've said, and think about how you feel."

"Your declaration did come as a surprise." Angela shook her head. "That does not alter my feelings, however. I admire you. I find your company agreeable, but that is all."

The vicar pulled a wry face. "I understand."

He looked so thoroughly mortified, Angela found herself wishing she *could* give the poor man some scrap of encouragement. No doubt he was correct in one thing—someone like her would make a far more suitable wife for the local vicar than for a peer of the realm.

"I'm sorry I cannot give you the answer you desire." She stooped to retrieve her fallen flowers. "I think you had better go now."

Mr. Michaeljohn gave a dispirited nod and let himself out through the gate. As she watched him walk back toward the vicarage, Angela fought the urge to run after him.

If he'd proposed to her the day before Lucius had, she might well have accepted, and counted herself fortunate to have attracted his notice. She would have reconciled herself to a marriage without any great love on her part as she had long reconciled herself to a life of toad-eating at Netherstowe.

Now that Lucius had made her believe she deserved more from life, would she ever know a moment's contentment again?

"How did it go?" Lucius hardly needed to ask.

One glance at the vicar's hangdog expression and sagging shoulders told him the interview with Angela had been less than a rousing success. Fighting down a traitorous flicker of satisfaction, Lucius reminded himself that he *wanted* Michaeljohn to succeed in wooing her.

"Disaster!" With a pitiful sigh, the vicar dropped into his accustomed chair on the opposite side of the chess table. "She admires me. She finds my company agreeable, but that's as far as it goes."

"Don't lose heart now. That's not such a bad start." Angela hadn't professed to admire *him* or find him agreeable company on the day he'd proposed to her. "This sort of thing takes patience and strategy. Rather like a good chess match. Let me pour us a couple of brandies. Then you can tell me everything you said and everything she said, and we can plan your next move."

"There isn't going to be a next move, I tell you." The vicar picked up the white queen from its place on the chessboard and used it to knock the white king over. "I've been checked, mated and tossed out of the game. Miss Lacewood told me she doesn't want to encourage my romantic attentions. She meant it, too. I've never seen her so resolved."

"I have," Lucius muttered under his breath as he poured the vicar a very liberal measure of brandy. For reasons he could not fathom, the notion brought a smile to his face.

He forced the corners of his mouth down. "You took her by surprise, that's all. She needs a little time to get used to the idea of you as a suitor."

"So I thought, at first." Seizing the glass Lucius held out to him, Michaeljohn bolted an ample draft of the brandy. "She assured me there was more to it than that."

Between drinks, the vicar repeated as much of his conversation with Angela as he could remember. By the time he'd finished, Lucius was shaking his head and rolling his eyes.

"Sincere admiration and regard?" He repeated the vicar's tepid endearments in disbelief. "You actually said that? No wonder she didn't give you more encouragement! And the business about her being your helpmate in the parish—why, you're lucky Angela didn't take off her shoe and pitch it at your head!"

"I told you this was a bad idea." Michaeljohn held out his empty brandy snifter. "What do I know about courting? It's not the sort of thing they teach one in the seminary, you know."

"You've been reading the wrong parts of the Bible, that's all." Lucius poured his friend another drink—less generous this time.

"Try studying the Song of Songs, why don't you? 'Rise up my love, my fair one, and come away.' 'Behold thou art fair my beloved, behold thou art fair. Thou hast doves' eyes.'" As Lucius imagined himself speaking those poetic words to Angela, his voice grew more and more impassioned. "'Stay me with flagons, comfort me with apples for I am sick with love!'"

The vicar stared at him in horror. "Are you mad? I couldn't say things like that to Miss Lacewood. Dear heaven, I can scarcely think them!"

Then perhaps the good vicar was not such

a worthy suitor for Angela after all, in spite of his handsome face and estimable character. No sooner had the thought crossed his mind than Lucius dismissed it with ruthless force.

"Nonsense! You need a little practice, that's all."

"How am I to get any practice?" The vicar rested his chin on the palm of his hand. "I told you what Miss Lacewood said. She won't tolerate my dropping by her cottage every day and trying a new approach until something works."

Lucius subsided into his chair. "I suppose not." He reached onto the chess board and pushed his king's pawn ahead two squares. "Let's play awhile. It helps me think."

"Only if you promise not to *let* me win." The vicar set his fallen king back up. "That's more humiliating than when you beat me outright."

"If you insist." Lucius took a sip of his brandy. "You've improved tremendously of late. I thought you could use a little encouragement."

The vicar pushed his own king's pawn forward. "I'd sooner fail on my own, thank you."

At the last moment, he pulled the pawn back, then advanced his king's knight instead. A bold move. Perhaps there was hope for the fellow yet, Lucius decided.

As a chess player, quite likely. But as a lover?

Lucius brought forward his king's bishop pawn a single space to protect the king's pawn from the vicar's rogue knight.

It seemed unfair, or at the very least ironic,

that he should be bursting with lavish endearments for Angela that he dared not speak, while poor Michaeljohn longed to win her, if only he could find the words.

"That's it!" The power of his idea lifted Lucius out of his chair and sent him scrambling to his grandfather's writing desk.

He almost tipped the inkwell in his haste to remove the stopper. Fortunately, he found a quill with a good sharp nib, or he might have cut off a finger in his haste to trim a fresh one.

"What's *it?*" asked the vicar as he gazed at Lucius, whose pen flew across the paper like a thing possessed.

Lucius did not reply. Instead, he continued to scribble as words and phrases welled up in his thoughts faster than his pen could render them.

Angel of my heart... His heart beat faster with every word. Something within him that had been caged suddenly escaped and took flight. *Have mercy on a man who worships you but cannot speak of it. I claim nothing from you, ask nothing of you, except that you read my words and know you are loved.*

On and on he wrote until he'd filled two pages, a sense of release surging through him, as potent as the zenith of physical lovemaking. He could make love to Angela with his words—quicken the delicate flutter of a pulse in the hollow of her throat, provoke a soft blush to her cheek, coax a sigh from her lips, and rouse all the sweet passions of her womanhood.

And he could do it at a safe remove, by proxy. That she would credit the vicar and hopefully come to care for him hardly mattered.

Though you may never be mine, Lucius concluded, savoring every syllable, *I will always be yours.*

While the ink dried, he slumped back in his chair, weak with relief. The explosive pressure that had been building within him was now safely vented.

At last he rose, scooped up the papers and handed them to the vicar.

"What am I meant to do with these?" Michaeljohn's golden brows bunched together as he attempted to decipher what Lucius had written.

"Take them back to the vicarage." Lucius drained the last of his brandy. "Copy them over in your own hand and deliver the result to Miss Lacewood tomorrow. Don't stay to talk or explain. Just hand over the letter, then go."

As he read further, the vicar began to shake his head. "I can't...."

"You want her, don't you?" Lucius bent his most compelling gaze on the other man. Now that he had committed his deepest feelings to paper, Angela *must* read them.

Desire and propriety warred openly on the vicar's expressive face until finally he bobbed a hasty, half-reluctant nod.

"Good." Lucius released his hostage breath. "Then do it."

Chapter Nineteen

"What's this?" Angela cast a dubious glance at the paper Tibby held out to her.

"Dunno, pet." Tibby's thin shoulders rose in a shrug and her sparse eyebrows arched high. "The vicar left it for you while you were out paying your call on Mrs. Shaw. I couldn't coax a word out of him. The poor man looked like he supposed I'd bite him. The two of you haven't quarreled, have you?"

Angela took the letter from Tibby's hand gingerly, as if *it* might bite her. "Me, quarrel with the vicar? Never."

She'd probably hurt his feelings dreadfully, though. The back of her throat tightened and her stomach began to churn. She hadn't meant to be so harsh in her rejection of his modest overtures. But the things he'd said about Lucius not caring for her had stung. For the first time in her life, she'd felt the need to sting back.

Now she regretted it.

How was poor Mr. Michaeljohn to divine the true extent to which his friend might or might not care for her, when Lucius took such pains to conceal his emotions? Even she, who knew the man more intimately than anyone, was hard-pressed to sort out the truth of his feelings from her own wishful speculations.

She turned the letter over and over in her hands, running one finger over her own name, written in the vicar's copperplate script. Knowing Mr. Michaeljohn, the letter probably contained an apology for presuming to speak of his admiration for her.

"Well?" prompted Tibby, her deep-set eyes fixed on the letter. "Aren't you going to read it? Then you'll know what it's all about."

"Y-yes, of course." Angela fanned herself with the letter. "First I must go take off my bonnet and gloves. Will you brew a cup of chocolate for me?"

Giving Tibby something to do, especially something to *cook,* always managed to distract her.

"Indeed I shall." Without another word about the letter, Tibby turned toward the kitchen. "Will you have a rusk with your drink, pet? I just took a pan from the oven. That's quite a walk out to the forge and back, and the wind's cool today. You'll need something to warm you up."

"A fresh rusk would be lovely, thank you, Tibby." Angela tugged at the strings of her bonnet as she mounted the stairs.

The crispy strips of toasted cake always tasted so good when dunked in a cup of rich chocolate.

She might need the comfort they would provide after she'd read the vicar's letter.

At the top of the stairs, Angela pushed open the door to her bedroom. It was smaller than the one she'd had at Netherstowe, tucked beneath the sloping eaves of the cottage, with a single gable window looking out onto the village square. But it was truly hers in a way the other never had been.

Tossing her hat and gloves onto the bed, she settled into a small armchair near the window. Autumn sunlight, filtering through the curtain, cast lacy shadows onto the vicar's letter. Angela drew a deep breath to nerve herself, then broke the dark wax seal and unfolded the paper.

Angel of my heart... With a groan, she let her arm fall, the letter still grasped between her fingers. Had the man not heard a thing she'd said to him, yesterday?

Only a lingering crumb of guilt kept her from starting a fire in her tiny hearth and consigning the vicar's letter to the flames. Reluctantly she glanced at the next sentence.

Have mercy on a man who worships you, but cannot speak of it. This time, instead of groaning, Angela growled. Why must he appeal to her greatest weakness? Perhaps he knew her better than she'd realized.

I claim nothing from you, ask nothing of you, except that you read my words and know you are loved. Quite against her will, Angela's breath caught in her throat. She read the words a second time. Then a third.

Her pulse quickened and a warm blush rose in her cheeks as she continued to read the rest of the letter. *You glow like the sun, warming everyone you touch, making good things grow, and bringing light to all the dark places.*

As he continued to praise her beauty, her courage and her caring, his words fed a raw hunger that had gnawed inside her for years. He seemed to see her, not as she truly was, perhaps, but as everything she'd ever aspired to be. How had Mr. Michaeljohn come to know her so intimately when he'd never been more to her than a familiar, taken-for-granted fixture of her little world?

Though you may never be mine, I will always be yours.

A soft knock on her door made Angela start as if she'd been caught robbing the parish poor box.

From out on the landing, Tibby called, "I've brought a tray with your chocolate and rusks."

Angela bounded from her chair to throw open the door. "You needn't have gone to all that trouble, Tibby. I was just getting ready to go down."

"Walking up a few stairs is no trouble to me." Tibby entered the room with a tray, from which the mouthwatering aromas of chocolate and toasted cake wafted. "You're the one who needs to put your feet up after walking out to the Shaws' and back. Why don't you take a bit of that money the earl left you to buy a horse and cart?"

"The walking is good for me." Angela cleared some books off a small, three-legged table by the window so Tibby could set the tray there. "It keeps me from getting any more plump on all the sweets you cook for me. Besides, a horse would just be one more thing for us to look after."

"There is that." Tibby wrinkled up her nose, probably imagining herself mucking out after a horse. "Besides, the vicar's always kind enough to drive you when you ask him."

She nodded toward the letter lying on Angela's chair. "Speaking of the vicar, what did he have to say for himself that he couldn't have waited to tell you in person?"

"N-nothing dreadfully urgent." Angela plundered her mind for a plausible falsehood. "Just a question…about the earl's bequest to St. Owen's. I can't imagine why he thought I'd know."

"I see." Tibby did not sound convinced, but for a wonder she let the matter drop without further comment. "Well, enjoy your little bite and have a rest. Will you be going to Helmhurst this evening?"

"Yes." She'd intended to, but… "No. Perhaps. I haven't made up my mind."

What would Lucius say if he knew she'd received such an ardent letter from his friend, the vicar? And how could she persist in her engagement to Lucius when another man's declaration of love stirred her so?

"You seem distracted this evening, my dear," said Lucius as he and Angela strolled through the rose garden at sunset. "Is something the matter?"

Lit by the rosy hues of twilight, she had a soft,

pensive look about her that he found far too appealing.

Since his grandfather's death, Lucius had fortified himself against the gentle seige she'd mounted on his resolve, fearful that she might strip all his masks away, if he gave her the chance. Tonight she had drawn back, lulling him to lower his guard a little.

"The matter?" His question seemed to startle her out of her winsome bemusement. "Not in the least. Why do you ask?"

He shrugged. "You're quiet, tonight, that's all. As if your mind were a million miles away." He pointed off to the east, where a few of the brighter stars had begun to twinkle into view. "Off consorting in the heavens."

Lucius liked the sound of that. It gave him an idea for something he would like to tell her in his next letter. He hoped he could hold the thought until Angela had gone and he got an opportunity to write it down.

"I was thinking of your grandfather. About the last time I walked in this garden with him."

Angela drifted toward one rosebush, now bare of its fragrant, transient blossoms. The jagged-edged leaves, sharp thorns and sour bloodred rose hips were all that was left to face the coming winter.

Was she telling the truth? Lucius wondered. He had rather hoped her faraway look might have something to do with his letters. Not that he expected her to admit it.

He had interrogated the poor vicar in an effort to learn what her response had been. But Michaeljohn knew too little of women to decipher the subtle cues Angela might be trying to send him about the change in her feelings.

How Lucius wished he could become an unnoticed shadow, haunting a quiet corner of her room while she read his letters. To watch the movement of her eyes as her avid glance darted along each line, greedily digesting his words. To hear her breath quicken or catch as some phrase, delved from deep in his heart, pierced hers.

He longed to know beyond doubt that he was making her fall in love with him. The true *him*— neither beau nor beast, but the perverse medley of fancies and fears, wit and wonder, sweets and sorrows that made up the genuine essence of a man, behind whatever mask of flesh he might wear.

Genuine essence. Lucius savored the words in his mind as he watched Angela retreat deeper into her own thoughts. Love in its genuine essence was what he wanted to stir in her. Pure gold, untainted by the dross of pity or duty.

"I'm sure Grandfather would approve of that trim little cottage of yours. You seem happily settled there."

Again his implied question seemed to call her back from wherever her mind had wandered. "I beg your pardon? Oh, the cottage. Yes, it's very cosy."

It had grown too dark for Lucius to read her

eyes, even if he'd been standing close enough. But her tone had a subtle edge, at odds with her words.

Then, as if she'd guessed his thoughts, Angela added, "Your grandfather hoped I'd be mistress of *this* house, someday."

So, her show of withdrawal had only been a feint to lure him out from his citadel. Though he rebuked himself for his lapse in vigilance, Lucius could not suppress a flicker of admiration for such a worthy adversary. Even if she was capable of mangling his heart worse than French shot had mangled his face.

"Not at the expense of your happiness." He lobbed an answering blast from behind freshly reinforced defences.

"And what makes you certain I could not be happy here...with you?"

For so softly spoken and wistful-sounding a question, it was a well-aimed strike. Did she sense how badly he wanted to pretend such a thing were possible?

But he was a practical man, and a proud one. He would have given up his fortune, his title, and anything else to make Angela happy here with him. But he could not surrender his pride and his practicality, for they were part of him. Too large a part, perhaps, but he could not help that.

"I know it!" Lucius tapped his fist against his chest, the way his grandfather had tried to do before he died. "Damn it, Angela, don't you understand? I'm trying to protect you!"

"Protect me from what?" She strode toward him with sure, purposeful steps. "From you?"

"Who else?"

He wanted to grasp the pliant flesh of her upper arms in his hands and shake all the naive illusions out of her. But he dared not reach for her in case he might end up gathering her into his embrace, instead.

Lucius spun on his heel and marched away. When he was certain she'd gone, he returned to the house and sat up in the library until dawn, composing a letter filled with the words he so wanted to tell her but didn't dare.

Oh, that man! Angela massaged her temples as she descended the stair of her cottage after a sleepless night.

One minute he infuriated her to the point where her palm itched to strike him. The next, she longed to gather him to her bosom and rock him as if he were an injured child. Later still she wanted to fling herself into his arms and beg for his touch.

The soft crackle of frying fat and the savory aroma of sausages lapped over Angela in a warm, comforting wave when she reached the bottom of the stairs.

"Good morning, Tibby," she called.

"Morning, pet. Not that it looks much good. The wind's blown up and I fancy we'll have rain before noon. If you've calls to make today, you should get about as soon as you've eaten breakfast."

Angela glanced out the window before making her way into the little dining nook. The sky did look unsettled, if not downright threatening. "Perhaps I'll do that."

As she drew out her chair to sit down, she caught sight of a letter propped against her teacup.

"When did this one come?" Angela called into the kitchen, certain her housekeeper would know what she was talking about.

Tibby bustled in from the kitchen, wiping her hands on her apron. "The vicar stopped by about an hour ago. Looked like he'd just rolled out of bed, poor man."

In a tone of vastly exaggerated innocence she remarked, "There must be a great mix-up about the earl's money to call for all this letter writing."

"It's *not* about the earl's money, Tibby, as I expect you've guessed." Angela reached for the letter. "It seems the vicar has some…feelings for me. He'd like me to jilt Lucius and marry him, instead. There, is that a rich enough helping of gossip to satisfy your appetite for the day?"

A little too rich, perhaps. Tibby pulled out one of the dining nook chairs and dropped into it with a surprising impact for one of her light weight. Perhaps her pretense of innocence had not been exaggerated after all.

"Oh my word," she repeated to herself several times. "This is a pretty pass."

"If you dare say Lucius will put a curse on the

vicar over this," cried Angela, "I'll sack you at once without character."

She didn't mean it, of course, but she couldn't stand the notion of Tibby pressuring her to accept the vicar when his letters tempted her too much already.

"Do you *want* to marry Mr. Michaeljohn?"

"No! I mean, I don't know." Angela turned the letter over and over in her hands. "I don't think so…but…"

Tibby stared at the letter. "Have you told him to stop writing to you?"

A helpless sigh gusted out of Angela. "I've tried."

"And he keeps writing anyhow?" For once Tibby looked incensed with someone other than Lord Daventry.

"You don't understand." Angela looked at the sealed, folded paper in her hand with a powerful mixture of inclination and aversion. "I haven't been able to bring myself to tell him."

"Oh."

Angela ripped open the seal and read a few lines to herself. It wasn't a letter this time, but a poem…a sonnet. Pirated a little from Shakespeare, but not so bad for all that.

Shall I compare you to an autumn day?
My angel, you yourself invite compare,
More to ripe October than to budding May,
When hues of sun and cornsilk ripple in
your hair.

There was more about her eyes and lips, her voice, her laughter and finally, *Your nature, like the best of nature, generous and kind.*

She stirred from her reading to feel a dreamy smile on her face, which she hastily stifled. Shaking the sheet of paper at Tibby, she demanded, "How can his words touch me like this when I feel nothing in his presence?"

"I dunno, love," Tibby admitted. "Been in service since I was so high." She held up her hand to a stature little more than half her present one. "Never had a beau or any of that. All I've seen about marriage was the master and the mistress out at Netherstowe—what a body should steer clear of."

"I'm so confused, Tibby. Lucius makes me feel so many things for him—not all of them good, as I suppose you'll agree. All the same, I can't help believing he needs me in a way Mr. Michaeljohn never will. Perhaps that's the problem. I want a man who needs me, but he can't stand needing anyone."

She glanced down at the letter again. "When I read the vicar's letters, though, I find myself wondering if he might need me after all."

Tibby suddenly sat up very straight and sniffed the air. "The sausages are burning!"

She rushed out to the kitchen and returned a few minutes later in a more composed fashion, as though the minor domestic crisis had somehow restored her confidence.

"You won't likely have much success sorting

out a tangled heart on an empty stomach." Tibby spoke in her accustomed brisk but fond tone as she placed a heaped plate before Angela.

"Now you set that letter aside, and put it clean out of your mind while you eat a good breakfast. Then go for a walk or do a bit of work in the garden. Say a wee prayer, maybe, and think on what'll make you happy. For, heaven knows, if you aren't happy in a match, the gentleman you choose won't be, either."

Pushing the letter to the opposite side of the table, Angela inhaled a deep breath of the savory steam rising from her plate. "I believe that's the most sensible advice you've ever given me."

"Get away with you." Tibby smiled, in spite of herself. "I've given you plenty of sound advice over the years."

She started back toward the kitchen, then stopped. "I'm beginning to wonder if my advice to you about Lord Daventry mightn't have been the best, though. I still think he's a queer fellow and all, but you've changed since you took up with him…in good ways. Not that I mean to sway your decision, mind. I think the world of the vicar. If you're happy, I'll be content."

Angela sprang from her chair to gather the older woman in a swift embrace. "Thank you, Tibby. I declare you're as wise as old King Solomon. I do believe you've given me the answer!"

She darted for the stairs to fetch her bonnet, gloves and wrap, while Tibby called after her,

"Here, now, that's all very well. But you need to come eat your breakfast first!"

Angela glanced back for an instant, a delicious sense of hope and assurance nourishing her spirit. "Oh Tibby, I couldn't possibly eat at a time like this."

While she tied her bonnet strings and pulled on her gloves, Angela rehearsed in her mind what she would say to the vicar and to Lucius.

First she'd ask each man if he trusted her judgment. Then she would ask if they wanted her to be happy, a question to which she was tolerably certain she knew the answer. Finally she'd inquire if they were willing to do what she judged would make her happy.

If both men gave positive answers to all her questions, she would tell the vicar he must stop writing to her and give up any notion of making her his wife. Then she would tell Lucius he must stop trying to protect her from him, or him from her, and solemnize the union they'd already consummated.

Buoyed by a novel sensation of assurance, Angela flew down the stairs. Ignoring Tibby's reproachful look, she dropped a quick kiss on the older woman's cheek in passing. A gust of wind caught the door when she pulled it open, almost wrenching the latch from her hand. She made sure to pull it closed good and tight behind her before setting off toward the vicarage.

The village square was all but deserted that morning. Those who ventured out of doors were blown on their way by the wind, along with the bright autumn leaves it had torn from the trees. Ordinarily Angela would have considered it too early in the morning to pay a call, but since the vicar had come to her house over an hour ago, she couldn't see any reason not to reciprocate.

The vicar's housekeeper answered Angela's knock with a puzzled expression on her ruddy face, as if she wondered who would be abroad at this hour on such a blustery morning.

"Come in, Miss Lacewood. I hope nothing's the matter. The vicar was yawning so over his breakfast, I bid the poor man go back to his bed for a while then begin the day over."

Angela fought down a qualm of disappointment. She had so wanted to resolve the matter before her present mood of confidence faltered.

"Don't wake him, please," she insisted. "It's nothing urgent, truly. I can come back later."

Had poor Mr. Michaeljohn sat up until the wee hours of the morning composing that sonnet for her? Now that she thought of it, his handwriting had looked less pristine than usual. "I hope he was not awake very late last night."

The housekeeper shook her head with an exasperated look that reminded Angela of Tibby. "Woken early this morning, you mean. Really, miss, you should remind the new earl that not everybody keeps his queer hours."

"His lordship called here, this morning?"

"Aye, Miss, with some papers. Gave me a right

turn, he did. Not that I ever credited the gossip about him, mind you."

Papers?

"You mustn't go, miss. The vicar told me to call him if he slept more than an hour, and it's been all of that. I'm sure he'd be vexed to hear you'd come then gone away again."

"V-very well. Perhaps I'll wait." The questions she had intended to put to the vicar suddenly yielded place to a more pressing one.

The housekeeper beckoned her down a corridor that ran beside the staircase. "You bide a minute or two in Mr. Michaeljohn's study while I go fetch him for you."

"Thank you." Angela stepped into a cramped little room that reminded her of the library at Helmhurst, in miniature.

Three walls were lined with shelves, crammed full of books. The floor was strewn with books and papers, while the writing desk held more stacks of paper. It surprised Angela that a man as fastidious as the vicar could work in the midst of such disarray.

Was it here that he'd written his letters to her? Angela wondered, curiosity getting the better of her.

She glanced at his desk. There lay an early copy of the poem he'd composed for her. As she picked it up for a closer look, the paper beneath it caught her eye. The spiky scrawl was familiar to her from the letters Lucius had sent to his grandfather during the war.

Shall I compare you to an autumn day?
What?

Angela rifled through the rest of the papers, her breath hastening, the way it had when she'd first learned of the old earl's bequest to her. By the time she had uncovered four more letters in Lord Daventry's familiar hand, her head was spinning and her heart pained with every lurching beat.

She heard feet descending the stairs in a clamorous rush, and a moment later the vicar appeared in his study door.

"Miss Lacewood…" He spied the sheaf of papers in her hand. "Please, I can explain."

The flutter of disbelief and distress within Angela exploded in a tempest of fury. She strode toward the door, daring the vicar to stand in her way. Perhaps he anticipated the danger, for he fell back to let her pass.

"I'll deal with you later." She shook the papers under his nose. "But first I have a few words to say to Lord Daventry."

Quite possibly the last words she would ever address to that heartless beast!

Chapter Twenty

Lucius pummeled his pillow, half wishing it were his own face.

Off in the distance he could hear all the muted sounds of daytime activity that should have lulled him to sleep—faint footsteps and the soft murmur of voices. This morning they had lost their soothing power. Yet neither were they sufficiently loud or unusual to provide a distraction from the thoughts that worried at him.

For the first time since he'd hit on his plan to promote a match between Angela and Mr. Michaeljohn, Lucius found himself wondering whether he might be doing the right thing but for all the wrong reasons. A very soft voice from deep in his conscience even dared to question whether he'd done the right thing at all.

He did regret harrying the vicar out of bed this morning, at an hour when most people other than himself were still fast asleep. But he'd so wanted Angela to read what he'd written. He could not bear to wait until Michaeljohn's next visit to Helmhurst. It had been all he could do to keep from skulking outside her cottage, spying in a window to watch as she read it.

On the drive back to Helmhurst, the left wheel of his gig had hit a rock. Luckily the mishap had occurred very near Shaw's forge, where the blacksmith was awake and hard at work despite the early hour.

"Morning, sir." The ex-gunner had given the former colonel a jaunty mock-salute. "Good to see ye out and about."

Shaw had looked over the damaged wheel and announced he could repair it in less than half an hour.

"Did I ever properly thank ye for what ye and Miss Lacewood did that night, sir?" The blacksmith tossed the question off while he concentrated on working the bellows and heating the bent wheel in the forge.

Lucius muttered some rubbish about no thanks being necessary.

"Ye may not feel the need of it, sir, but I do." Shaw pulled the iron from the fire with a massive pair of tongs and transferred it to his anvil. "The wife'd had just about as much of my carrying on as she could stand. She'd about decided to take the boy and go away."

"I'm pleased to hear it all worked out."

"Indeed it has, sir." The blacksmith hefted his hammer and began to pound the red-hot metal back into its proper shape with sure, powerful strokes, sending off a shower of sparks.

He raised his voice to carry above the noise of his work. "Just talking to ye that night, sir, it helped. Made me see I wasn't the only one as good as went to hell in the war. Damned if I'd let it keep me there for the rest of my life or drag anybody else down for company."

Lucius replied with a polite nod, but inwardly he reeled as if the blacksmith had cast his soul into the fire then hammered it with the truth.

The war, that last battle in particular, had cast him into hell. When Angela had reached down to pluck him out, he'd resisted, because he feared he might end up hauling her down with him. That *had* been why he'd resisted, hadn't it?

Apparently satisfied with his handiwork, the blacksmith dropped his hammer, then lowered the glowing part of the wheel into a trough of water to cool it. Watching the water bubble and hiss, Lucius felt a similar turmoil raging in his own belly.

Two hours later that turmoil had not subsided.

He was too tired and confused to decide what he must do. If he could only sleep for a while, perhaps everything would look clearer when he woke. At the moment, he was sure of only two things. One, that he loved Angela. The other, that he wanted to be with her and to make her happy.

What he could not decide was if it might be possible to accomplish both at the same time.

As he made one last, desperate effort to sleep, Lucius sensed discordant notes in the distant domestic hum of his household. A raised voice. A door slamming. The soft but ominous thunder of rapid footfalls on the stairs.

Before he could rally his wits, the storm broke upon him.

His bedroom door burst open, followed by a further hail of footsteps. Then someone tore the heavy curtains of his window open, unleashing the daylight upon him in a blinding flash.

"What in blazes is going on?" Lucius bellowed, raising his arm to shield his face from the light, and from the sight of whoever had committed this assault.

"I'd do worse than this to you if I could, Lucius Daventry!" cried Angela. "You must have no conscience at all if you can sleep soundly after what you've done to me, you brute!"

Lucius felt the mild sting of several sheets of paper slapped against his arm.

Oh, damn!

"How dare you?" She flogged him with the papers again. "Did you want to be rid of me that badly? Enough to trick me into falling in love with a man I care nothing for?"

"Please, Angela, let me explain!"

"Your friend Michaeljohn told me he could explain, too." With a shriek of vexation, she began to tear the papers to pieces. Lucius felt as if she were tearing part of his heart along with them.

"How do you two learned gentlemen propose to explain why Mr. Michaeljohn has copies of the letters he sent to me, written in *your* hand?

You must think I'm completely daft to have been taken in by this disgusting little scheme of yours in the first place."

"Angela, I'm sorry. I never meant for you to find out." Lucius groped on the bedside table for his mask.

Before he could locate it, Angela knocked the contents of the table onto the floor with a violent swipe of her hand.

"Don't bother trying to hide yourself!" Grasping his wrist with savage power beyond anything he would have imagined her capable, Angela wrenched his arm down.

"Those scars on your face aren't nearly as ugly as the ones on your soul, Lucius. And don't fret yourself that I'll feel sorry for you. After what you've done, I shall *never* waste another moment's pity on you!"

He should have welcomed those words. But hearing them from her lips in that harsh, anguished tone tore at Lucius.

"I shouldn't bother in any case." She thrust his arm away from her as if it were some particularly disgusting variety of vermin. "I couldn't begin to feel as sorry for you as you feel for yourself."

"You're right."

Squinting against the light, Lucius fumbled for his dressing gown and pulled it on. Angela was seeing him at his most broken and vulnerable already. Such pride as he had left insisted he must face her clothed, at the very least.

"I a-am?" She froze for a moment, then rallied.

"I mean…of course, I am. Do you have any idea what you did to me with this cruel trick of yours?"

Lucius shrank from hearing her call it that. He had meant his letters to be so much more. A release for the emotions he had not dared express to her. A means to convince Angela of her own beauty and merit. A spark to kindle her love for a man more worthy of it.

"I'll tell you, shall I?" she challenged him, when he did not reply. "You almost pulled my heart in two, that's what. You made me imagine myself falling in love with a man I've never cared for—and feel guilty on account of it."

Lucius had never seen her so overwrought. Much of it was anger, he could tell. Anger he deserved. But behind the blast of fury he sensed grief, caused by the battle he had set off within her. A battle too much like the one he'd fought with himself over her.

"I'm sorry, Angela, I only thought…"

"You *didn't* think!" She balled her fists, as if to keep from striking him. "What if you'd kept on until I ended up married to the man, then found out it was all one great lie?"

Her anger had almost spent itself, but beneath it ran a bitterness that would endure for a long time. Never had Lucius wanted to take her in his arms more than he did at that moment. But he'd forfeited any right or ability to offer Angela comfort.

"Don't blame Michaeljohn." Lucius could not beg her pardon for himself. "The whole idea was mine from the start. He only went along with it very reluctantly, because he loves you and wants you but couldn't find the words to tell you how much."

"I'll blame who I please," flared Angela. "There's plenty to go around without stinting either of you."

Lucius quailed before the revulsion in her eyes. She looked at him as though his entire countenance were hideously mangled, not just that one corner of his face.

"How dare you do this to me?" She demanded again. "How dare you?"

"How dare I?" Lucius shook his head. "I *didn't* dare, Angela. Don't you see? If I'd dared, I would have seized the chance to love you, and to hell with anything else. Instead, I took the coward's way."

It wouldn't make any difference, but somehow he must convince her that he reproached himself no less than she reproached him.

"Seized the chance?" Angela loosed a barrage of bitter laughter. "I gave you dozens of chances, Lucius. Hundreds. A fresh one every day I came to see you. And you turned up your nose at all of them."

She moved toward the door. "Well, no more. If you are so desperate to be rid of me, I'll be delighted to oblige you. I'll make certain everyone knows that our engagement is broken. Congratulations, your lordship. You are free of me at last."

That final word came out on the ragged edge

of a sob, but Angela did not break down in tears. In fact, she retained enough self-possession to march out of the room with her head held high.

There was something strangely cleansing, Angela decided as she left Helmhurst for the last time, about allowing herself to get really angry and indignant on her own behalf, then giving those explosive emotions full release. All her life she'd swallowed slights, neglect and insults, like some foul-tasting tonic she must tolerate for her own good.

Well, no more!

She had never imagined Lucius Daventry looking so unnerved as she'd just seen him. Angela might have been inclined to feel a little sorry for the man, except that she'd sworn never again to take pity on him. With good reason, too, she reminded herself. If he'd ever cared for her in the way she'd foolishly imagined, Lucius could not have hurt and deceived her in so cruel a fashion.

During her walk to Helmhurst, the wind had howled through the trees, tearing off their remaining leaves and lashing the branches about. It had all but picked Angela up and carried her along the road. She'd gloried in its violence, so well matched to the tempest raging inside her. Now, as she headed back toward Grafton Renforth, the wind had eased, but the clouds it had blown up were beginning to spit fat drops of rain.

Angela resisted the temptation to weep with them. She was well rid of Lucius Daventry, and thankfully cured of her foolish romantic fancies. Perhaps, now, she could recapture her old contentment with life and close a door on the past few months, as if they'd been no more than a dark dream.

More and more drops of rain began to fall, splattering on the road. Angela muttered curses under her breath. She should have ordered one of his lordship's carriages to fetch her home. The man owed her that much at least.

No help for it now, though.

Picking up her skirts, Angela began to run, hoping she would not be soaked to the bone by the time she reached the Shaws'. She could take shelter there until the rain eased.

To her surprise, it was the blacksmith, not his wife, who answered her frantic knocking. "Miss Lacewood, come in out of the rain. Lizzie's off to the village with the boy. Did you not meet her on the road?"

"No…Mr. Shaw," gasped Angela, winded from running. "Must…have missed her. I was…on my way back…from Helmhurst."

The blacksmith cast her a questioning look, clearly wondering why a man with as many carriages as his lordship could not spare one to drive his fiancée home on a day like this.

"Do sit down, miss, and take off that wet wrap. I was just about to have a mid-morning bite when I heard you knock. The tea's hot if you'd care for a cup."

On her recent visits to the forge, Angela had

seldom seen Mr. Shaw, except at a distance. Though she hadn't spoken with him since the night he'd threatened her, she was not frightened of him now. Mrs. Shaw insisted her husband was a changed man since then, a blessing for which she thanked Lord Daventry.

"I'm most grateful for your hospitality, Mr. Shaw." Angela hung her wrap and bonnet on a hook by the door, then took a seat at the table. "I apologize for barging in on you like this."

"No bother, miss. I'm glad of the company."

The blacksmith set a steaming mug on the table before her. Angela wrapped her hands around it to warm them.

He offered her food, which Angela declined, urging him to eat his own before it got cold. They exchanged a few remarks about the weather, punctuated by long awkward moments of silence. When they had exhausted that topic, Angela asked about Mrs. Shaw's errand in the village. That kept them in conversation for a while longer.

Finally, after a sustained, uneasy pause Mr. Shaw said, "His lordship was here early this morning. Had a spot of bother with his gig driving back from town."

Angela nodded and tried to appear interested in the information. Lucius must have been rushing home after having left that poem for the vicar to copy. Whatever had happened with the gig, it served him right!

The blacksmith toyed with his fork. "I finally had a chance to thank him for talking some sense into me, when I was in such a bad way, that time. Now I reckon it's past time I thanked you as well, miss, and begged your pardon for acting such a lout."

The whole apology was clearly an ordeal for him. Angela couldn't have held a grudge against Mr. Shaw if she'd wanted to. "I'm glad to hear you and your wife are doing so much better. Sometimes it's hardest to get on with the people we love best, isn't it?"

"Aye, that's so, miss," agreed the blacksmith. "I hope you and his lordship will have every happiness together. You're fine folk, both."

Those plain, kind words struck Angela a harder blow than Mr. Shaw's brawny fist ever could. She tried to summon the forceful indignation that had carried her to Helmhurst, only to discover she had expended most of it.

"Thank you." Angela forced herself to continue. Since she would have to repeat the news often in the days to come, she might as well get some practice. "I'm sorry to say, his lordship and I will not be getting married, after all. I've broken our engagement."

For a moment Mr. Shaw digested her news in silence. Then he rubbed his blackened knuckles against his chin. "I'm sorry to hear that, miss. Potted as I was that night you both came here, I recollect, clear as can be, the look in his lordship's eye when I…raised my hand to you. I mind he would have done anything to protect you."

Something in the blacksmith's earnest gaze

prompted Angela to give a more candid reply than she'd intended. "Unfortunately, Mr. Shaw, he could not protect me from himself."

After a long, pensive pause, the blacksmith asked, "Are you sure of that, miss?"

He rose abruptly and began to clear his dishes from the table, leaving Angela to ponder his question.

Time and again she had tried to save Lucius from the demons that haunted him. Was it possible he'd tried to protect her from them? Or was she, once again, imagining what she wished to be true?

A restrained but insistent knock on the Shaws' door made Angela start. Had Lucius come after her?

The blacksmith hurried to answer the summons. "More company today than we often have in a week."

He pulled open the door to admit the vicar.

"Sorry to disturb you, Mr. Shaw. By any chance did Miss Lacewood—?" He caught sight of her, seated at the table. "Ah, so she did seek shelter here."

"Don't stand out in the rain, Vicar." Mr. Shaw stepped back to let him enter. "Come in where it's dry."

Doffing his hat, Mr. Michaeljohn stepped over the threshold. He cast Angela a chastened look, almost as if he were begging her permission to take refuge under the same roof.

"You were looking for me?" Angela managed to rouse a flicker of her earlier indignation.

She might have suspected Lucius capable of doing what he'd done. But a man of God should have known better than to deceive her in such a way.

He gave a guilty-looking nod. "Mrs. Tibbs came by the vicarage looking for you. I thought you might have gone to Helmhurst, so I drove out to fetch you. When I was told you'd left already, I hoped you might have elected to wait out the storm here or at Netherstowe."

"Does it surprise you to discover I have the sense to come in out of the rain?"

"Why, no, of course not." The vicar gave a patently false chuckle, perhaps hoping to convince the blacksmith that Angela had been in jest. "I am pleased to find you safe and dry."

"Mr. Shaw has been a very kind host."

"Will you come have a cup of tea with us, Vicar?" The blacksmith glanced back and forth between his two guests, clearly aware that he had landed in the middle of something he'd prefer to have no part in.

"Thank you, no. I have some business back at the vicarage." With the look of a man mustering his courage, Mr. Michaeljohn glanced at Angela. "It's not raining very hard, now, if you would like a drive back to town, Miss Lacewood?"

Considering the circumstances under which they'd parted, Angela conceded it must have taken some fortitude for him to make such an offer.

"Thank you, Vicar. I believe I would."

She rose from the table and collected her wrap. On the way out the door she turned to the blacksmith. "You've been a very gracious host, Mr. Shaw."

"I'm glad we had a chance to talk at last, miss. I hope you'll think about what I said."

"I will."

The vicar's weather report proved true. When Angela emerged from the Shaws' cottage, not only had the rain stopped but the wind had blown some of the clouds away, creating little pockets for the sun to stream through. Off in the distance, a pale rainbow shimmered.

They had not driven far when Mr. Michaeljohn cast her a sidelong glance. "Can you *ever* forgive me, Miss Lacewood?"

A sharp answer rose to her lips. But the vicar looked so miserable, so crushed by the weight of what he had done, that to have scolded him more would have been like beating a wounded animal. Rather than swallowing her anger, as she'd done so often, she released it with a sigh.

"I suppose I can forgive you, but it'll take some doing. Perhaps I ought to be flattered that you cared for me enough to do something like this, but I'm not. If you truly loved me, I think you would want to see me happy in whatever choice I made."

The vicar flinched from her rebuke but nodded to acknowledge the justice of it. "Like Daventry, you mean. He loved you enough to want you happy, but he believed you had a better chance of finding that happiness with me."

"You're mistaken, Vicar. His lordship is a man who cannot bear having anything out of his control. Not even his own emotions…or mine. He hated the fact that our engagement gave me power over him, so he set about to make me break it, without a care for how much it would hurt me, or you. Or himself."

Mr. Michaeljohn mulled over her words in silence for a few moments, then he spoke. "There is a great deal in what you say, but I believe there's more to it than that. At first I thought Daventry only wanted to be rid of you…or perhaps in my selfishness I made myself believe it. But when I copied those letters, and when I saw the look that came over him when he wrote them, I knew in my heart he meant every word. I've never committed so grave a sin as when I blinded myself to that truth."

Though part of her still wanted to throttle him when she remembered what he'd done, at the same time Angela sensed a new warmth of feeling bubbling up in her heart for Mr. Michaeljohn. He wasn't a flawless paragon, after all. Just a fellow creature who, like her, had made mistakes.

As the vicar's gig came to a stop in front of her cottage, Angela reached over and patted his hands, which clung so tightly to the reins. "I believe there is a lady somewhere who will love you for who you are. Promise me you'll keep your eyes open for her."

He gave a glum nod.

"Good." Angela climbed out of the little buggy. "And don't be too hard on yourself. Everybody makes mistakes."

If Mr. Michaeljohn replied, Angela did not hear it. For at that moment the cottage door burst open and Tibby came rushing out.

"So the vicar found you, did he? Thank heaven! What a fright you gave me." She pulled Angela toward the cottage. "Get inside at once and change out of those wet clothes before you catch cold. Rushing out of here without breakfast. I imagine you'll be ready to eat, now...."

As Tibby's motherly fussing washed over her, Angela found herself thinking over what the vicar and the blacksmith had said about Lucius. Both suggested he'd done what he'd done in a misguided effort to protect her and help her find happiness.

So many opposing thoughts whirled in her mind, so many contradictory feelings played a savage tug-of-war with her heart. How she wished the old earl were still alive so she could talk it over with him and have the benefit of his wisdom.

"Is there anything more I can do for you, pet?" asked Tibby, after Angela had changed clothes and eaten.

A notion that had been slowly taking root in Angela's mind suddenly blossomed. "Bath."

"That's just the thing!" cried Tibby. "I'll go heat some water."

"No, Tibby." Angela began to laugh, her spirits

lifting for the first time in weeks. "I don't want you to draw me a bath. I want you to start packing. We're going to Bath!"

Chapter Twenty-One

"Bath?" Lucius asked, as though he had not heard the vicar perfectly well, or there had been some ambiguity about his news. "Angela has gone to Bath?"

The two men sat in the library at Holmhurst, a neglected chessboard between them.

Nathan Michaeljohn gave a glum nod. "A few days ago, with no word when she expects to return."

"*If* she expects to return," Lucius corrected him, "which I doubt she does."

He'd finally succeeded in driving Angela away. Never had triumph tasted so bitter. Even the faint hope that, in Bath, she might secure a husband worthy of her love did not avail Lucius. For he knew she could search the world over without finding a man who would *love her* as he did.

"Now, now." The vicar tried to force a smile, but failed. "Don't lose hope, my friend. If Miss Lacewood could consider forgiving what I did,

I'm sure she can do the same for you. Your motives were more noble than mine."

"They weren't. You're too charitable, Nathan, especially considering how ill I used you in all this. I don't deserve Angela's forgiveness and I don't want it."

He could bear her contempt far more easily. Forgiveness smacked too much of pity.

The vicar picked up the white queen, turning it over and over. "It's true, then, what everyone in the village is saying, that Miss Lacewood broke your engagement?"

"The most sensible action she's taken in quite some time."

Any crumb of satisfaction Lucius might have taken from it was poisoned by the regret that Angela believed he had wanted to be rid of her.

The vicar glanced toward the old earl's writing desk. "You'll miss her."

"I do." It sounded pathetic, but to deny his feelings would have been a desecration.

"So will many others in the parish." The vicar sighed. "Miss Lacewood asked me to visit several of her particular friends in her absence. I believe she enlisted Mrs. Shaw as well. It won't be the same, I fear, but we will endeavor to fill her place and hope it may not be for long."

Since Angela had walked out of Helhurst a free woman, a weight had settled on Lucius's heart. He'd assumed nothing could make it heavier. The vicar's words proved him wrong.

Being deprived of Angela's companionship was

no more than he deserved. But to have cheated
others of her company, when they'd done nothing
to merit such punishment, sickened Lucius with
shame. Was there anything he could do to atone?

"You have plenty to occupy your time, Nathan, as does Mrs. Shaw, I suspect. Could I help
out…or would visits from Lord Lucifer do more
harm than good?"

The vicar mulled over his question. "I imagine
that will depend entirely upon you."

No doubt it would.

Lucius had little experience making himself
agreeable to strangers…and less inclination. But
if it might compensate Angela's friends for her
absence, in some small measure, he owed it to
them, and to her, to throw his whole heart into
the enterprise.

In a voice he scarcely recognized as his own,
Lucius asked the vicar, "Could I prevail upon you
to take me around and provide proper introduc-
tions?"

"What? Now?"

Lucius shrugged. "No sense putting it off."

If he did, he might find some excuse to delay
the undertaking indefinitely. He owed Angela
better service than that.

"That was a pleasant evening, last," said Tibby,
one morning after she and Angela had been some
six weeks in the elegant spa town of Bath. "Mr.
Livermore seems a very nice gentleman. It's plain
he's smitten with you."

"Rubbish, Tibby." Angela glanced up from her breakfast. "You think every gentleman who invites me to dance is smitten with me."

The housekeeper shrugged. "One of us has to keep her eyes open. A gentleman could be swooning at your feet or fighting duels for your honor and you'd never pay any mind."

She bustled off to dust the sitting room of the small town house they'd let on a respectable but not particularly fashionable street.

"Don't exaggerate." Angela called after her. "I'm sure I'd have noticed a man swooning. You are right about Mr. Livermore being a nice fellow, though."

She'd met quite a number of nice men in Bath, as well as one or two vile ones. Contrary to what Tibby believed, Angela had done her best to pay attention to the nice ones. Just as she had done her best to enjoy herself in Bath.

There was always plenty to do, here—shopping, taking the waters, strolling in Sidney Gardens on mild days. In the evenings there were balls, concerts and private card parties for which her presence was in high demand.

Most people in town appeared to know she'd inherited a small fortune from the old earl, then broken her engagement with his grandson. Yet the mild scandal seemed to make her more sought after, rather than less.

Every so often someone would be tactless enough to let slip some remark about Lord Lucifer, which never failed to quicken her pulse in a way nothing else in Bath had been able to.

"Have you decided, yet, what we're going to do for Christmas?" called Tibby from the sitting room.

"At last count we had six invitations to house parties." Angela stared out the small dining room window at a few snowflakes drifting lazily down onto the street. "Unfortunately, I can't say I'm much tempted by any of them. Have you a preference where we go? Christmas is getting so close, I must make up my mind soon."

Tibby appeared in the doorway with her dust cloth in hand. "I was going to hold my peace, especially if you had your heart set on one of those house parties. But, to tell you the truth, I'm rather hankering to go home for Christmas."

"Oh, Tibby..." Angela gnawed her lower lip. "I don't know."

Part of her had been yearning for days to return to Grafton Renforth. Heaven help her, she was even homesick for the sight of Netherstowe. Had the vicar and Mrs. Shaw been calling regularly on her friends, as they'd promised? She longed to see them for herself. To pay surprise visits bearing the Christmas gifts she could now afford.

But...was she ready to face Mr. Michaeljohn again? Or Lucius?

Tibby pulled a much creased letter out of her apron pocket. "This came for me t'other day. From Lady Bulwick, herself, if you please."

She handed it to Angela, who read with growing amazement. "Clemmie has taken a fancy to the vicar? My word! And Aunt Hester supposes you and I could talk some sense into her? Why didn't you show me this before?"

"I didn't want to sway you if you had your heart set on going someplace else." Tibby gathered up Angela's breakfast dishes. "But I could tell by the look on your face just now, you hanker for home as bad as I do."

Tibby's words reminded Angela of something Lucius had once said, about her face being an open book for anyone who cared enough to read it.

At the thought of him, a foolish blush crept into her cheeks and her pulse sped up yet again. Why couldn't any of the nice, respectable, unmasked gentlemen of Bath affect her that way? Drat them!

"You know," said Tibby. "Reading between the lines, I almost think her ladyship misses the pair of us around the place. I know she and Lord Bulwick and the girls didn't always treat you as well as they might have when you were younger. For all that, they're the only family you have, apart from Master Miles way off in India. Don't you think it's time you made peace with them?"

Angela pondered the idea. "Perhaps."

Not denying her feelings or her rights in the matter, but acknowledging that the Bulwicks had made mistakes, too. "I'm not saying I've decided to go, mind you. But I will think on it."

She flashed Tibby a mischievous grin. "I rather

doubt Aunt Hester would approve the kind of advice I'd be apt to give her precious Clemmie."

A while later, when the aroma of hot gingerbread permeated every corner of the little house, Tibby knocked on Angela's door to find her sitting in the middle of the bed with a great many papers spread around her.

"Bless me!" Tibby shook her head. "I thought you were going to burn those letters before we ever left home."

Part of Angela had wanted to, but… "I couldn't bring myself to, Tibby. They say such lovely things about me, and when I read them, I can't help believe they're true, regardless of who wrote them, or why."

Tibby's disapproving look softened. "I reckon that's not such a bad reason to keep them, then. Will you come have a bit of gingerbread?"

"In a while."

As Tibby went away again, Angela began to collect the letters. She found herself wishing she hadn't torn up the original ones Lucius had composed. Perhaps if she could read them over in his own hand, she might be able to conclude, once and for all, if he'd truly meant what he'd written.

If he had…Angela mourned the life they might have enjoyed together.

In the middle of a concert at the Upper Assembly Rooms the previous evening, she'd found herself wondering if the constellation Orion was visible in the northern sky yet. During supper at

Lady Middleton's whist party, she'd helped herself to a delicious-looking little pastry that reminded her of the ones she and Lucius had shared at the masquerade ball. When she'd bitten into it, the delicacy had tasted so bland she could scarcely force herself to finish it.

Bland, Angela concluded, like her whole life here in Bath.

Her summer with Lucius had never been that way. Sometimes bitter, often tart, now and then sweeter than anything she'd ever tasted. Hard as she tried to deny it, Angela feared she would never love another man as she had come to love him.

If that were true, she decided, gathering the letters to her bosom, then perhaps she had nothing to lose by wrestling Lucius Daventry's demons for possession of his heart and soul.

Catching sight of herself in the looking glass, Angela tilted her chin defiantly.

Nothing but her self-respect, which had been too hard won for her ever to surrender.

A light, crisp shroud of snow draped St. Owen's churchyard on Christmas Eve, when Lucius paused there to lay a sprig of holly on his grandfather's grave. While anyone observing him might have thought the new earl a rather tragic figure, Lucius knew otherwise.

He found himself looking forward to evensong when he would listen to the familiar readings about men who had heard angels in the night, and others who had followed a star. For the first time in a great while, perhaps his whole life, he knew a sweet, melancholy sense of contentment, a gift more precious to him than any amount of gold or incense.

His only regret was that others had paid so dear a price for it.

"Happy Christmas, Lucius."

Those words wafted so softly from behind him on the still, cold air, Lucius wondered if he'd imagined them. He hesitated to turn around, in case Angela might not be there. But turn he did, for if there was the smallest chance, he must know, even at the cost of disappointment.

He was not disappointed.

As Angela approached him, she drew back the hood of her fur-trimmed cloak. Lucius knew she was no mere fancy, because her golden beauty struck him afresh, beyond anything he could have imagined.

His self-control, which he had too often neglected to exercise of late, deserted him. He knew his face must expose the wistful hunger that ached in his heart.

"H-happy Christmas. I hadn't heard you were coming home for the holidays."

"I didn't know myself until a few days ago." Angela seemed to have acquired all his lost composure. For once, her eyes gave nothing of her feelings away to Lucius. "You've been a busy fellow of late, I hear. All our mutual friends are full of your praises. At this rate, I fear you'll never resurrect Lord Lucifer."

Lucius shrugged. "Good riddance to him."

A chickadee whistled from its perch in an ancient stunted yew tree nearby.

"Why did you take up with my 'strays'?" Her voice sounded almost severe. "Was it some sort of penance?"

"Perhaps it began that way," Lucius admitted. "But it rapidly became such a pleasure that I fear it's lost all value as penance."

"Indeed?" One slender brow arched.

Lucius nodded. "I was convinced that pity and charity must go hand in glove with contempt. Getting to know your friends during the past few weeks, I've discovered they have more to do with…"

"Love? You may say the word, Lucius. I promise your tongue will not turn to stone."

"Very well, then…love. See here, did you want something with me?" He motioned toward his grandfather's grave. "Or did you just come to visit."

"Both." She took a few steps closer to him. "I have something to ask you, and I had a feeling I might find you here. This seems as good a place as any to settle what we left unfinished."

"I thought everything between us was finished." He barely managed to contain a sigh.

"Not quite," said Angela. "I have one question for you. After all you have put me through, I believe you owe me an honest answer."

Though her words had a rather ominous sound, Lucius nodded. "I suppose I do."

Snowflakes began to waft gently down around them—soft, beautiful and cold. They settled on Angela's hair like a veil of the most delicate lace.

"Now that I have no power to compel you to marry me, will you admit you once loved me?" Gazing into his eyes in the falling darkness, she must have seen something to make her add, "And still do?"

Pride demanded he deny it, but Lucius could not bear to burden his conscience with another lie to Angela.

"I did love you, more than I ever let myself believe." It tormented him to speak those words aloud, with Angela so near, having abdicated the right to take her in his arms. "I love you now, and always will."

Might as well make a clean breast while he was at it, for he might never get another opportunity to tell her. "The letters I wrote were a far more truthful account of my feelings than any words I ever spoke to you until now."

In his shame, he wanted to avert his face. But that would cheat Angela of her due. "It was wrong of me to desecrate those expressions of my deepest feelings by using them to deceive you. I deceived myself into believing I had noble reasons for doing what I did. Now I know a great part of it was cowardice and arrogance masquerading as concern for your happiness."

No doubt she'd recognized the sordid truth for herself.

"I will not ask your forgiveness." He turned away from her. "We both know I don't deserve it, any more than I deserved the love you once offered me."

A light tug on his sleeve detained him. "Hold a moment, your lordship. I'm not through with you, yet."

What more could she do or say to wound him? Given the power she wielded over his heart, Lucius dreaded to think. Still he turned back to accept his just punishment.

"I fear your arrogance is not as well cured as you may believe."

In a bewildering contradiction, the hand that clutched his sleeve now trailed downward to wrap around his fingers. "Remember what your grandfather said, *there are some things of which even an earl cannot have the ordering.* Well, forgiveness is one of them. You cannot command my forgiveness if I choose to withhold it, but neither can you deny my forgiveness if I choose to grant it."

All his life Lucius had sought and treasured control, even of his own emotions. From the moment she'd stumbled into his arms, Angela Lacewood had led a quiet rebellion against his authority. Little had he guessed that her object was to liberate *him* from a tyranny of his own making.

"I have already forgiven you," she announced

in a tone of gentle defiance. "Otherwise, I would not be here."

Cool, soothing and cleansing as snow, grace settled over him, baffling and beautiful.

Slowly Angela lifted her gaze from their joined hands. "Nor would I be here unless I loved you, still. I've decided I would rather remain unwed than give my hand where I cannot give my heart. That is…unless…you are willing to make me your bride."

From the folds of her cloak she drew out a pair of spectacles and placed them in his hand. "An oculist in Bath made these for me. The dark glass will protect your eyes in daylight. Much as I enjoy the occasional night of stargazing, I need a husband who can take part in the daylight world with me."

Lucius turned the spectacles over and over in his hand. True, they would shield his eyes. But not his scars.

This was the bride-price Angela demanded of him.

"Have you become so enamored of gloom and darkness that you cannot abide the warmth of sunshine, Lucius?"

Had he?

His dark demons called to Lucius with a siren's song. They would never desert him or disappoint him, never elevate him to great heights only to cast him down even deeper. They would hide him from the scorn and pity of the world.

The struggle must have shown on his face, for

a dignified sadness settled over Angela's features. It put Lucius in mind of an army commander whose troops had fought valiantly but who must now accept defeat. Slowly she turned to go.

Lucius watched, unable to break the stubborn spell that bound him.

Then some force propelled him forward. Like the push of a frail but loving hand.

He dropped to his knees in the snow. "Angela, wait!"

She stopped.

Lucius wrenched the mask from his face and felt a single snowflake kiss his mangled flesh. "Will you be my wife? Please."

As she turned her vulnerable gaze upon him once more, Lucius braced himself for the aversion he would see in her eyes.

Instead, he saw only love—hers and the reflection of his own.

She held her arms open to him. "If you promise I will not have to endure a long engagement."

Rising from the ground, Lucius fumbled to put on his new spectacles. But when he swept Angela into his arms, a bracing sense of his old assurance welled up in him.

"I'll arrange for a special license at once." He savored every sensation of their embrace. "You'll be Countess of Welland before the New Year."

"There is one thing more..." She pulled off her glove to caress his cheek.

Lucius did not flinch from her touch, nor her request...whatever it might be. "Name it."

"Naturally, I shall expect a poetic love letter on every wedding anniversary."

"I'll stock up on plenty of paper and ink," Lucius assured her as his lips closed over hers in a kiss that held all the beauty of twilight and all the promise of a fresh new dawn.

* * * * *

A sneaky peek at next month…

HISTORICAL

IGNITE YOUR IMAGINATION, STEP INTO THE PAST…

My wish list for next month's titles…

In stores from 4th October 2013:

☐ A Date with Dishonour – Mary Brendan

☐ The Master of Stonegrave Hall – Helen Dickson

☐ Engagement of Convenience – Georgie Lee

☐ Defiant in the Viking's Bed – Joanna Fulford

☐ The Adventurer's Bride – June Francis

☐ Christmas Cowboy Kisses – Carolyn Davidson, Carol Arens & Lauri Robinson

Available at WHSmith, Tesco, Asda, Eason, Amazon and Apple

Just can't wait?

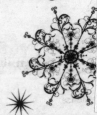

She's loved and lost — will she ever learn to open her heart again?

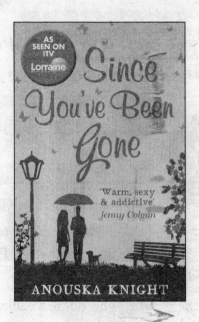

3/MB438

  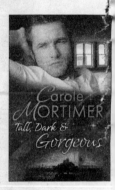